THE SECRET OF YS

Harold Nottridge

© Copyright 2004 Harold Nottridge.
All rights reserved. No part of this publication may be reproduced, stored in a retrieval system, or transmitted, in any form or by any means, electronic, mechanical, photocopying, recording, or otherwise, without the written prior permission of the author.

Printed in Victoria, BC, Canada

Note for Librarians: a cataloguing record for this book that includes Dewey Decimal Classification and US Library of Congress numbers is available from the Library and Archives of Canada. The complete cataloguing record can be obtained from their online database at:
www.collectionscanada.ca/amicus/index-e.html
ISBN 1-4120-2657-1

TRAFFORD

This book was published *on-demand* in cooperation with Trafford Publishing. On-demand publishing is a unique process and service of making a book available for retail sale to the public taking advantage of on-demand manufacturing and Internet marketing. On-demand publishing includes promotions, retail sales, manufacturing, order fulfilment, accounting and collecting royalties on behalf of the author.

Offices in Canada, USA, UK, Ireland, and Spain
book sales for North America and international:
Trafford Publishing, 6E–2333 Government St.
Victoria, BC V8T 4P4 CANADA
phone 250 383 6864   toll-free 1 888 232 4444
fax 250 383 6804   email to orders@trafford.com
book sales in Europe:
Trafford Publishing (UK) Ltd., Enterprise House, Wistaston Road Business Centre
Crewe, Cheshire CW2 7RP UNITED KINGDOM
phone 01270 251 396   local rate 0845 230 9601
facsimile 01270 254 983   orders.uk@trafford.com
order online at:
www.trafford.com/robots/04-0485.html

10   9   8   7   6   5   4

Harold Nottridge was born in London and grew up in Australia. He read History at Cambridge and became a teacher then a college Lecturer in History and Sociology.

Published work includes poetry, short stories, a book on The Sociology of Urban Living and a Life of Joan of Arc for children.

This is his first novel.

AD 1926

From the Journal of Ann Davies, student of languages at London University

January

I could not sleep after the telegram arrived. I moved around preparing for my departure, wrote a letter to my tutor, a note with keys for my future flatmate who would arrive when I was away and another note to Mr Goodheart who lived in the flat above and to whom I would carry my cat at dawn. After checking the times of trains and finishing my packing, I sat down before the dying fire with Ginger on my lap. I read and re-read the telegram.

"Aunt Gwyneth died unexpectedly. Come home at once. Will meet your train. Dafydd."

I was deeply shocked and felt as though the bottom had fallen out of my world. My aunt had always looked after my brother and me since the accidental death of my parents when we were very young. She had been a mother to us. She had planned our education, made me learn French and Breton and above all had insisted that I go to University. The hours passed until at last daylight reminded me that I must start on my journey.

It was cold on the train. I had a compartment to myself and time to reflect on what was to come. My thoughts were as bleak as the wintry landscape but I did think a little about my new flatmate. Her name was Captain Mary Smith and she was a Social Worker in the Salvation Army. I had some misgivings about her as I had been told that she was a little eccentric. Eccentric? In what way? I only hoped that she would remember to feed Ginger when she had charge of him.

My thoughts now focused on Gwyneth and on her life as a young woman when she had worked as a midwife and nurse in France and other countries, but especially in Brittany. She was reticent about her work abroad and only rarely spoke freely about Brittany. It seemed to me to be a closed book.

The rail journey came to an end and I was relieved to see Dafydd waiting on the platform and to feel his arms around me. I was glad to know that I would sleep in my old bedroom with its Breton lace curtains at the little window and the massive Welsh Bible by the bedside.

Downstairs some village people had come to pay their last respects to Gwyneth. Gwyneth's physician and her lawyer were also present. When I had settled in they accompanied me and Blodwen, Gwyneth's maid, up to my aunt's bedroom as I wished to see the place where she had died. It was a small room but had a Celtic Harp by the window and an artist's easel, paints and brushes, pencils and paper by the bed. Blodwen's eyes were red with weeping as she described what had happened.

On the day my aunt died she was apparently quite well and having no commitments told Blodwen that she wished to be undisturbed, play her harp and do some painting. She was pale Blodwen said. Working downstairs Blodwen clearly heard the sound of the harp at first quite gentle but gradually growing louder and fiercer. "Like a storm" Blodwen described it. Then came a lull of some length and Blodwen thought Gwyneth would be painting, but after about half an hour she heard a sudden, heavy sound from the bedroom. Something had fallen. She rushed upstairs and found Gwyneth lying on the floor. Blodwen felt for her pulse but there was none. She ran and fetched Dr Meredith who lived nearby and though he came at once and did everything possible, he could not revive my aunt.

The picture was still on the easel. My aunt could paint well and I studied it for some time. It was a seascape in which the land seemed to have almost vanished. It was a dark night, the darkness of the sea relieved only by a great band of moonlight. A black rock projected from the sea and standing by it was the figure of a young woman. The face could not be seen as the head was turned away. One white arm was stretched out over the rock as if in evocation. "It's a strange picture and it isn't really finished" remarked Dr Meredith. He then took his leave.

Just before Dafydd and I parted for the night he said he had something to give me. He produced a small bag and a note from Gwyneth which said – "in the event of my death this must be given to my niece Ann." I opened the little silk bag. Within rested a silver cross and chain which were very beautiful. There were incisions on the side of the cross. "These are Ogam letters" I cried. "It must be very old indeed."

"It's a fifth century cross" said Dafydd. He seemed rather excited.

"It's a talisman and will protect you from harm. Wear it always."

I went to my bed and slept fitfully. It was in the small

hours of the morning when I awoke. The house was very quiet and outside a light snow was falling. I lit my candle in its brass candlestick, threw a cashmere shawl over my nightdress and slowly, barefoot, tiptoed down the stairs. Something was drawing me to Gwyneth's workroom known as "The Sanctum". The candlelight softly picked out objects. There were rows of books in Welsh and Breton, a piano, and a "pardon" costume which she may have worn or have had given to her when she was in Brittany.

I sat down and remembered what had happened in this room one June night. My aunt, usually a woman of few words, had spoken at greater length about the far distant past of ancient Brittany. Her eyes gleamed, her pale cheeks became flushed as she related the great Breton legends. So vividly did she speak it were as though those legendary figures were people living today. Guenolé, the loving yet formidable saint, King Gradlon, Princess Dahut and others. Then she said "I have experienced so much that was strange and secret in Brittany." She paused for a long while lost in thought. A smile radiated her face as she gripped my hands in hers.

"You too must learn what I have learned in Brittany. You shall share my experiences too. Do not forget what I have said."

We had been together all night and the June sun was touching the window with gold as I left her.

I closed the door of Gwyneth's room and went down to the front room where they had put the coffin. I pulled the shroud back gently and gazed at the face so composed in death. I looked at her lips so firm. Would she take her secrets with her? I am not a religious person but I knelt by the coffin with my hands clasped in prayer. I asked God to give me wisdom and guidance in the years ahead when I would be standing on my own. While I was on my knees I glanced at the other side of the coffin and saw a young man standing there. I saw clearly his shock of hair, his huge torso, his immense arms and his leather cincture. I had no fear for he was a vision not a human being and in a moment he had melted away.

I remember the funeral which was held the next day. The sermon and encomia in the little church, the burial, the open grave dark against the dazzling white of the fresh snow, the mourners in black, the handfuls of earth that we cast on the coffin below and the words "pridd I pridd" ashes to ashes "llwch I llwch" dust to dust.

I had an uncomfortable journey back to London. The weather was very cold and the train was delayed. I found some solace in examining closely the silver cross. When and how was it made? Why did it have the power of being a talisman? Was it really a Christian symbol?

As the train approached London I began to feel once more anxiety over my new flatmate. Perhaps it was because I was tired and depressed after the funeral. I need not have worried so much. When I arrived at the flat Ginger was purring away with the self-satisfied look of a well fed cat and his old, shabby collar had been replaced by a new leather one.

I thanked Mary for all her trouble. I found her to be a quiet spoken person of few words. She had baked scones for me which I could not eat but I gratefully sipped the hot tea. As I got up to go to my bedroom she grasped my hands warmly and said "if you need any help in the night wake me at once."

I slept soundly and was late in wakening. Mary had already gone to work. I suddenly noticed two unfamiliar objects in the sitting room. One was a portable organ and the other a sewing machine. I hoped that the use of these would not be an interruption to my studies or I would have to shut myself away in my bedroom. As I was passing Mary's room I glanced through the open door and noticed on the wall a photograph of a young man in khaki tropical uniform. There was a gigantic eucalyptus tree in the background so I guessed the picture must have been taken in Australia. At about teatime Mary turned up, she hung up her bonnet and sat down close to the fire with her feet stretched towards the flames. She drank the tea I offered and then looked at me with a twinkle in her eyes.

"You can be certain I'll not play the organ except at the weekends and then only when you are out. As for the machine, it's a hobby. I make clothes for the needy." She looked at the little organ. "Would you mind if I just tried it out to make sure it's not out of tune after the train journey here?"

She sat down at the organ and after touching a few keys began to play "Eine Kleine Nachtmusik." It was Gwyneth's favourite! I burst into tears and sobbed and sobbed. I felt her arms around me. "Let it come" she said. "You've bottled it up long enough."

Looking back to that evening it was the time when we began to learn to live together. Then for about three weeks I was very ill. I had come back from the funeral with a severe cold which developed into near pneumonia. Mary devoted herself to nursing me and I could not have recovered without her. One day when I was still convalescent Mary mentioned that in my delirium I had talked about a voice and a harp. I thought for a few moments and then I told her what I had suddenly remembered. I had been on my way back from a lecture when I heard my name "Ann" called. There was no one in sight. It was a man's voice, very strong but not an English voice. Then I heard a few notes played on a harp and silence.

Fit again I went back to my studies. In the early spring I was surprised to receive two letters, both in French. Each bore the postmark "Douarnenez" and had been forwarded by my late aunt's solicitor. The first letter was from a Pension in Douarnenez and from the tone of this letter it appeared that my aunt had stayed there several times. It said "we will hold the bookings for you and your niece for August and September but we would like you to confirm the reservations." The second letter was from the curé of Douarnenez saying "I would be very happy indeed to help your niece with conversation practice in both French and Breton as there are always people here in the evenings. I myself will also be glad to tell her about those aspects of our local history in which you yourself were so profoundly interested."

I was puzzled by both letters. My aunt, while insisting I must go to Brittany, had never mentioned Douarnenez at all. Why not? And why this particular Pension? On the stairs I heard Mary's footsteps and as she entered the flat I decided to explain to her the gist of the letters. What was in my mind already was the thought that I must go alone to the place chosen for my work that summer. I knew I couldn't procrastinate and must make a firm booking.

After I had explained the contents of the letters to her, Mary looked at me thoughtfully.

"Ann", she said, "you must remember that you have just recovered from a severe illness. I don't think you should go alone. If you like I could arrange for some leave and come along with you."

I hesitated to say anything. I could not make up my mind on the spur of the moment. For Mary it would be a holiday. For me, apart from my French studies, it would be the fulfilment of Gwyneth's wish that I would probe the historic mystery that was Brittany. This idea was dominating my mind more and more. Would a companion interfere with my outlook? Mary felt my hesitation. Then she said "think about it."

I made my decision in a week. I made all the arrangements and by the beginning of August exams were over and we were almost ready to leave. On the last evening before our departure we sat reading.

"You are concentrating very hard on that book" remarked Mary.

"It's only because it is about the fourth and fifth centuries in this country and in Brittany. Yet I am interested in more than books. In Wales I used to look at the gravestones of people who had died during those centuries. I would stand on lonely hillsides and touch the inscriptions. I tried to visualize the lives of these men, women and children and wondered about their languages and customs. Does not something apart from their gravestones survive today? We are not conscious of the past yet I do believe it does intrude into our lives. You know the poet says 'for every age is a dream that is dying or a dream that is coming to birth'. Everything is linked together. Though we live within history we must feel free within it not chained down to our own times. I feel that if there were someone from many centuries ago whom we might love deeply we could briefly be with them, feel their love, even understand them to some extent."

Mary looked intently at me. "Do you think it is possible in person to go to the past? To live then? You don't mean reincarnation?"

"Not at all. I'll put it this way. My spirit lives within my body. I believe that it is possible for my spirit to leave my body as in a dream. It could then travel in time into the body of someone else and might be there a while before it returned. But look. It's getting late and we have a long day ahead of us. Let's get some sleep."

1st August

We have arrived in Brittany. I find the land full of mysteries. Our pension at Douarnenez has green shutters fast closed to keep out the sun or deter prying eyes. It crouches back from the access lane as if it feared contamination with a world beyond. La gerante, lace-capped, is welcoming but speaks little. She hardly mentions my aunt. Black Nose, the dog, is very quiet.

After unpacking Mary said "You look pale. Do go out and look around. I've got letters to write home."

I wandered round and looked out over the sea. I found the footpath by which we would go down to the plage to bathe and I could understand why my aunt came here as the bathing was so accessible. I became interested in an enclosure off the footpath. Here the garden had apparently been neglected for a long time as it was like a small jungle. Trees, bushes and grass fought for mastery but in the centre, almost completely overgrown, there was an upright stone.

My curiosity aroused, I stepped over the enclosure wall and forced my way through the tangled undergrowth until I was right by the stone. I could make out some letters and set about clearing the surface to see what they said. There was no date but the inscription ran "In memory of Annette, a young woman drowned when bathing alone at the Black Stone."

I moved out of the enclosure and walked slowly down

to the plage. Looking at the sea I noticed a black rock which very much resembled the painting my aunt had left. I stood thinking hard. Was there such a spiritual connection between my aunt and this girl who had died, apparently so long ago, that she had tried to express her feelings in her painting? Certainly the rock itself was not far from the pension. I even noticed there was a cleft on one side that my aunt had faithfully reproduced in her painting. Perhaps because I was brought up among mountains I had no fear of rocks and the huge ones on the edge of the plage appeared to me to be pleasant, friendly, strong giants.

After tea we walked to Douarnenez. It is a fishing port full of Breton voices. From the women repairing nets, their speech as fast as their fingers on the needles, to the argot of the sailors. I am so happy at being here and I feel that Brittany will become my land.

The next day, before breakfast, Mary starts giving me swimming lessons. I learn quickly. She has also taught me to float and I love to do so face down looking at all the wonders of the sea below. During our afternoon bathing she shows me exercises which are good for me and whatever I do she is close by my side holding out a hand to help me. I feel like a captive but say nothing. I just want to be alone in the sea.

7th August

Time is passing. At last I have met a true Breton. Yves is a fisherman who launches his boat near where we bathe. He crosses himself every time he pushes the boat off. We often bathe near the black rock partly because on one side – the eastern side – it is almost free from wrack.

One day I noticed Yves was looking intently at me while I bathed. When I emerged from the sea he came up to me. How strong the man was! He did not look at my body but pointed at the rock which rose so sharply from the waves. He looked into my eyes with a gaze that frightened me so severe it was.

"Diwall" he cried, "Diwall".

"What does it mean?" asked Mary.

"It means 'beware'" I replied.

The man stopped pointing and gazed at me again. He went on "Dangerus eo – it is dangerous to bathe to the west of that rock. Mesdemoiselles do not bathe there as you value your lives." I grasped the meaning of his gestures and his limited French. The bathing was doing me good and the swimming made me feel stronger. I did not like his interference but I asked, in Breton, "Why not?" He replied in the same language:-

"Lady, I have seen too many corpses come from that sea. I assure you that it is dangerous on the west side of that rock. There are unpredictable currents and more serious happenings too. Enjoy your swimming but keep to the east side of the rock where there are no hidden hazards. I must tell you that my mother and I call that rock The Rock of Calvary for it symbolises for us the deaths of my father and many other fisherman in the sea and the suffering that comes to those that mourn them." He turned sharply away and we did not see him for days.

19th August

We are enjoying our evening visits to the curé. Mary sits in an armchair with her knitting on her lap and four inquisitive cats watching her. I talk in Breton and we often finish our sessions there with songs in Breton, French or Welsh.

One evening Mary and I were alone with the curé and he said "I'll tell you about our local history. I mean the part in which your late aunt was so interested." He pointed to the sea. "The Bay of Douarnenez. Under those waves is hidden the secret of our greatest legend. On clear nights, so it is said, you can hear the bells of Ker-ys ringing beneath the waves.

Ker-ys, Ys, the city that for the sins of its people was sunk beneath the waves in the fifth century AD. The impression is that the city may have been both rich and powerful. Legend and history are interwoven in the story.

When Rome fell, barbarian peoples attacked and town life in this area may have declined. There were external pressures too. The Franks, in what is now eastern Brittany, and sea raids by Saxons and others. Parts of West Brittany had become like a vacuum so the Gallo-Romans who had lived there had either died or gone elsewhere. So people from your country came here to settle. They brought their own language with them which partly displaced speech of Latin origin. The same language was spoken in Brittany as in fifth and sixth century Britain."

There was silence, then the curé said "You've been very quiet Mademoiselle Ann. Have you fallen in love with this country and its ways?"

I felt my cheeks go red when he spoke. He went on. "What a pity you have to depart so soon. You are a very thoughtful young woman. Please do not be embarrassed if I tell you that when you go back to Wales you'll remember your experiences here as the great crossroads of your life."

28th August

We are to have a wonderful experience in a week's time and I do want Mary to enjoy it. She has worked hard at looking after me and teaching me to swim. We have not got much time left so I am glad she will at least see a Pardon in a great church.

The curé was delighted. "The Pardon is a religious manifestation bound up with Breton life and tradition over the centuries. You will stand outside with the onlookers and watch the Procession come out of the church. The Procession is an integral part of the Pardon. You will understand our religion better after you have seen one. I'll say a prayer for you."

I returned to Mary and told her the good news. She looked dubious.

"It's a Catholic church service?"

"Not really. We stand with the crowd and watch a Procession. That's all. Call it a joyous occasion. Like your own Festivals."

4th September

Before setting off for the church two letters arrived for Mary, one from Melbourne, the other from International HQ. Her face was grave as she set them aside for later perusal. We continued on our way and soon we could see the magnificent mediaeval church with the needle of its spire reaching up to the clear, blue sky. We hastened to join the others flocking to the church. Both sides of the pathway to the entrance were already lined with people but we managed to secure a place from which we would be sure of seeing all that went on.

People chatted quietly while waiting, then ceased altogether and turned their eyes expectantly towards the church door. It was beginning. We saw them and it was beautiful!

Three young Breton women advanced at the head of the procession. They were tall, slim, fair haired and richly clad. They wore over-dresses embroidered with flowers and edged with lace. On their shoulders were draped long, silk shawls. On their heads they wore high lace bonnets. They halted, proud and calm, in front of us.

The woman in the centre bore a long, upright pole from whose crosspiece at the top depended an embroidered banner depicting the Virgin Mary. The needlework was superb. More was yet to come. Emerging slowly from the church entrance came eight sturdy men whose shoulders bore a framework of shining, polished oak poles. Swaying above them gently was the sculptured image of the Virgin. There was a subdued murmur of acclamation. Men gravely removed their hats in reverence, women bowed their heads.

Suddenly Mary was clutching desperately at my arm. Her face beneath the sunburn had gone quite pale. "My God!" she cried hoarsely. "They're idol worshippers! They adore an image instead of the one true God. They're heathens!"

"Don't you understand what's happening?" I whispered, worried lest someone should hear what she was saying. "This is how people showed their devotion to God in the Dark and Middle Ages. They loved pilgrimages and processions. Here and now they have preserved that tradition. Look at their faces! How lovely they can be in their affection for their patronal church. How kind they are towards people not of their type of worship. That is true Christianity. Can you not accept them and their Pardon?"

I had unwisely not realised when I suggested seeing the Pardon how strong Mary's reactions would be to a religious practice different from her own. Yet why did differences between us suddenly surface at an event which was to me wholly pleasurable? Mary was a woman devout in her own particular faith.

She rounded on me. "Ann, I think sometimes you just live in the Dark Ages whose history you have studied and you will slip back there. You mustn't accept these Pardons. People bowing to an idol!" Incredible anger was rising in her. Her eyes flashed, her voice shrilled.

"Such rubbish! It's the blood of Christ that saves

us! What this country needs is converting. I'd like to wander through France, tell them about Jesus at every crossroads and market place and save them from the Devil. But – I haven't got the language." Her face fell and there were tears in her eyes.

"It's a big country, France" I whispered. I had no more to say. The crowd was moving away and we dropped down on two abandoned seats. I closed my eyes. I was sleepy with the warmth of the sun and I felt wretched. It wasn't that we two were so different. I liked Mary. The problem as far as I could see was that she could not accept the tolerance I had in my nature and learned from my aunt. This division between myself and a woman whom I cherished for her warmth and kindness to me when I was ill, hurt me, and it brought to mind now Gwyneth's words. "Go alone or with a companion exactly with your own interests." Perhaps it was also a difference in personality although we had lived together for eight months in perfect amity.

I felt now, as things were, that I really wanted to creep silently away from Mary and everyone else. Was I part of a religious past? Not living in the present? I wanted to be by myself at those gravestones on Welsh mountains or to see a Pardon in Dark Age Brittany with my own eyes. Such were the very odd thoughts that came to me.

I opened my eyes. I looked at Mary, then we both rose and walked away from the scene and everyone there. Neither of us would ever speak of the Pardon again but, thank God, we could still talk together freely as before. I reflected on our holiday. For weeks I had been in close touch with a great civilization and its people, and it had changed me both in mind and heart. Mary too had met people in another country and learned something of their ways. Our holiday had altered us physically too. The daily swimming had made us both much fitter and I suggested a swim when we returned to the pension.

Mary appeared happy swimming but when we returned to our room and she read her two letters, a look of sadness and disappointment came over her. She said nothing but that night she tossed restlessly in her sleep and I wondered if she had some special anxiety.

Next morning Mary said "Have you enjoyed your holiday?"

"It's been marvellous" I replied. "I am so grateful for your help and friendship and for teaching me to swim. I've enjoyed it so much."

Mary regarded me kindly. "You're a nice woman, Ann, and highly intelligent. I feel sure you will have a great future."

"Me? I just get along as best I can."

10th September

The weather changed and the skies were overcast and presaged rain. The plage, except for Yves and his boat, was deserted. The night wind howled round the cottages and shook the heavy shutters of our pension. The days grew shorter, the nights longer. We took walks and visited Menez-Hom and the hills.

The atmosphere became heavy and brooding. We still bathed, for the sea remained warm. Mary always touched my hand as if she wanted to be close to me, though I now swam and floated well. Once we went walking in the twilight and noticed that the trees over Annette's grave were swaying in the wind as if paying homage to the dead. One smaller tree, old and moribund, waved its withered arms wildly, as if in horror at Annette's drowning. The Bay waters were troubled by subtle currents which reflected the fading light, though the sea by the plage was calm.

Suddenly, in the near darkness, almost hidden in the long grass by the grave, we saw a human figure. We could just make out a middle-aged woman with long hair and wearing dark clothes kneeling close to the gravestone. By her side was a bunch of wild flowers. She was bending over the grave, her head bowed low, her hands clasped in prayer, and as we drew a little nearer her anguished voice reached us in the still air. "The dead return! I see them always. They arise! From the deep of the sea they arise! Annette! My son! They arise and I see their faces! The dead of Ys too arise when the bells sound from that accursed city!"

Mary, taken aback, whispered "Couldn't you comfort her?" The woman, rising to her feet, turned and stared into my face with pain filled eyes. All I wanted to do was to be close to her in her trouble.

I put my arms around the woman and held her gently while whispering in Breton "Yea, though I walk through the valley of the shadow of death I will fear no evil."

"Who are you that speaks Breton so? Are you from the dead? A woman risen from Ys?" The name of the lost city was hissed through tight clenched teeth. "No, my dear, rest assured that I am truly from the living. I am a real person who comes to you in this year of our Lord, 1926. I am Welsh but speak Breton too." I felt her hands for a moment clasping me round my neck. Then she drew away from me, shuddered, and murmured in French. "I will go to my own dwelling and pray there for my son and for her" she pointed to the grave. She grasped the bunch of flowers in her thin hand, placed it across the grave and without speaking or looking at us, walked slowly away towards Douarnenez, her thin figure disappearing into the sea mist.

Next morning at breakfast we mentioned our strange encounter to la gerente. "Ah, yes" she said. "Madelaine. A very pleasant, well educated widow who lost her only child, a son, at sea and occasionally it affects her mind. Then she says the dead will return including the dead of Ys. She is not quite herself when she has these spells and her appearance changes."

After breakfast Mary went off to swim and I opened my books but could not study. I was thinking about death, of Gwyneth's passing and the deaths of Annette, Madeleine's son, and the many Bretons who had lost their lives at sea.

I closed my eyes and murmured. "Lord I am just a student. You have given me the gift of languages, grant me also a greater gift – compassion for those who suffer and mourn for their loved ones drowned at sea."

Two days later Mary, on waking, said she had a headache and thought she would rest in bed. "You'll have the day to yourself Ann. Do go out and have a long walk." I made Mary comfortable, warned the femme de chambre not to disturb her, and set out on my own for the first time since we had been in Douarnenez.

I knew what I had to do. Visit Madeleine. Her cottage was by the sea and her dinghy rested on chocks nearby. She was standing by the cottage door, a tall, slim figure in a fine black dress and I was astonished at the change in her. Her hair was covered neatly by a snowy white head cloth. She smiled and looked at me as if she had waited many years for this meeting.

"I knew you would come to me. Do come in and sit down." I sat on the bench she indicated and looked around at the room. Lace bobbins, fishing nets and lines, books and on the wall a Kodak print of a young sailor with a telescope under his arm. Below it was a large crucifix. She clasped my right hand in hers and pointed my fingers at the photograph and the crucifix. Then with the tip of her finger she touched the old silver cross on my breast as if linking all three objects together, and thus asking me to share her sorrow. My tears fell and she gently wiped them away with her fingertips.

After a few moments Madelaine said "you must be hungry." She brought a brass tray on which was a beaker of water and a tartine, knelt down and offered it to me. I gratefully accepted the refreshment and appreciated her warm hospitality. We sat in silence gazing at each other. I was conscious of a flood of new thoughts and the wish that I could spend some years in Brittany surfaced. I even wondered if I should marry a Breton fisherman.

As if reading my thoughts, Madelaine pointed to the nets and said "Life is hard here for the fisherfolk, especially the women. You've seen the beautiful side in the Pardon but to know us you must also share our anguish. Suffering would be your lot as a married woman here. For a young woman you were very understanding when we met at Annette's grave. You appear to love Brittany and want to know its people and I think that when you leave Douarnenez to return to Wales you will find that you have left part of your heart in Brittany." She smiled and there was a twinkle in her eye as she said "If you do

come back remember my home is always open to you."
My heart warmed to her words.

Madelaine talked with me about my French and Breton studies and she listened intently as I told her of Gwyneth's death and how it had brought me to Brittany.

The shadows were beginning to lengthen and I had to return to my companion. I got up to go. Then Madelaine said "I have never told this to anyone else. I sometimes fish at night and once, at midnight, I rowed out a long way. The sea was mirror calm and I was casting a line when I heard the sound of bells, not ringing melodiously but jangling together. It lasted barely a second then the night became tranquil again." We were outside now. Her face was pale. She leant on my arm and pointed to the waves. "It was that very night when the bells of Ys were ringing that my son was drowned at sea! She clasped my hands in hers and said "Come back to me Ann, and to the Brittany you love."

"I'll return" I said. I walked away then looked back and waved.

Madelaine was standing still, a figure dark against the white cottage. I turned off onto the shore path and could no longer see her. I felt a great sense of liberation and felt that I could no longer live only my cloistered life as a student. I would be independent. Above all, in Madelaine I had found a true friend and it seemed appropriate that some words of Gwyneth came back to me. "You are destined soon to have a great adventure." As I continued on my way I decided I would not tell Mary about my visit to Madelaine. It would remain part of my own life.

I assumed that Mary and I would have another year

together in the flat though I realised that the Salvation Army sends officers to do social work elsewhere. If so, we would meet sometimes and holiday together. What I did not know was that all our plans for the future would be destroyed by a piece of paper.

I found Mary fully recovered and cheerful. "We must return by mid-September" she said. "But let's relax now and enjoy the rest of the holiday. No more study for you!"

Our last days passed very pleasantly and the weather changed and was hot. We swam daily, once in the evening, and even bathed on our very last day at the pension (September 12th). That day the sea was so smooth and we laughed as we frolicked and splashed each other. Mary was still laughing as we returned to the plage and she raced ahead of me to reach the pension. When we were nearing the pension la gerante appeared waving something white above her head and calling "Mademoiselle Mary! Un telegramme pour vous!"

Mary vanished into our room and I followed. I found her, still in her wet swimming suit, standing by her bed, her face ashen. She was clutching the telegram. She gave it to me.

Bewildered I stared at the words "Urgent Smith Douarnenez. Posting achieved satisfactorily. Embark T.S.S. Moreton Bay Sept 28 1926 for Melbourne. Return London immediately."

My heartbeat quickened as I looked into her eyes and saw a woman dominated by her religious beliefs but swayed also by love. I murmured "I'll make some tea, then we'll talk."

As we sipped our tea, Mary talked as she never had before. She told me how in childhood she had developed a devotion to Christ and how, as an adult, she had the desire to do His work in the Salvation Army in Australia and had applied to be posted there. Nevertheless she had been very happy in London, particularly after she had met John, a visiting Australian Salvationist whom she hoped to marry. After he returned to Melbourne she had badgered Headquarters for a posting there but now that it had come she was beginning to have doubts. "Oh Ann" she cried "I never thought of what I would be leaving behind. I shall probably never come back to England, my relatives or you. John and I won't have enough money. Once in Australia the "Tyranny of Distance" will keep me permanently there. Yet, it's God's will!"

I too was saddened at the thought of perhaps never seeing her again and I put my arm around her and drew her close to me. Mary closed her eyes for a few moments and murmured "Father, if it be Thy will, let this cup pass from me."

We sat together through the long afternoon until Mary, exhausted, slept on my shoulder. It was then that I felt keenly the pain of loneliness when I realised that soon I would be watching the liner sailing away with her. She stirred and I spoke to her. "There is no need to be so upset. You will have a great future in Australia. You have an ardent faith and you and John will be doing God's work there. You will rejoice in marriage. Then there will be letters. I'll write about my studies and my prospects and you'll tell me all about your work and the winsome ways of your first baby." Mary smiled a little. "I know, Ann, but it's hard to part from people. It will be sunny in Australia but I shall miss the cat by the hearth and the young friend who brought me tea."

Tears trickled down her cheeks. I wiped them away and wished I could do more for her but deep within me was my own pain. We were just beginning to know each other when fate intervened to separate us. So we sat on until dusk descended and we were summoned to dinner.

We were both very quiet during the meal but when we had finished Mary whispered "I'd be happier if we could sing together." She took my arm and led me to the empty lounge where there was an old and mellow cottage piano with candles in its sconces. We lit them and Mary seated herself. We sang "Guide Me, O Thou Great Jehovah." Then Mary said "Let's sing a little more." Mary had a sweet voice and so we continued with our favourite hymns. Then we sat and talked for a while. "I'll miss you Mary" I said "and will think of you often."

"I'll pray for you Ann. It's the distance that's intimidating. 13000 miles from England!" She stifled a yawn.

"Go to bed and get some sleep Mary. We've a long journey ahead tomorrow. I'll come later. I'd like to go up to the Tower Room one last time." We said "Goodnight" and I moved towards the stairs leading to the Tower Room. They were steep but the effort rewarding. The Tower Room was circular with wide views over the sea. The ideal place in which to be alone to think. I felt as though my feelings were being pulled in opposite directions. Mary was going away and that was very hard. Yet I had to leave Brittany. I thought of Madelaine who had aroused such strong desires in me to stay that the thought of leaving the country saddened me almost as much as losing Mary. Yet the words of Gwyneth came once more into my mind. "You are destined soon to have a great adventure." What adventure could there possibly be in losing my friend and leaving Brittany?

I went over to the window and gazed for a long time at the Bay of Douarnenez. There was a full moon and the sea had not even a ripple on its surface. It was mirror calm.

I returned to our bedroom and found Mary fast asleep. It was 9.30, the house was quiet and the golden yellow moonlight was beginning to touch our room. I thought of the moon shining brightly over the Bay and as it was so hot I suddenly decided to go for a swim. Then I remembered the curé's words "This will be the great crossroads of your life."

I had the feeling that something or someone was pulling at me mentally and I recalled a friendly Gaelic saying, "The sea says 'come and visit me! Come to my bosom now!'" Some great force beyond me was beginning to compel me to go and bathe at night in the sea alone. I have no fear and it is no sudden impulse. During our weeks of swimming I have learned the position of every hollow, every rock in the sea nearby and I long for the bodily freedom of the waves. I murmur "Let me do the right thing now, Lord."

I looked at Mary slumbering peacefully. I did not want her to be worried about me so I found a piece of paper and wrote "9.30 pm – gone for a dip in the sea. Be back in about thirty minutes. Don't worry. Ann." I put the note by her bedside.

Again the curé's words came back to me. "This will be the great crossroads of your life."

I am nearly at the end of my journal entries. The night candle flame is burning low and I must stop writing before it is completely dark. When next I take up my journal I shall be writing a new chapter in my life. Yet for my last entry before I get up to go for my swim (as if she were by my side speaking to me) I add the final word, the name of the aunt who taught me I must act and live – alone – "Gwyneth."

... ...

There was only a tiny click as Ann locked the journal away. Her feet made no sound on the outside stairs and she moved quietly on until she reached the shore path. The moon bathed the Maritime Pines in a soft light and the only sound was the gentle lapping of the waves on the shore. On the shingle bank she stopped and looked around. From Douarnenez came a yellow glow and a lighthouse winked a stern warning. The moon cast a bright track over the sea and on the far side of the Bay white cottages reflected the light. The beauty of the evening enclosed her and she felt completely at one with this lovely land. Would she return she wondered? A feeling of sadness came over her at the thought that she might not.

Opposite was the islet, shaped like a toad, and halfway between it and the water's edge a gleaming object broke the surface of the sea. The Rock of Calvary! They had always obeyed Yves' warning and never bathed to the west of it. Ann knew that at this time of night the tide at the Rock would not have risen far and might only be up to her elbows. She felt she must wade out to it and felt a shiver of excitement at this solitary adventure.

Everything that night seemed in perfect harmony, even the huge bulbous face of the great boulder on the shore that towered over her as she crossed the beach.

Contented and happy she flung her towel and shoes onto a ledge and barefoot made her way slowly to the sea over the soft, cold sand. She shivered a little as a slight breeze arose but then was overcome by the deep urge to enter those dim, mysterious waters. She touched the silver cross on her breast, feeling its smoothness and the Ogam letters incised on the edges, then boldly dipped her toes in the surf and waded into the sea. She gasped with pleasure as she plunged into the water which surged over her shoulders.

She looked back. The massive face on the shore seemed to be watching her. From Douarnenez came the faint clip-clop of hooves and the rattle of trap wheels. All else was calm. She waded out further and the Rock that was her objective drew closer. She quivered with excitement but an inner, warning voice said "I had better not go far. Only just to the Rock and back." The cold water was, inch by inch, creeping possessively up her body. She smelled sea wrack strongly and the islet was nearer. On that eastern side of the Rock the currents were swirling and Ann had to step cautiously to keep her balance. Her heart beat faster. Should she retreat now when she was so close to the Rock? No! She would not let fear master her.

The Rock of Calvary was a great magnet. Ann stretched out her right arm which glistened like marble and touched the Rock and felt its firmness. She rested, panting for breath, overcome by wonder. Now she had the impression that eyes were looking at her from the Rock while at the same moment she heard the beat of oars. That would be Yves coming in on the flood tide.

Ann felt a strange drowsiness coming over her and

almost sleepily she looked at the western side of the Rock. She must go there! Holding on to the Rock itself she slowly waded round though the water grew deeper until it was almost shoulder high. Everything now appeared to be bathed in a brilliant light. Her ears tingled and she heard a voice call out "Come here!" Bells were ringing; a harp was playing!

That was all Ann could hear now. Her senses no longer responded to any external sounds – the splash of oars pulling desperately the voice shouting in Breton "Come back! Come back!" The clatter of hooves and a woman's screams. All was silence as she felt herself being sucked down into a great darkness and with that darkness came an overwhelming loneliness.

AD 495

PART 1

THE FISHERFOLK AND THE PLOU

CHAPTER 1

It was twilight when Jahaan The Fisherman reached his secret harbour. He was a fair haired, powerful young man, clad in a wolfskin and with eyes that had the look of those who gaze constantly over wide seas.

It was calm with no boats in sight. Round the cliffs, near his harbour, was a labyrinth of rocks jutting up like fangs from the waves and the unceasing swirls of water warning of reefs below. Above this deadly shoreline was an intricate pattern of natural Leading Marks which only Norah and he could interpret. No one could approach his landing place or even get into the ravine where they lived. He and his grandmother were secure from foes. From the sea even the keenest observer could discern only a high, bare cliff towering up into the sky, the perilous waters at its base.

Jahaan collected his fish hooks and the boat lantern for which he had come and was about to leave when his attention was drawn to what looked like a long object lying on a nearby rock ledge. He walked over. His bare feet made no sound as he approached but abruptly he halted and became motionless as the rock itself while his huge hand slid down to the knife in the girdle round his waist. After some moments he called out in the Breton tongue.

"Norah!"

A figure appeared in the narrow fissure through the cliff. It was swathed from head to ankles in a brown cloak, the feet bare.

"Merch!" he explained.

"A woman? A dead woman?"

"Come!"

Sure footed as the man, his grandmother joined him and cautiously they approached the body. They stared wide-eyed at this intruder. It was incomprehensible to them. How had she come there? The limbs were bare, the body clad in blue cloth. It was now dark but the moon, hitherto obscured by clouds, suddenly shone onto the woman's neck. There was the gleam of metal. Norah whispered "hold your lamp closer to her head." The flickering light barely showed the white face of a young woman. The eyes were closed and her dark hair was spread out on the rock.

"That's a silver cross on her neck" cried Norah. "She may be a Kristion!" She slowly made the sign of the cross and looked up to the stars above as if asking God for help. Then she crouched down and placed her hand on the woman's breast. For minutes she stayed thus her lips trembling. Suddenly she cried "Holy Virgin! Her heart's beating! We must take her to warmth – to our hut!" A dark look clouded the man's features yet he spoke in perplexity rather than anger. "Someone from There may notice that the body's gone and thus know that we live in the ravine." "I doubt it!" Norah spoke vigorously. "Ys people don't even have a harbour. I think it was a rogue wave that left her there. Anyway, if she dies on our hands we can at least give the poor woman Kristion burial by our hut." "I'll get the litter" said Jahaan and silently they carried her to their home several hundred paces through the fissure and into the ravine. As they left Jahaan glanced back but there were no craft on the sea.

The roof gave out a wisp of smoke. "Build a good fire!" ordered Norah as she made up a bed of heather and straw. "I don't like the chill in those limbs. She may have been in the sea a long time. We had best strip her and wrap her in a blanket. Hold her up." As Jahaan held the naked torso against him, Norah quickly pulled off the brief garment and wrapped a blanket quickly round her. They laid the form in front of the fire. Norah took a wooden cross from the wall and held it over the woman. She said loudly, "Lord! Let Thy servant be healed and made whole again!"

Norah poured hot water over some herb leaves and held the vessel to the woman's lips, raising her head as she did so. The liquid moistened the lips but did not enter the woman's mouth. Norah shook her head, "A bad sign" she said. Then she put heated stones in the bed and added blankets. The woman was still breathing but almost imperceptibly. Was she sinking into that sleep, familiar in Norah's experience, from which there is no awakening?

Only the glow from the fire and the tiny rushlight flame lit up Norah's furrowed brow. She waited to succour this unknown life. Jahaan settled himself by the door, a spear close to hand, a grave look on his face. Norah threw dried plants on the fire. Smoke emerged and she muttered incantations. "Let the healing vapours from the sacred herbs drive away the evil ones of the night." It was a long night watch. Norah stirred only to mend a rushlight. Jahaan gazed at the figure on the palliasse then at their fragile door. In his mind lurked the dread that their unknown guest might be a woman from the sea and that the monster Sea God would rend that feeble barrier apart and claim his own. Yet when he looked at that still face on which rested the shadow of the great wooden cross suspended from the roof, compassion for this woman welled up in his heart. There was a calm about her features though it might be that of coming death.

As Norah crouched by the palliasse her unwinking gaze on the woman, her thoughts were sombre. She recalled a vigil held for a Kristion woman. They had encircled the sheeted corpse, said prayers, chanted hymns for the dead. Jahaan had got up on to his feet and was staring at the stars. Norah joined him. "It's midnight!" she said. "The tide's almost on the ebb."

"Then we'll know if the woman is to live?"

"Then we'll know if she will live, or die with the ebbing tide." Norah's eyes sought some message in his. He whispered almost inaudibly "We know nothing of her except that her hands show no callouses and she has never walked barefoot. She is different from our women. I have never heard of her in That City when I have been there." He frowned.

"We must find out! Would that Guenole were here! I feel certain that he could bring her to life. I have only my herbs and my prayers. God help her!" She resumed her close observation of the pale countenance. Day was almost night and still Norah watched. Unexpectedly a gentle sigh escaped the woman's lips, her eyelids fluttered and her eyes opened. Norah clasped her hands together and looked up at the cross. "Jahaan" she called "Praise be to God. She lives! She lives!"

... ...

Time passed slowly until at last a speck of light appeared in the darkness. The light gradually grew stronger and the face of an old woman emerged from the gloom. The woman spoke but the young woman did not understand what was said. It was the gestures that told her to drink. Her lips were moistened by the liquid in the vessel held to her mouth and she took a few small sips. The woman smiled approvingly. As she was drinking the young woman felt the warmth of a powerful hand against her back. It was a man holding her up to drink. Her head fell forward in her weakness and as weariness overwhelmed her she thought she was slipping back into the darkness. The pitying voice of the old woman came to her. "She's exhausted Jahaan, but she will recover. Then she'll be able to tell us all about herself."

The young woman could not understand what these people were saying but as the darkness cleared she was aware that she could interpret their gestures. Yes, she would drink again. The bitter tasting draught was healing her. The woman now pointed to her own lips, closed them, then placed her finger there. The young woman knew what the gesture meant! She must not try to speak yet. "Lie still!" those old eyes commanded. Nor could she move in her exhaustion so she lay as though chained to this bed that emitted the fragrance of leaves and wood smoke.

Hitherto, the man had been silent. Now he said in his own strange language, "Who are you?" The woman interposed.

"She's not fit for questions yet. We must tell her our own names before she tells us who she is. Let her lie there in peace." She took the young woman's hand in hers and placed it within the bosom of her own dress pressing it against her. The stranger felt warmth creeping into her fingers as the old woman exclaimed "Safe! You're safe with us! We'll look after you!" The stranger understood. The old woman pointed with her free hand to herself, "Norah! Norah!" she cried. She stabbed with her fingers at the man. "Jahaan!" Tears welled up into the young woman's eyes and she sobbed. Norah took her into her arms to comfort her then she repeated her own name and the man's over and over again, pronouncing the syllables carefully. The young woman was beginning to realise the great affection Norah was showing her. Yet there was a deep terror in her mind now that she understood her own position. She did not know who she was and she had forgotten her own language! She did not know theirs! She could not reply to them. All she now knew were that lips were imprinting kisses on her brow and that the old woman's wrinkled face was giving out reassurance. These people would not harm her she thought, as she fell into a deep sleep.

When she awoke darkness had gone and beams of sunshine were penetrating the hut. Thrushes were singing joyously and Norah was pottering in and out of the hut muttering and humming to herself. Then she turned and saw her patient trying to raise herself. She pointed to a brown shift, smiled, and said "I am going to dress you in that if we can get you up. It's only a simple garment but it's better than nothing and that unusual dress you were wearing is not really suitable. But what is important to me is your cross. It is finely wrought. Perhaps it can tell us something of your past if it awakens an echo in your memory?"

The young woman shook her head. There was a blank, tired expression in her eyes. A shadow of doubt flickered across Norah's face and for an instant her eyes grew hard. Yet she would not give up easily and now she pointed to the cross in the hut centre. On it was a sculpture, a naked man hanging by his hands from the cross-trees.

"Do you not see the likeness to your own cross? It's almost the same as yours?" Again that baffled shaking of the head. "Well, well, we'll find out all in time. Let me dress you." Norah pulled back the blanket to reveal the young woman's bare torso. She was about to hold her up so that she could slip the shift over her head, when suddenly her attention was riveted to the young woman's body. She had a normal figure but below her left breast were four moles, well spaced and set in the shape of a cross. In their centre was a third breast and nipple! Norah drew back in astonishment but made no comment, although tears rose in her eyes. She bent her head in reverence as she said to herself "Oh God, what a gift you have sent us from the sea!" She went and knelt down before the cross, her eyes fast closed and hands raised in prayer. "Dear loving God! Once you gave us Guen whose triple breasts did suckle saints, even Guenole himself. In your wisdom you have given us this woman to succour, cherish and nurture. If it is Thy Will, she will be a Kristion. Then we will wed her! Her womb will bear good men whom she'll nourish at those three breasts for Thy glory!"

"Norah!" whispered the young woman.

"Ah!" exclaimed Norah smiling "So you can speak after all, even if you can't say the name in the way we do. I recognised it. What a blessing is language! Let's dress you now and then you can get up. Take it slowly."

Helped by Norah, the young woman sat up and the old shift was slipped over her head. She moved to the edge of the bed. Her bare white feet touched the floor and she wriggled her toes in the ash before staggering up onto her feet. She was led to the door and here she breathed deeply of the fresh air before sitting down on a log seat. She could see Jahaan standing by a great oak with a fish creel. Norah left her and hurried towards Jahaan. They whispered together. "I've seen nothing at all" said Jahaan "no boats, no footprints by the marsh. They could not have brought her in that way. How is she?"

"She's better and much brighter, Jahaan. She soon picked up my name and can speak it, though with a different accent. It's difficult to follow. I wonder if she is a Kristion. When I showed her the silver cross she made no response to it."

"We can be sure of nothing. What do you think of it all?"

"I believe that she has lost her memory. It must be very frightening for her not to know where she is or who she is."

His eyes darkened and he pressed his lips together like a man pondering a riddle. "We must find out who she is for our own safety as well as hers. Who are her kin? Was she shipwrecked? The only explanation I can see why she was on the rock ledge. Guenole will make his usual visit to us in about two moons' time, perhaps less. I hope we will see him soon." He shrugged his shoulders. "Meanwhile, we must try and get some information from her. She should learn our language quickly. Let's eat now."

That first meal with them was an ordeal for the young woman though she instinctively felt that their hospitality was generous. Norah pulled out the breadcake from the ashes and took the fish from where it had been broiling. She broke the bread into three portions. Jahaan skilfully stripped the fish flesh from the bones and gave their guest the largest piece. Norah said grace. Then they all ate with a good appetite.

Jahaan was next to the young woman. He noticed her appearance. The small, neat feet, the plump cheeks and the full bosom. She glanced timidly at him realizing the power in his arms when he moved a huge log for her to sit down. The fish was good and she munched hungrily at it and her warm crust. Jahaan held the water pot of spring water to her lips and she drank from it thirstily, looking up into his eyes. He talked although she understood nothing. Then he said Norah's name and she smiled. She repeated the name and smiled again. She seemed encouraged by the great strength flowing from him. Then he said his own name – Jahaan – and she repeated it trying to copy his pronunciation yet still using that strange accent of hers.

Jahaan stretched out his arm, pointing at her. She did not quite understand what he wanted.

"What is your name?"

His meaning suddenly burst upon her. The man and woman were both watching her intently. Norah also pointed to her and asked the same question. "What is your name? Tell us if you can remember it!"

What happened now was unforeseen. The woman gave a great shudder and a wave of anguish distorted her features. The eyes dilated. The lips gaped wide and the tongue flickered sinuously in and out. She gave a sigh and sweat drops glistened on her brow. Then sounds, like a death rattle, burst explosively from her.

Norah, taken aback, shrank away as the rattle was thrice repeated. Yet, tough and fearless, she would not be defeated but came close and grasped the young woman's hands in hers while looking for some clue in those pain filled eyes.

"Don't be frightened. You are with friends. You are trying to tell me your name. What is your name?"

"A – N – A!"

Worn out by her efforts she sank back into Norah's arms. "Ana!" cried Norah. "Now we know your name and it is indeed a mighty bond between us. It is a good name – the name of the Virgin's mother. Why, you could even be a Kristion! Praise be to God who sent us Ana from the sea to help and cherish!"

From that moment of revelation onwards, Norah and Jahaan began a new relationship with Ana. It was a period of growing acceptance of her. She, who bore such a holy name, became a warm-hearted human being to them, not an unknown from the sea. They were never to know anything more about her past life from her lips except that one word, but her name was enough to dissolve any barrier that might have developed between them.

So they used her name often. They would call out "Ana" and she would hurry to them with a smile. Moreover, she had a very good ear, and rapidly began to recognise the sounds of their speech.

Ana was indeed a willing young woman but there were so many things in their life to learn the hard way. Her thighs ached at night from hours of squatting over the quern, and her back ached from the backwards and forwards rhythm as she ground the grain. Norah taught her how to carry heavy loads on her head in a basket and to sing a Breton chant at work. Yet no singing or work could rid her of the crushing burden of amnesia that was so hard to bear. Sometimes the flour in the quern would be moistened by her tears as she wondered "Who am I, woman without a past? Where is the home I have lost, the family I have forgotten? What strange chance has flung me upon these rocky shores?" She was grateful to Jahaan and Norah for having saved her but she longed for a glimpse of her past.

Ana knew that for her security she was not left alone. Norah told her of certain perils in their life. In the woods there were wolves and sometimes the more dangerous wild boar. She now knew there were no other people in the ravine nor could strangers ever penetrate into their fastness so guarded was it by nature. At one end was the only outlet to the sea hazardous with its rocks. At the opposite end of the ravine was the great marsh. Once Norah took Ana to it. She showed her the waters, in places of a sinister slimy green and told her of the treacherous bogs that lay in wait for the unwary. "There is a route across it" she said, "but only four people know that secret pathway. No one else can cross it without us as guides. They would perish in minutes." Ana shuddered.

She had excellent hearing and once overheard them talking when they were away from the hut. She caught fragments of conversation. "She will have to go to the plou as soon as possible ... Jahaan, I've caught her weeping when she is alone. It must be so hard for her." The voice became gentler ... "Jahaan, she's such a pleasant person that I feel almost as if she were my own daughter" ... "We can only make a decision when he comes and tells us what to do."

The long days came and went. Ana knew a tension was building up in her two companions. It was because they were expecting a certain "he" to come to them and help them. They were uncertain about something but always pleasant to her. Meantime, they all just waited and went on with their ordinary lives. She did not know that it was her future that mattered so much to them.

Once when she and Ana were alone together, Norah spoke of Guen. "She was of noble birth, also called Teirbron for her three breasts with which she suckled her children. Guenole, her noblest son is a saint whose work today will overcome the triple-headed pagan gods! Blessed was Guen and blessed too is her son Guenole." She paused for a moment and sighed as she put her hand on Ana's shoulder. "I hope that you will soon meet Guenole." She glanced for a moment at Ana's bosom then they silently resumed their work.

With Jahaan Ana's relationship was otherwise than

with Norah. At that time he appeared to her to be a reticent man hardly speaking to her when they were alone together. She was more in his company soon for she had to help with the fish which she carried to the smoking huts for smoking or salting for the winter months.

One evening Norah told Ana to go to the harbour to carry back fish to the smoke huts. It was beginning to rain and there was a rumble of thunder in the distance but the fisherfolk were indifferent to such weather. She wore only a thin and ragged linen shift. When she reached the harbour she found that Jahaan, as usual, had placed her creel filled with silvery fish on a rocky ledge in the cliff which was at the height of her shoulders. This made it much easier for her to swing the creel onto her head. Meantime, in the fading light, Jahaan was busy packing another creel with fish for the next trip. They had no time to lose for if the fish were left unattended they would vanish in seconds into the maws of the voracious gulls. A black thunder cloud overhung the sea and lightning was flashing over the rocks.

Ana was about to swing her creel up onto her head when her attention was distracted by something far out at sea. On the horizon dark clouds were gathering and against this gloom there appeared a tiny sail. The vessel itself, hull down on the horizon, did not seem to be moving. She stood quite still engrossed as she looked into the distance. Suddenly she felt powerful hands gripping her shoulders like a vice and Jahaan cried brusquely, "my God, do you know that ship? Have you seen her before? Whence does she come?" She jerked herself out of that grip and swung round, half facing him so that he felt the power of her sideways look. Her face was white with an anger and reproach in it that he had never noticed in her before.

"Jahaan, Jahaan, I swear to you by all that is sacred to you that I know nothing of that vessel! All I know is that I owe my life to you and Norah!" With both hands she clasped her left breast. "My heart beats in my bosom today, Jahaan, only because you two rescued me and carried me to your hut! You saved me! Why should you ever doubt me? Why should you harbour suspicions of me? I don't know where I came from. I wish I knew! That's all I can say to you!" She bent her head low for a moment to try and hide her tears then she tossed the creel onto her head and turned to go. Suddenly there was a great clap of thunder and rain, unheeded by both of them, fell down in torrents, soaking Ana's light shift until it clung to the contours of her body. There was a great flash of lightning and Jahaan saw this womanly figure as never before. The high round breasts, the curve of the full hips and the dignity as she walked away, swaying from side to side, yet holding herself upright like a queen. Her small, bare feet made deep imprints in the wet mud of the path.

Jahaan frowned and muttered to himself. "I'm a fool! Of course I believe her. Why did I speak so harshly to the maid? I must always remember what she has been through and be more patient with her. It is hard for her knowing nothing of her past. What will her future be? What will it be?"

It would be a mystery to him and Norah and Ana.

Until the coming of Guenole himself.

CHAPTER 2

"Who is it? Who could it possibly be in our quiet ravine?" she wondered. Ana sat back on her haunches glad of a break from her toil at the quern. She rubbed the flour dust from her eyes and listened intently. It could not be Norah hard at work inside their hut. Jahaan had gone down to the harbour but would return shortly. Who is it? A stranger?

Then suddenly singing came to her ears. "*Quoniam tu es que extravisti me de ventre* ... Thou art he that took me out of the womb." The joyful sounds echoed from the rocks and rang through the trees.

He appeared.

She rubbed her eyes again and looked.

The newcomer was a thin, tall, broad-shouldered man. A crude tonsure showed up amidst his wild grey hair and he carried himself with dignity. He wore a goatskin cincture and a cross depended from his neck. In his hand he carried an ash stick. Ana thought "How can he defend himself against wild animals?" he looked keenly about him as he strode. Norah emerging from the hut ran up to him and Jahaan, hurrying, joined her. They knelt down before him, Norah bending very low and touching the ground with her forehead. The man raised her up. "Peace be unto you and to your household. Kristos gives blessings to you and all who dwell with you! And who is this young woman so busy at her quern? I did not know you had a stranger living with you."

"We will tell you later, Father. But first let me wash your feet. Then you can speak with her."

Ana bent once more over her quern. Intuitively she knew that Jahaan and Norah wished to be alone with Guenole for it was He. They talked a while in low voices so that she caught no word. Then alone he came up to her. She stopped grinding but still knelt, her meal-whitened hands clasped together. He gazed at her for a few moments then held out his hand and raised her to her feet. He took a pinch of the flour which he sifted with his fingers as if to test its quality. Yet she detected a deeper purpose behind the action. He would sift through the secrets of her life and find out who she was! ... He straightened up and looked her full in the face.

His eyes! Against his brown cheeks they were as blue as the deep of the sea. Young as she was she saw the power in them. The tremendous strength of a leader who led men not by weapons but by spiritual strength. He was a man who struggled against evil and had overcome devils and demons. His keen gaze pierced right through her body, her mind, her soul as if he read every thought, every impulse of her heart. It was a power that was beyond himself, and she felt that Guenole would give his own life for what he believed to be the truth. Yet, though that gaze was so penetrating it was the look of one who had a warm love for humanity. He smiled encouragingly at her, accepting her, but his gaze never left her face for an instant. "It's hard work grinding corn but you have some fine flour there."

"I do my best" said Ana "but I'm not yet very used to this labour. My fingers are clumsy compared to

Norah's." With a rueful smile she raised her palm upwards.

"We Bretons" he said pointing to her, to Norah and back to himself, the gesture meaning that he was bringing her into his own sphere, "We Bretons" he repeated "all have to work hard to get our food whether it comes from land or sea. It never comes without great effort but still we say, rejoicing at every sunrise, "Give us today our daily bread!" How tender his smile was! He took her right hand in his clasping it firmly. Meantime Norah had come up with Ana's former possessions. The small blue garment, the cap, the silver cross. What did they mean to him?

"They have told me that you remember your name – Ana?"

"Yes, that's my name."

"Apart from your name you say you have no memory of your past life. I mean your life before Jahaan and Norah rescued you." Ana began to cry bitterly but she felt his hand clasping hers reassuringly.

"Nay, nay, do not weep! I realise how sad it is for you that you cannot remember your past life. Give thanks to God that you were washed up by the sea so close to the dwelling of Jahaan and Norah. It saved you from slavery or death."

Guenole spoke to her in clear Breton so that she could follow almost every word. Sometimes Latin slipped its way in. Her keen intelligence could often interpret these interpolations though she could not translate them word for word. Guenole took up only the silver cross. Ana comprehended that the cross would be a test for her that was also a challenge. He gazed at it intently, his brow furrowed. He held it up looking at it from different angles. The sun was reflected back brilliantly from the polished silver. He even placed it edge on to examine the incised edges.

"Do you notice that this metal object is like the one I am wearing?"

"Yes. I can see that the shapes are similar."

"Do you know what is the true meaning of that shape? Of what event it is a symbol?" He gazed intently into her eyes. Puzzled, she shook her head.

"Are you sure that you don't know the meaning of the cross? Think carefully. Have you the slightest recollection of something connected with it?"

"None at all."

He sighed. "Ana, I believe you. Sometimes ignorance is better than false knowledge. Whoever you may be I must tell you the meaning of that symbol, the cross. It was once the worst death that men inflicted on others. The Romans made it punishment for slaves. They nailed them naked to a cross then hanged them up to die. Yet one man whom they crucified was the Son of God. His cross of pain, Ana, has become the emblem of hope to all who are Kristion – who follow Kristos – for he rose again from the dead. I do not know where you were before you came here but you might perhaps have had some contact with someone who was Kristion. So think of Kristos who was crucified almost five centuries ago. His power is everywhere." Guenole fingered the cross delicately poring over the tiny scratches. Then he nodded. "See, that's the Ogam script on your cross – those lines cut into the chamfer of the long upright. The word engraved there is 'Kristos'." Slowly he made a movement with his right hand up and down and across his bare chest to reproduce the shape of the cross.

"Are you satisfied with your life here Ana?"

She hesitated before replying. His scrutiny of her was searching. "Yes, I'm so glad I am here. Jahaan and Norah have been very good to me."

"You will not stay here all your life. In the land beyond this ravine there is a settlement – a plou - and a church of the Kristion. We shall baptise you and so you will become a Kristion. Also you're a young woman and must marry. We will find a husband for you and you will bear his children."

Ana's cheeks reddened. Was there compulsion in his words? Whom must she marry? "I'll do whatever you think is right for me" she said. "You understand that I'm still distressed by my loss of memory."

"I'll talk to Jahaan and Norah about your future. One thing more. Norah tells me that you bear the mark of the cross on your body. I feel sure that God destined you to be a Kristion."

"Where is your own home, sir?" Ana asked. Guenole looked up at the blue sky. "Home? Apart from a hut I've no home. If benighted a cavity in the bole of an oak or a rock overhang suffices for shelter. I was called to work among all Bretons whether coastal fisherman or forest dwellers. I love this land and the people who dwell in it. My task is to bring to them the message of Kristos the Redeemer. I've always, too, a warm feeling for homeless strangers who come here. For people like yourself!" His smile was comforting as the embers in the hut. He left her to talk to the others. She could only surmise what was being said though she knew her future fate was being weighed in the balance. The discussion was lengthy.

Guenole set the tone. "I have thought deeply over

this matter. I am convinced that Ana is neither a ghost nor a dead person who has come back to life – only Lazarus or Kristos could do that. I believe that she is some unfortunate woman who either fell overboard from a ship or whom some rogue attempted to kill by drowning. The strange clothing? I do not know. Yet I cannot understand, if she's a pagan, why she has a cross. In spite of her apparent inability to recognise it, I feel it may be her own. Some people may think she is a Woman from the Sea. Never listen to such nonsense! She is a healthy young woman. She will marry and have children."

Norah spoke. "I've grown so frightened. I couldn't even tell her why. Suppose that her kin, if she has kin, get to know that she is here and come to snatch her from our keeping?"

Guenole raised his hand protesting "It won't happen! After all you have the best claim on Ana. You saved her life! Who's going to drown himself in the marsh to reach her? She's safe here! If she goes to the plou, even as a stranger, she will be under the protection of the chief and his brave warriors. Moreover, the Church will look after a baptised woman."

The voices grew softer ... the watching woman heard fragments of speech. Guenole was insistent. "Innocent ... a blow to the head ... she must go to the plou ... to the church ... the cross on her bosom ... we must respect it." The talk continued even more quietly. "You'll have to tell her who we are and why we've settled here" said Guenole. "Tell her, too, about Ys and your relationship to that city. Norah, you do the talking. When you go through the marsh you'll have to guide her. Later on tell her the secret of the pathway."

The discussion was over. Ana saw Norah and Jahaan were kneeling before Guenole. He held out his cross to them. Their eyes were closed, they were grasping the cross and they were repeating words after Guenole. She did not understand what they were saying.

"Ana!" Guenole spoke quietly as he beckoned her. His eyes were welcoming. The other two were smiling, holding out their hands to her. All doubts had gone. She felt confidence come to her. She was trembling, not with fear, but with joy for the suspense was over for them as well as for herself. Guenole, this great religious leader, had exorcised those unknown spectres, those evil ones who had flung her on the Armorican shore.

Ana came slowly toward them, her eyes cast down, meekly as a suppliant, her hands clasped together in front of her. She would have knelt but Guenole took both her hands and held them straight out before her so that Norah and Jahaan could grasp them in their own warm palms. "Now" he said "Norah and Jahaan have each sworn solemnly by this cross that they will protect and defend you Ana. They will nourish you as one of their own family, they will consider you from this moment on as one of their own kin." "We have sworn this oath" they both declared gravely. "We will give our lives for her if need be."

Relaxed and happy they sat down to their simple meal which Guenole blessed. He could not stay much longer for he had to return to the little community of monks that he was founding by a distant river. He broke the bread for them, keeping the smallest piece for himself and took the tiniest fish. When they had finished, they all three knelt down before him and he placed his hands over them in benediction. Then, accompanied by Jahaan, he set off on the path that led to the marshes. Ana stood with Norah's arm round her while they watched the saint walking through the trees. Once he turned and waved to them with his stick and made the sign of the cross. Then suddenly he was out of sight.

CHAPTER 3

"It is a long story" said Norah "and it concerns the life of women here in this land, my own life, and that of others close to me."

It was evening and Norah and Ana were alone together.

"My people have not always been in Armorica. When the Romans left Britannia there was then conflict with the Saxons and others. A few people from South West Britannia came to see this Armorica land the other side of the Channel. They liked it and settled. Others followed, mostly crofters used both to fishing and farming. I was just a child and I travelled with my kin. I'll never forget that sea journey. There were two small ships and several curraghs filled with many people. In mid-Channel we ran into bad weather and lost two curraghs. Those who were in them we shall see at the Great Awakening!" Norah wiped away the tears, sighed and went on. "Let me tell you more about my people. We were close-knit groups all speaking Breton. We lived together in settlements each of which was a parish (plou) with its own little church. I love our church, simple as it is." Her eyes grew bright with happy memories. "Even as a young girl I used to creep alone to the church and pray. I prayed that God would give me children. I grew up rapidly and was soon given in marriage to a man of adventure. He had, alone, at terrible risk discovered this almost inaccessible ravine. On our wedding night

I got myself with child. The baby was Jahaan's father. Other children followed. I had a large family."

Norah suddenly put her arm round Ana's shoulders and glanced into the young woman's eyes with a look of kindness and love. "From the moment we rescued you" she whispered "I asked God to give me the wisdom to help you in your life. You have good health. I believe it is God's will that you will marry and, like myself, bear children."

So pleasantly did Norah speak that Ana felt only a slight infringement of her own natural reticence. She knew she had to learn a social code strange to her. A nubile female was "given" in marriage. Was there no more personal choice possible? As if she had said enough on marriage Norah changed the subject.

"Beyond our plou we had problems like everyone else. There were the Franks and the fear of coast raids by Sea Wolves. Then there could be the menace of the Bagaudae, bands of lawless men, who sometimes attacked settlements to rob them of food and women to sell as slaves. Yet all might have been well but for that accursed city!" For moments she was distant from Ana, lost in the bitterness of her memories.

"Perhaps it had to happen! My first born grew to manhood and became an excellent worker in both stone and wood. One day while selecting trees he met a man in long robes embroidered with double dolphins, the insignia of Ys, who spoke to him in Breton. Ys is a fortified pagan city on the coast and, once prosperous, it had declined over the years. This official, after talking with my son, invited him, and others who were willing, to come to Ys and help restore buildings which had fallen into disrepair. Since they were

Kristions he said they could build a small church for themselves but they must not visit the temple of Ys. It was a tempting offer and a number of young men accepted. My son and one of his friends were betrothed so they married and their wives accompanied them to Ys where they settled.

Time passed. The two wives became pregnant. The men repaired houses. They were prosperous. But the official had not told them that the people of Ys, xenophobic, were cruel and as unstable as their dwellings. Suddenly the marsh fever erupted. The populace attributed this to the Kristion foreigners. There was a riot which the authorities ignored. The mob killed all the men. Of their wives, both in travail that day one, badly beaten, succeeded in expelling a baby before she died. No one knows the fate of the child. My son's wife, dying, gave birth in the woods. A passing Breton found the baby and brought it here. We named it Jahaan." She wept for some moments.

"We sent messengers to seek restitution. The rulers expressed regret but said the deaths were accidental. They explained their future policy. Henceforth they would not permit settlement by strangers in Ys. People might visit the city but unless given special permission would have to leave before sunset under pain of death. Guenole, alone of the Breton clerics, has visited Ys and spoken with Gradlon their King. Even the heathen priests dare not lay a finger on Guenole. Years ago when my husband died, Jahaan and I came to this ravine to live. It is isolated but quiet and healthy and the fishing is good. It is true it is close to Ys but we are safe. Sometimes Jahaan will go with fish to Ys but returns before sunset. No one has molested him." She pressed her arm around Ana. Her brow had lightened and she smiled.

"That's our story but there's something that I have not yet explained to you. When we found you lying unconscious we thought at first that you were from Ys, placed there to trap us if we removed your body. Common sense made us immediately change that view. The people of Ys are not now seafarers." Her lips curled in disdain. "Moreover you wore a cross – not a pagan symbol. With Guenole we believe you were a castaway, washed or pushed overboard from a ship. Perhaps a head blow caused your amnesia. You are safe with us. We'll protect you against all enemies and help you when we go to the plou."

Ana grew white, then red, then white again at Norah's words. Surprise, sorrow, gratitude overwhelmed her. This was the secret that she had unconsciously penetrated when they found her lying so helpless on the rock. Notwithstanding their doubts they had accepted her, had taken her right into their home to revive her and had made her one of their family. They would defend her with their lives if need be!

Mingled with her deep feelings was also the effect of the tragedy unfolded in Norah's story. The murder of Jahaan's father and the other men reflected the bitter if dormant conflict in Armorica. On the one side the Breton Kristion totally opposed to pagan faiths. On the other, their implacable heathen enemy, enmeshed in an ineluctable struggle for existence and to maintain a heathen religion intact.

Where did she stand in this dark conflict between two religions? One fact was clear to Ana. She could not remain aloof. Her future life – or death – would be linked up closely with the kindly pair who had befriended her.

Norah went on speaking. "You'll appreciate that now Kristion and heathen cannot live together in Ys it is becoming cut off from the real world. Closer to it swirl the flood tides of Kristion peoples. Soon it may only be an islet surrounded by Kristion. Then one day perhaps God's power will destroy that city and its heathen temple will be razed to the ground. The Cross is all-conquering! God forgive me, Ana, I shouldn't say bitter words. 'Vengeance is mine' saith the Lord. I don't wish harm to those suffering women and children in Ys only that they may give up their evil ways and pagan beliefs. God grant that this may be so! Look, the sun is sinking! Let's rest before we cross the marsh and go to the plou."

Ana rested little that night. The sleepless hours were spent in thinking about her own position. Of late she had felt closer to Jahaan. One evening he had brought her a honeycomb. He smiled broadly at her pleasure when he saw her eat it. She had also helped him. She found him once at the harbour with blood dripping from a knife cut in his arm. He shrugged his shoulders. "It's nothing!" he said as he grimaced with pain. Norah always insisted Ana must carry a strip of clean linen round her waist. She cut pieces off this, washed and staunched the wound with leaves, and bound it up. It soon healed.

That night she pondered deeply over what Guenole and Norah had said about marriage since she surmised that the matter might well be raised again when they went to the plou. She owed her life to Norah and Jahaan. Wasn't it her duty, wasn't it right to accept what they would propose for her? Yet there was a stubborn vein of independence in her which made her want to control her own life and make her own decisions.

Ana fell asleep at last, only to waken from a vivid dream of the perils of the marsh! Yet her faith in Jahaan and his ability to cope with the worst dangers in water was very great. She knew it was indeed a hazardous crossing. This great stretch of bog traversed by certain routes known only to four persons. At night the danger was even greater for then the Will o' the Wisp appeared. These were evanescent blue lights which flamed up here and there to baffle the senses of the unwary. They were goblins who dwelt in the marsh waters to confuse and entrap people to their doom. Some even said they were the souls of people who had lived wicked lives. For Ana the marsh was the gateway to the world outside. Another door to pass through in her life.

Dawn was breaking as they approached the marsh. The cliffs widened out to form a gigantic basin, the marsh, enclosed by precipices. They could see a lofty cliff opposite which was their aim.

To Ana's eyes the marsh offered a variegated landscape. There were stretches of vivid green on which grew the warning bog myrtle near treacherous ground. There were reed beds in the distance. Two humps of rock, well spaced from each other, were the only solid ground. It was a fearsome sight but Jahaan stepped out boldly onto the grassy stretch. Norah, agile for her years, guided Ana to the grass tufts to which she must jump.

After about an hour they arrived at the first rock and rested before the crossing of the great pools. They stripped, put their clothing into bags round their necks, and stepped into the shallow water following Jahaan exactly. They splashed onto the second rock and rested before the last and worst ordeal, the walk on rocky ledges concealed beneath the waters. Since the ledges were nearly invisible they had to feel their way, their feet interpreting every inequality, each crack on the surface of the rock beneath. Here Jahaan's memory, like Norah's, guided him with astonishing accuracy. So many paces along one ledge, a half turn to give another measured trudge through mud on the rock. Often the foul marsh gas bubbled beneath them. Twice Jahaan stopped completely to check his position by secret Leading Marks on the precipice opposite.

Ana was trembling with nervous strain when suddenly she felt herself lifted bodily up in Jahaan's strong arms and tossed over his shoulder. Thus, borne by him, she crossed the great pool. They clambered up, dried themselves, put on their clothes, and set out on the journey through the woods.

... ...

Deep in the great forest a massive boulder mounted guard over a footpath below its base. On its peak stood a watchman. Beyond, the trees receded to leave an open space and fields. On lush grass browsed cows, flanks branded with crosses. Boys yelled at striped swine hunting for acorns and sheep wandered lazily from one grazing to another. Through meadow and cornfield alike flowed a stream of limpid water.

At the edge of the wood axemen were hacking away at the limbs of a felled oak. In the near distance was a beehive chapel grey against the greening trees and surrounded by a garden where shaven headed men paced up and down, lips moving in prayer.

The major part of the buildings in the plou was within a perimeter fence of stout wooden stakes and a ditch. The little wooden huts crouched back behind this protection as if they feared an enemy. In the artisans' work huts blacksmiths toiled at the bundle of iron rods that their skill must convert into pattern-welded swords. Close by, a horse turned a big quern from which women carried away flour for bolting. In the centre of the plou was a square and its focus was a high wooden cross by which hung a bell. An old man standing by made low reverence to the cross. Close to the cross stood the villa. It was old but only the lower courses of brick had escaped devastation by fire though they were still smoke-blackened. On these courses had been built a new timber house which at the front took the form of an open gallery. From this gallery there was a broad view of the plou.

Within the gallery three people were silently looking at a fourth seated on a tripeccia. He had been talking to them. The tripeccia was on a floor mosaic depicting a child clasping a plump duck in his arms. The stranger on the three-legged stool had cast his bag carelessly on the mosaic to show his indifference to such pagan vestiges. His neat tonsure emphasized a high, dome-shaped head. There was authority in his gestures and in the gold pectoral cross he bore. One of three facing him was also a cleric but his robes were muddy and his red, curly hair crudely shorn. He stared at the newcomer. He was the priest of the plou and his speech, though polite, was forthright.

"Holy Father, our interpreter Claudia will translate as the woman is Breton speaking and does not understand Latin fluently. It seemed right a woman should be present. You will speak with her about the conhospitae!"

"I'll interpret not only the words but the sense" said Claudia. "You will find her a fine person and an excellent nurse to the sick. I commend her."

It was a voice as clear as a silver bell to the ears of the stranger priest opposite. He shifted uneasily on his stool. Some instinct warned him to be careful how he spoke to this lady. His voice rasped like a file on iron.

"You have altars on which you celebrate Mass?"

"*Non habemus aras* – we have no altars of stone or marble" growled the Breton cleric. "I've seen altars of polished marble in southern Gaul. Here, we kneel on the bare earth and that – that is our next altar." He pointed at the axemen struggling with the felled oak.

The other priest held up a white hand appeasingly. "I know. It doesn't matter to God whether his altars are marble or wood but I've come here to speak of a heresy that you must extirpate like a poisonous weed." He jerked out a document from his bag. "I carry this to all churches in Armorica as a warning." He glanced at the Latin. "It states that in certain churches, women – 'conhospitae'" – he spat out the word – "are actually assisting the priest at the Mass and even handling the chalice and administering the blood of Christ, for this purpose coming right up to the altars of God. If this is true it is an appalling state of affairs!"

"For our church here you're mistaken" riposted the redhead. "I've never even heard of this heresy! Our deaconess disrobes women for their baptism – that is proper. If you wish, speak to her about the conhospitae!" He called out in Breton. The deaconess came and knelt down for a moment at the feet of the stranger priest though her manner was not subservient. Through Claudia, as interpreter, the stranger interrogated her.

"Have you ever neared the table on which stands the bread and wine?"

"Of course! I take bread and wine to be blessed by the priest."

His brow darkened and his words were as quick as dagger thrusts. "Where is this table – altar – which you actually touched when you put the bread and wine there?"

"In our church – on the right. I'll show it to you if you wish! We women go there with food and drink so that they may be blessed. Then we carry them to the sick who are too ill to come to church. They find this such a wonderful consolation. I know, for I nurse them." She stared hard at the priest as if she found something repulsive in his manner. Claudia was even bolder. "Don't you understand? She speaks the truth. I too do what she has described so well. It is such a joy to share in this rite – the eulogia" – the Greek flowed smoothly from her lips – "to partake of food so blessed, the 'pain benit'. Surely you would allow us to take food so sanctified to the sick? I assure you no woman touches chalice or paten. We Bretons are not barbarians but Kristion! Take back my words to your metropolitans whether in Lugdunum or elsewhere!" Her eyes were fiery as she looked at him.

The stranger priest coloured and slightly bent his head. "That is well. You have reassured me and my journey has not been wasted. Yet remember that this heresy must be wiped out. Let me tell you also" he smiled and his voice softened "that the metropolitan does not want to constrain the growth of your Breton church. He realises that you are faithful worshippers and your church could be the finest in the whole country. Yet be on your guard always! Satan waits to seize souls in his rapacious claws." He seized his polaire and stood up. The others rose. "I have to thank you all and especially Claudia for your help. I must hurry for my horse travels at a speed that suits his age, not my wishes."

"I'll provide an escort for you Father. Armed horsemen. Six good German swords in the right hands are an excellent argument against those gentlemen who travel the ruined Roman roads looking for easy prey. My wife will give you a glass of wine for the nights are still chilly." Thomas, a stockily built man, grinned affably as he spoke. He wore buskins the worse for wear and an old Roman military buckle gleamed on his belt. Claudia poured a clear, golden liquid from a square glass bottle that bore the legend "Julius fecit". The priest watched her appreciatively and sipped the wine delicately. "That's from the north bank of the Garumna! It pleases me that my birthplace was there too, lady Claudia." The wine mellowed him. Thomas chatted on in a brisk soldierly way, his speech interlarded with Breton idioms.

"You shaven heads have problems but you're not the only people with them." The priest strained his ears to try and comprehend what was said. "We lack iron, tools and above all men. Our women are fertile but it takes time to train men to fight. The Saxons when they raid are adept at finding weak spots in the defences. They're creatures of marsh flats and tidal waters! Up an estuary they'll creep, even in storms, for they're heedless of weather. Thirty or so boats crawling into the belly of the land. A sentry asleep, a night attack – that was Aquilonia – then they're in to kill and be off with the gold and silver. And women slaves bound fast whose bodies they'll use for breeding new warriors. I'm trying to create my enemy's type of swords but it's tough work."

The priest had finished his wine. He put his hands together in prayer, while the others knelt, and blessed them. Clumsily he mounted his horse and escorted by hard faced men armed with spears and shields as well as swords, rode off. The darkening forest swallowed them up.

Thomas yawned. His wife put her small hand in his. "You're weary! All that patrolling in the forest for brigands who never appear and then that priest."

"There's that other matter of the young woman too." Claudia nodded but it was the redhead who spoke. "Guenole has been to the ravine to see the young woman. He insisted that she must come to the plou to be baptised. We know nothing of her background as she's lost her memory. Apparently she was a castaway. She's learnt Breton – remembers her name 'Ana'."

"We must stamp out any idle gossip that's arisen." Claudia's lips were firm. "See, they're coming now! They're on the forest path. It's Jahaan, Norah and the young woman."

The three neared the square by the big quern. Women dropped their flour sacks and stood, gaping and gossiping. Their voices were as the sound of many birds. One wench whispered "Who is she? Shall we have mischiefs with our crops?" Ana felt the glances full of curiosity.

Geese hissed furiously at the newcomer. An old fisherman said "Welcome to the plou and here are six fine trout for your supper." He smiled pleasantly at her.

They reached the villa. Ana, conscious of her mud-spattered garment, saw before her a young woman clad in pure white linen. She felt the warm grasp of a friendly hand. Claudia smiled and said in Breton "I give you a warm welcome to the plou!" Thomas, too, was smiling and shaking her hand but he turned to the swordsmith and his fellows who stood staring and said "Don't stand there gawking when you've work to do! Get those swords finished!"

The men hurried off. Claudia, chatting, took the three to the hut which served as a guest house. When she returned she sat down on the tripeccia and looked at the mosaic of the child with the duck. The smile had left her lips. She was very pale and her cheeks were streaming with tears. Thomas put his huge hand on her shoulders. "It's very hard for you, Claudia. Remember, if you can, that the child was baptised. He is now with the angels. Perhaps you'll have other children." "It's so strange, Thomas, but when I first saw Ana's face it all came back to me. That night he went from us. Why, why should the face of this young woman stranger, her hair, her very presence, evoke such thoughts in me? At this moment I see his little face again!" Thomas did not answer at once. He was silently gazing at the work being done in the plou. The priest had left them. Then he spoke. "In this life we never know when tragedy will strike us. Life is so short and so very hard." He paused, gazing with affection at Claudia. The two, though of different backgrounds, were very close to each other.

Claudia dried her eyes. "What will happen to the

young woman Ana now? Work in the fields with the other girls? Yes, she must not at present receive special treatment. But you are hungry, it's time we supped." She went to the doorway and waved several times to the woman waiting to receive orders. Her bare feet noiseless on the flags as she brought the dishes the woman came in. She grunted quietly and throatily making no other sounds. Martha, as they called her, was quite dumb but a faithful servant. They knew nothing of her parentage.

CHAPTER 4

The summer night was fast receding when Ana woke to hear Norah's morning prayers. To her ears came other stranger sounds. The blacksmith calling for fuel, a lamb bleating, a child crying. The sky was blue but over the forest hung a grey cloud. All was so different from the cherished quiet of the ravine. Her curiosity about what was to come to her was overshadowed by some apprehension about the future.

Norah never had doubts! Cheerfully, she clad Ana in her work tunic of coarse cloth which covered her only to below the knees and left the right shoulder and arm bare for work. Norah smiled "You're toiling with the others, so you'll meet young women from the plou. God be with you!" Outside, the plou was already a scene of activity and bustle. Herdsmen led out oxen, hunters slipped into the woods, smoke spiralled upwards from cooking fires.

"Ana!" The doorway was abruptly darkened by a huge figure. A massive hand grasped a long stick. "You're on field work this morning! Follow me." Ana followed him.

In a nearby meadow the young women waited. They chatted in low voices which ceased when they saw the newcomer. One nodded in welcome. The overseer explained the work. Half were to uproot weeds, the rest were to break up clods with heavy hoes. He waved his big stick – his symbol of office – as a signal that the work must begin and waited until they started. Ana saw Jahaan helping another young man to drive a team of oxen. It was so good to see him, to know that he was near her.

Ana had thought that the young Breton women might ignore her since she was a stranger, but they worked with such absorption they scarcely ever spoke at all, even to each other. Their natural leader appeared to be a tall girl, full-breasted and fair-haired, whose tresses flowed out like liquid gold. Like the other girls, she seemed to be one with the soil on which she worked and nothing distracted her. She had finely cut features, keen eyes and firm lips.

The girls worked on until the plou bell tinkled. They dropped their hoes, crossed their hands in reverence over their breasts, then flung themselves down to rest and munch their food, rye bread, dried venison and tansy leaves. The fair girl said to Ana "Drink from my water pot. You're one of us now." Ana drank, her lips at the place where Breton lips had been. It was a symbolic action. It meant the beginning of the life she was to share with the Bretons of the plou.

Daily, they trudged out to work. It was not always in the fields. Sometimes they would collect faggots in the forest. There they would see horsed patrols suddenly appear or hunters, bleeding from struggles with their quarries. The fox, the wolf, or the formidable wild boar. Some carried their booty. Hares, still twisted in the agony of snares, the carcasses of deer, black with flies, Game birds, feathers matted with blood.

To the companions of Ana, the forest appeared a more insecure place than the placid fields near the plou. Their talk revealed the hidden dread in which they regarded the remote woodland glades. The trees, they would whisper, were peopled at times by strange spirits who bore a perpetual grudge against humanity. "The corrigans are wicked and mischievous" said the fair girl in a low voice as if she feared the spirits might hear what she said. "They are full of malice and guile when they come out at night. I've seen milk soured right through from their evil work and sows who dropped abortions instead of healthy piglets when the corrigans were abroad. Look at my stick! Yesterday it was all right. Today it just fell into two pieces when I touched it."

"There's a worse demon in those thickets up yonder on the hill" said another speaker, shivering in fear. "If a woman is unlucky enough to meet him, he'll invite her to a dance. The dance will be wonderful but at the end she'll either drop dead from exhaustion or wake up from a very long sleep to find that a hundred years have passed and she's all alone in this world."

Ana wondered greatly but said nothing. She could not understand why the forest which provided food, fuel and shelter was supposed to have evil beings there. Somehow she guessed that she must learn to accept her companions' fears and inner thoughts. At night, especially, their nerves were taut as bowstrings and only an urgent errand would compel them to walk through the woods when the corrigans were abroad.

One evening as they returned from work the fair girl was talking about the Evil Eye and its effects on people when footsteps interrupted her and a strong voice came from behind them.

"There's a sure remedy for the Evil Eye and for all demons too, however powerful they may appear. Against the Cross they are weak." It was Guenole who had come to see Ana and the girls. Claudia was with him "The Cross is always the mightier power! Kneel, girl!"

He said these words to a girl bruised by a falling branch. On her painful shoulder he gently placed his right hand while his lips moved in silent prayer. His other hand was extended upwards in invocation to God. For a while he remained thus, motionless. Gradually the pain furrows on the girl's brow faded. The saint placed both his hands in a benediction on her head then removed them; the swelling had gone nor was there bleeding from cuts in the flesh.

"Praise God for His Almighty power manifest in the healing of His servant. This is the only power that can heal, the only power that is triumphant, before whom the demons that you fear are feeble charlatans!"

He turned on his heel and vanished along the pathway. Claudia had come to invite Ana to eat with her after her work was over. When Ana had gathered faggots and had carried the bundle to the old woman who needed them she went up to the villa. Martha set out the wholesome food. There was cold roast pork, bread baked in segments, each marked with a cross, elm bark and a dark honeycomb. When they had finished the meal Martha brought out the Burdigala then crouched in a corner. Her eyes glowed and Ana felt it was a great comfort to sit close to Martha. Her very presence, silent though it was, would warm one's own heart.

Claudia began the conversation "You must pardon me if I appear to speak Breton slowly for it is not my native tongue. I was born in Burdigala and my speech was of the Latin idiom. One day, it so happened that I was standing at our port when a trading vessel arrived, towing three curraghs behind her. The curraghs had been blown right off course in a storm and the trader had taken pity on them. My father and I gave the castaways shelter and they recovered their health. Often I talked with one of them, Thomas who was a chief among his own people. Bathed in that rich sunshine we sat in my father's vineyard and spoke about that island of mist and rain from which he had come. In time he asked me to marry him and we were wed in the old church by the archway. Soon after we sailed for that part of Armorica where his own Bretons had settled. Our sailors were a tough lot and they sailed their craft superbly in the rough seas we encountered. We evaded the Sea Wolves and landed at a bay near here. At first I found his Breton kinsfolk reserved but quickly we learnt to accept each other. There's nothing more to tell you, nothing but good – except for the child."

"The child? What child?"

Claudia had gone very pale. For a moment she turned her head away then looked Ana full in the face. Her large eyes were dilated and there was a strange glow in them. It was a glow that might have been on the face of some supernatural being, an angel perhaps. She got up and paced up and down with short steps.

"When we arrived here I was already with child. The Bretons looked forward very much to my bearing a male heir who would take Thomas' place later and become their leader. The baby, a healthy child for his first two years, was strong and plump but in his third summer the humid weather struck the children with the bloody flux; he was one of its victims. He fought for days against the enemy but one night – a fine summer night like this – he died in my arms." Her agitation was increasing. She looked still harder at Ana.

"I know – I know that it's fitting I should show you where he is buried. Will you come with me now?"

"I'll come." Ana hardly knew what to think or say. During this talk she had been drawn much closer mentally to Claudia. That was all she understood for the present.

"As is seemly I'll wrap your hair in this black dominical and we'll go barefoot in reverence to God." She took Ana's hand in hers and led her, unresisting, from the villa to the entrance gate in the palisade. It was starlight with the crescent moon just creeping up into the sky and small ghosts of clouds were drifting in from the west. On the grass sparkled the heavy dew. She gripped Ana's hand more firmly. "Let's walk beneath the moon, secure in our faith and in the peace of God."

The gate watchman looked enquiringly at the veiled women. "We go to pray at the burial place." The gate swung back, the wooden wards creaked sullenly. They moved quietly, their bare feet making no sound on the wet grass. Behind them lay the plou, bathed in a great tranquillity. Claudia led the way past the stream, heedless of roots that irked her feet. Soon they came to a clearing in the woods, in which logs lay in symmetrical lines and there was a high wooden cross, its gaunt arms nailed to a great oak. "The church" whispered Claudia.

There was a long drawn out howl from a wolf nearby. At the same moment a tall, hooded shape rose up from the grass and glided straight at them. The skeleton hands outstretched in front with claws about to seize them. Ana, momentarily taken aback, halted and clutched at Claudia's arm, her dominical floated away from her face but she remained still. The other woman stolidly stood her ground. It was a human voice steeped in anguish that issued forth from the cowl.

"Who are you that desecrate the peace of God and disturb the prayers of His chosen ones as they keep vigil in the darkest hours of the night? My God, why do you torment me with demons that take the form of women?"

"We are not demons, Holy Father, and we won't disturb you" said Claudia in a voice that enshrined a warm compassion with a gentle measure of severity. "We go to pray to God by the grave of one who died in the faith."

"And you would take an unbaptized female with you there where the saints rest?"

"It is right that she should know how Kristions live and how they die in the sure and certain hope of the resurrection. Our prayer will ensure that evil spirits and demons that lurk in the darkness are driven away from the resting places of the holy dead."

The lonely monk turned away and threw himself face down at the foot of the cross. They continued along by the side of the church until they came to a path that branched off at the foot of a mighty cypress. A few paces more and they were in another clearing. Ana could see irregular shapes set in the ground.

"The burial place." Claudia was shaking like one with ague. She took Ana's hand still more tightly in hers. They passed on between the lines of stones until they arrived at the corner of the ground. Here the stones were much smaller. "Young children" muttered Claudia hoarsely. "Here it is."

By the roots of a gigantic oak whose branches overshadowed it with a misty green canopy was a small standing stone facing towards the moon. Dark marks on the stone glistened with the dew drops. Claudia and Ana both knelt down. Before them was a tiny mound where fresh blades of grass pushed their way upwards to the light and air. Moisture diamonds, sparkling and twinkling, crowned each blade with beauty.

Claudia stretched out her hand until it was touching the surface of the hard stone as if it were a human being that she felt so gently. Her fingers, bone-white, pointed softly to each mark.

Ana bent down closer and saw that letters were incised in the granite.

> *Hic jacit*
> *Valerius Filius*
> *Thomae et Claudiae*
> *Anni 2 In Pace*

"My son, Valerius; two years old. May he rest in peace!"

"My son, no longer dead. He has gone to Heaven – that great world beyond me – that world of the future in which you also shall live." There was no sorrow in her gleaming eyes, only exaltation, triumph and a deep, burning love for all who lived or had ever lived or would live. While she spoke the stone had changed in appearance. It began to glow – a vivid white colour against which the cut letters burned as if traced in fire, becoming a bright violet hue. Claudia's own face shone with that same unearthly light, her hands were held upright in communion with God. For a long time she remained thus until the light faded from the stone and from her features. Then she shuddered.

"We'll return to the villa now."

... ...

Only the twin-beaked oil lamp was burning there. Claudia lit a honey-wax candle whose perfumed smoke emitted a great fragrance culled from the flowers of field and forest. Breathing deeply, she motioned Ana to the tripeccia but herself remained standing. Her long cloak worn over her white dress was a warm wine colour in the candlelight. Her face was calm and only the eyes betrayed her thoughts and feelings. Sometimes she turned to look at Ana, sometimes her face could only be seen as a dark profile against the glow of the candle burning away in its bronze sconce.

"I did not make the decision to take you to the burial ground on the spur of the moment. I have spent long hours on my knees supplicating God that he would grant me wisdom in whatever action I asked from you. My final decision was determined as much by my heart as by my mind. Ana, I realised that we were linked by some bond as close as that which they say unites identical twins. My thoughts were your thoughts, your thoughts were my thoughts. You're a young woman, Ana, but I perceive that we love the same things. Do you regret that unknown life that was your past? I don't know but I can tell you, my friend, that occasionally I do think back to my beloved Burdigala. Something tells me that I shall never see it again. The old Roman arch, the streets of the merchants, the vineyards, they're mine no longer any more than what you experienced in your unknown life is yours. I do not forget them but

I must not brood over them." She looked intently at Ana. "You've three articles that appear to have come from your former life?"

"I blush to say what they are. A strange cap, an odd-looking garment and the silver cross whose past significance I still cannot quite grasp."

"Don't try to, Ana. They're only bare, stark elements in the process by which we all first got to know you. After all, we do know your own name."

How powerful was the look of the woman! Ana was held by her gaze! Claudia went on, "I can, you know, from one point of view, regard this matter just from my common sense. Like Norah, I hold that your loss of memory could have been caused by a blow to your head, either accidental or deliberate. Yet what was your past, Ana?"

Uneasily Ana moved her bare feet around feeling for the firm, cold tiles with her toes. There was something enduring in their relation to her. She looked up at Claudia. Her voice was husky. "I'd like to know one fact above all else." She struggled with the Breton idioms, almost stammering in her attempts to make her meaning clear. "You're a shrewd person, Claudia. You're kind and intelligent beyond the majority of women. Who am I? Have you formed already some kind of picture of my unknown background?"

Claudia did not speak. There was a wooden box beneath the oil lamp. She put the lamp to one side and lit another honey-wax candle which she set with its fellow close to the box. Then she unlocked the box and took from it a vellum parchment which she spread out under the light. "Just look at this."

Ana, at first baffled, could only see blurs on the

age-yellowed sheet; these became regular columns of figures. She was mystified.

"You see the accounts of a Burdigala wine merchant. On this vellum he noted down the moneys he received for his wares. That's of no importance to us! Now look hard at the blank space between his figures. Do you see anything more now?"

To Ana's eyes, very faintly, writing appeared. Fragments of letters, even whole words.

"You see much older writing than our merchant's accounts." Claudia touched the manuscript lovingly. "Some scribe very long ago penned down these verses. Our merchant, short of vellum, scraped away at the surface, hoping to destroy the older letters and use the vellum for his accounts. What an oaf he was! Virgil is far more important than this money bag! Still, luckily, we can read a line or two. Look! 'Date lilia' – scatter lilies with lavish hands. It's about the funeral of someone who died young in that pagan world of the Latin poet. Let me tell you what this manuscript means for me and what its value is for your own life, too."

"The manuscript lying before you is a palimpsest – a manuscript on which something fresh has been written. To me, Ana, you are a palimpsest. Long before they found you lying unconscious on the rock, the mark of your childhood and previous adult life had been etched on your body which is healthy and beautiful. On your warm heart and your quick mind, too. Your past life was a good one, like those words of Virgil lying there. God gave you certain gifts; they are the older part of the manuscript which cannot ever be erased even if you do not remember who your kin were."

"What about my present life? Surely that is the most

important aspect for me just now?"

"Only in part. It is true that you're having the Breton speech impressed on you, while your hands are marked by hoe or quern. Your belly is still that of a virgin but if God wills, you'll marry and know child bearing and rearing among us."

Claudia looked from the candles to Ana and back again. She leant over and grasped Ana by the arm. It were as if a sudden, nervous shock had come to her.

"I took you to see that stone because I knew that it would mean more than the burial place of my son, precious though that is to me. That stone may outlast many centuries. That is its power and its meaning – to you. It glowed in sympathetic rapport with you. Yes, the very granite knew the strength of your personality. There is a saying '*Sunt lacrimae rerum*' – 'things have their tears'. I knew the rock felt with you. Somehow, too, I perceived that you had seen such burial stones before and pondered on them." Her speech had become gradually slower with an emphasis on each word. Her eyes glowed with an extraordinary intensity.

Ana grew white with emotion. "Are you revealing something to me of my other life which I have forgotten?"

"Only in a very general sense. Shall I put it in these words? Someone in the fullness of time may see that stone, may read the inscription, may learn that it marked the resting place of a little child. We, the human race, are moving forward, always forward in time. Some move more quickly than others. There are even a few who have the power to see into the future."

"You mean the Second Sight?"

"Yes, but by no means in a limited way. In the plou an

old woman may see the Banshee washing death clothes and connect this event with a young girl whom she knows. Then days, weeks later the girl dies. No, definitely, I'm thinking rather of someone different whose sight may span many centuries. I cannot express this easily but I believe that I may have this kind of sight as yet undeveloped. I must confess that I have not seen anyone in the far future but when we knelt by the stone and it glowed, my heart as much as my mind told me it might happen. Yet whatever happens to us, remember '*Quis separabit?*' – who shall separate us from the Love of God – the Love of God that reaches over the long centuries."

"I, too, am groping for understanding, Claudia. I find certain things here that are baffling. What to me is most strange about my companions is their fear of those they call corrigans. Who really sees these demons? Do they actually exist?"

Claudia released her arm and looked hard into her eyes. "You don't believe in these mysterious powers, then? ... *Odi profanum* ... you don't go with the crowd?"

"I saw the terrible tusks of a dead wild boar today. It can inflict ghastly wounds and should be feared as well as fought. But – but – these demons are so vague."

"I advise you to keep close counsel in these matters. Some beliefs are relics, persistent survivals of old pagan faiths against which the church is struggling still. We Kristions must oppose the Cross to the Powers of Darkness. You're a wise person, but watch your words lest you should be misinterpreted. Be patient with your companions."

"Don't think that I ignore illness. Your people are

healthy but I hear tell of plagues that come quickly on them to kill, such as the marsh fever."

Claudia looked out in the direction of the burial ground. Her eyes grew misty with sadness. "It's painfully true. There'll always be 'the pestilence that walketh the darkness, the sickness that destroyeth at the noontide.' We must not fear them. Ultimately death has no terror for us. It's the gateway to another world, to life eternal." Her face was transfigured. The hair round her head a halo. Her smile was full of affection and understanding. It inspired Ana. Its memory was to encourage her in all the days that lay ahead of her.

It was growing late; the moon no longer shone in a clear sky.

"There's one last thing I must tell you. If you sincerely desire to become a Kristion and be baptised into the Kristion faith, it is essential that you give some proof that you have lived a worthy life, helpful to others in certain ways. The care of the sick and elderly is one of these. We think that you should now help the deaconess with the invalids."

"But if I'm not yet a baptised Kristion someone might object."

"They won't object, knowing that it is part of your preparation for baptism. You're shy and modest too, Ana, but we won't let you hide the gift that God has given you. Norah has already told Guenole that your hand healed her when she was scalded by very hot water and Jahaan has described how skilfully you bound up his cut arm. Guenole himself is a healer of great repute and is also a good judge of character. He has an instinct for finding talents in others and thinks firmly you should be a healer. To you this work may seem almost like living in a new world. You are very capable of doing it and doing it well. Your mental horizons will broaden."

"When will that be? I feel conscious of my own shortcomings!"

"Never fear! The opportunity will come quickly of its own accord." She said these last words on the steps of the villa gallery as Ana was departing. Halfway to the guest house she looked back. The plou was immersed in darkness, the air had become calm. Claudia stood on the steps, a candle in each hand. Her white dress and bare feet glowed like a dove's plumage. All else was in gloom. The two candles burned with a steady light and in Ana's nostrils still lingered their sweet scent.

CHAPTER 5

The morning after her meeting with Claudia, Ana took her belongings over to the hut of Maura the deaconess. There she would begin the nursing that was part of her preparation for baptism. It was hard to leave Norah.

The hut was crammed with herbs of many kinds, bandages and even litters for carrying people. Only at one end was there room for two beds, a fireplace and a cross.

Her days and even sometimes her nights were filled with work. Initially she visited the sick and elderly with Maura but soon they considered her experienced enough to visit some patients on her own. There was always such joy for Ana when she found that her healing hands would relieve pain. Her work was not merely in the plou but also in the great forest. Here lived woodmen, charcoal burners, hunters. Everywhere people grew to like the young woman who spoke Breton with an odd accent and who worked so hard. Women at their laundry would wave to this girl who stood singing, up to her belly in the chill waters of a rock pool while she scrubbed away at garments or linen soiled by blood or ordure.

She learnt much and discovered that she had a great love for those suffering. She had no time to brood on her forgotten past. She made friends. One was Maria who lived in the plou and sometimes would come with her when she attended sick children. There was Azenor who lived miles away in the depths of the forest. She was a typical forest dweller, tough, adaptable and outspoken. She was expecting her first baby and Maura tried often without success to persuade her to have the birth in the plou. Another friend was an Irish wolfhound that sometimes went with her when she visited the forest folk. They were all people whom she got to know well and whom she liked.

There was only one cloud on her horizon. Avel, the deacon. His religious duties included reading lessons in church. He visited the sick with food and medicines and to the seriously ill he brought the viaticum. He was an expert with herbs which he brought to Maura in the hut. He spoke briefly and then with a foreign accent, for he came from the South. Sometimes he would chat in the hut with Maura who respected him very much for his austerity, for he fasted rigorously and went barefoot even in winter. He hardly ever even glanced at Ana and avoided her gaze. She sometimes met him during her work, especially when he brought food to the ill.

Once, when Ana was alone she wanted to change the blankets of a sick woman but could not manage on her own. He suddenly entered the hut and said rather abruptly "I'll lift this woman up so that you can change her." He placed his powerful hands under the woman's body and raised her up while Ana quickly changed the blankets. Their fingers momentarily were in contact. She felt as if she were touching heated metal so hot were his hands, yet on the way home she forgot all about Avel and thought only of the Wolfhound trotting by her side or the beauty of the trees in leaf.

Avel had to go to Norah about a cope she was sewing

for the church. Just then Norah was busy measuring Ana for a new shift. She asked him to hold her tablets while she passed her measuring string round Ana's neck. She would then call out the size of the neck and he would note it down on her tablets. Avel obeyed and it was over in moments. Yet as he went with Norah to talk about the cope, Ana noticed he had gone pale. Azenor was sitting on a log and had seen the whole incident.

"You don't seem to be at ease when Avel is near" she said. Ana told her about what she felt when she was changing the bed with Avel's help. "Why should you be bothered about the man? It's his duty to visit sick people. He's just a human being like yourself. Anyway, he's vowed to celibacy."

"The hot hands? A touch of fever perhaps! These people who immerse themselves in icy water to get rid of their sins can't do that without their bodies suffering from it."

"I've come to tell you, Ana, about something much more important to me than Avel. I'll have my baby in the plou after all. It was not the deaconess who persuaded me but you, you've got such a strong character. I make one condition. You'll deliver me."

She left. Ana tried not to brood over her strange meetings with Avel. She wondered if she were judging him too harshly in some way. After all, he was a stranger like herself. She was more affected by the fact that Norah and Jahaan would return to the ravine for the fishing. She found time for a farewell hour with Norah and they talked of Ana's work as well as of her baptism.

"You are happy in your work of healing?" asked Norah.

"Very happy. I've never been so happy since I came here. I am so busy. I wish you were here too."

"Be patient. Just before your baptism we'll have you back with us in the ravine. Remember one thing, the most important thing in your life. When you're alone pray silently to God to help you. Pray very often if you are in any difficulty of mind or body or in any great danger. Remember that God is with you. Say to yourself 'God. You are with me!' And also remember that what happens to us is the will of God. He is watching over us wherever we are or whatever we are doing."

"You spoke to me once Norah about slavery. You said 'if you were unlucky and got caught by slave raiders like the Sea Wolves you would have to accept that a master naturally uses his captive women for breeding. Thus he would fill your womb'. Is it the will of God that women should be slaves and bear children in slavery?"

"Yes, it is God's will and they are doing His work in their slavery. There have been great Christian slaves able even in slavery to tell their fellow slaves about Kristos."

"I shall miss you and Jahaan so much Norah."

"We both shall miss you very much Ana. Now before we depart let me give you two things which will be useful to you. Jahaan has made a polaire for your herbs, from me accept this woollen cap to wear at night. With every stitch I said a prayer for you. When you are away I shall remember those prayers and I shall be praying always for you. The cap ties tightly under your chin. It will keep you warmer than a wimple. I have also made a white cap which you will wear at your baptism."

On the day they left she accompanied the two of them as far as the watchman stationed on the great rock. Then they were off by the forest path and she stood looking after them with tears in her eyes. Ana suddenly felt very much alone.

Each night she had thoughts of Jahaan, especially of that time when he had carried her in his arms as they crossed the most perilous part of the marsh. She heard his voice again, full of encouragement. She woke only to hear the deaconess's snores. Then she realised how much she missed Norah and Jahaan. She knew that they would soon return but a yearning for their company was growing on her and nothing else could satisfy that yearning.

One day a charcoal burner, his face black from a night's watching, ran into the plou shouting for help. He had penetrated into a distant thicket and there found a man dying from starvation. Thomas at once collected a party of armed men and accompanied by Ana followed the man back to that part of the woods. The trees were tangled and the axemen had sometimes to hack a way until they came to a glade. They gasped with horror. On the grass was lying a man, almost a living skeleton. In Latin he whispered to Ana "Leave me! Leave me! Save them! Save them!"

"Who?"

"My wife – children – underground – there is a hole yonder!"

One of the hunters sniffed the air like a hound scenting game. "There's an open space over there! I can smell it." The men wriggled and pushed their way through the undergrowth. Truncated columns of white stone loomed up before them. Broken bricks fought a losing battle with the encroaching trees and shrubs.

"An old villa" said Thomas. There was a formidable

hissing. He transfixed a huge viper with his spear.

The trackers lost no time but moved on fast, casting about like dogs running game to earth. The spoor ended up in a flat circle of stone. Long marks on the edge showed where the unfortunate man had crawled away for help. A dark hole in the middle of the circle yawned up before the searchers. Two volunteers, knives in mouths, were lowered and vanished into the mouth of a tunnel at the base of the pit. They returned, white faced.

"Three dead! A woman and two children! Must be the man's wife! We'll have to bring them out." Thomas looked at Ana; she had already tied up her skirt to free her legs.

"I'll go down with the men." She swayed down the footholds, using their hand rope. The massive stones of the pit hemmed them in like a tomb. The three crawled into the chamber of death. The men held up their torches.

A young woman sat with her back against the wall. Her attitude was so peaceful that Ana for a moment thought the woman was asleep but the dead girl, with unblinking eyes, stared at the black embers of a fire as if she had once hoped that her own life might be rekindled thereby. Across her knees was slumped a baby's body and by her side, arms outstretched, an older child lay. The baby's mouth was stuffed with moss; the mother's last offering.

On the floor within reach was an earthen pitcher, two platters of fine Samian ware, a spear and a bronze mirror, highly polished. Ana felt bitter grief. She was witnessing not only human death but the end of the civilization in which they had lived. High up, the torchlight showed a finely sculptured figure on the wall. A woman with long hair flowing right back from her shoulders with the speed of her ride. She bestrode a proud, curvetting horse and her eyes looked into the distance but she appeared indifferent to the fate of the three dead beings below her. Ana looked again at the dead woman. Had she once bowed in reverence before this goddess? Had she sacrificed her poor food to obtain a divine blessing? She would never know. The Bretons with her crossed themselves and averted their gaze from the horse lest it should bring a mischance upon them. One said "That's a demon up there. One of those pagan goddesses! We'll have to break her up before she can do any harm to anyone."

His attention was distracted by his fellows who were examining a rectangular shape in the end wall of the room. Someone had bricked up a cavity. He thrust hard with his axe. The wall caved in to reveal a long passageway. The air within was wholesome and fresh as if a breeze were coming through a small aperture. The passageway extended for many paces, but though the men searched it carefully for survivors they found nothing except three large food jars which were quite empty.

Meantime, Ana had eased the baby away from the death grip of the mother and set it against her own breast. She put her hand on the baby's heart. She started. There seemed to be a weak pulse. "I think she lives!" she shouted. The cries brought the men back and one of them held the bronze mirror to the baby's mouth. A faint mist showed on the mirror. "The baby is alive" they cried. There were tears of joy in their eyes. One crawled back to get more help. Ana carried the baby, the men hoisted up the corpses of the woman and the other child and they were borne back on litters to the plou where the starving man had already been taken. Thomas and his assistant remained a long time below ground. They carefully examined the pit, the chamber and the long passageway. "I think it will do well for a refuge" said the chief. "It will give shelter to a hundred or more. We'll keep reserves of food and water there. Swear all the men who have seen this place to secrecy. It's better that no one else in the plou knows about this hiding place yet."

The baby, a girl, revived and was fed by one of the women in the plou. Yet Gaius – for that was the man's name – was another problem. He was extremely weak from starvation and when he learnt that his wife and child had died, he turned his face to the wall and would have given up completely but for Ana. She would not let him die. She told him that his baby still lived and he must live for her also and cherish her. A weak smile came to his thin face. However, there still remained a difficulty. The poor man was so feeble that he could not even take food from a cup.

At this juncture Ana had a helper who solved the problem. Maria had been standing by, her eyes full of pity for the sufferer. "I know how I can get food into him! I'll nurse him as if he were my own baby. I've plenty of milk!" Her face shone with joy as she clasped her hands together in prayer. "God, aid me to save this man! You, Lord, sent me here to help all who suffer." She opened her shift; her breasts plunged outwards. She knelt so that she leant well over him. The exhausted invalid saw the red nipples moist with milk erecting for their task. "Open your mouth wide!" ordered Maria.

She thrust her left nipple firmly through his pallid lips. "Drink deeply" she cried. "Suck hard from me! Empty my breast! I give you life! God gives you life!"

Her nursing did save his life and soon he was on to other food and able to tell his story. Marauding bands had burnt his farm which was some distance from the plou and all the food of the family had been stolen or destroyed. For a time, he and his family had wandered in the forest but, worn out, had taken shelter in the underground hiding place which they alone knew. Without food and ill, they had begun to die. He had crawled out to summon help; it had come too late for two of them.

Apart from his story he spoke little at first but as time passed it was clear that he was an intelligent man, able to read the Gospels in Latin and also to speak in a Latin idiom. By birth he was a Gallo-Roman and his eyes would grow sad as he told of the devastation of the land. He became good friends with several in the plou. With Claudia with whom he read Latin, with Maria who had suckled him back to health. With Ana, too. He would sit with her as the red-headed priest explained the first rudiments of the Kristion faith. He found these of great interest but there were special difficulties for him that did not affect Ana.

"What you say is very good" he said in his deep voice, "The teaching and life of Kristos are wonderful stories. I understand that if I undergo your baptism and become one of the Kristion I shall know fully the resurrection which is promised to all who believe in Kristos." The priest smiled gravely. He looked straight into the eyes of this thoughtful neophyte. "You find some difficulties?"

"There was a very close bond between my wife and myself. What of her? She is dead. She died in loneliness and misery. Ana, you saw the goddess' image – Epona – down there. My wife believed in a goddess that you might call a demon. What of her fate?"

Ana held Gaius' baby in her arms, fondling her and holding her tightly to her bosom when the child chortled with joy. A song thrush above them raised its hymns of praise high up in the trees. The priest pointed to it.

"Listen to God's creatures as they adore Him and be thankful that there is one God whom we all worship. Gaius, before Kristos there were good men who lived as he would have wanted them to live. Socrates the Greek lived a noble life. Also, do remember that your wife was a loving mother to her children – even unto death!"

Tears rolled down the still pale cheeks of the Gallo-Roman.

"We have given her an honoured grave close to that of the Kristion. Try not to grieve for her overmuch, Gaius, but pray for her soul and that of the child that died with her. Your baby there shall be baptised into the Kristion faith. Let Ana help you to understand the Paternoster while I go to pray with a sick monk."

It was lovely to sit there in the sunshine and render into Breton the Latin words of the Paternoster which she had been taught. Sweet to feel the tiny fingers of the woman-child touching her breast. To know, in a great fullness of spirit, the love of God and of humanity. Above all things, to experience peace.

She had seen little of Avel recently. People said that he spent long days in retreat in his lonely hut in the woods, praying and fasting. Once, they met by chance and she was surprised at the change in his appearance. He had gone thin as if from fasting and his eyes were blood red as if from night vigils. She never met him now when she was visiting the sick but he did once visit the hut which she shared with the deaconess, to ask about herbs. It was the evening before the night when she would be left alone in sole charge. He gazed hard at the herbs, examining all of them carefully and touching them with his fingers while he held a bowl of warm water in his palm. He glanced at the lamp and her palliasse, then he rejoined the deaconess outside and they went off together to make a night visit to a woodman whose wife was gravely ill and to whom Avel would take the viaticum.

Twilight was slowly falling on the plou. Ana sat at the door in the fading light looking round at the huts where people were already settling down for their night's rest. The gates of the plou had just been locked and the dogs had been fed. There were two Molossians, huge mastiffs. There were also two Irish wolfhounds. One of the latter had adopted her as a friend. It came up to Ana, as she sat there. It rubbed against her and licked her. She stroked it, enjoying the feel of its coat, the nose that pushed at her feet, sniffing up her own special smell in its canine way. Then it ambled off to seek a comfortable resting place for the night.

Ana prepared and ate her simple meal, then set a pot of water on the embers of her fire so that warm water would always be available. She lit the small lamp that would burn slowly through the night, giving out a tiny, subdued light. The door was always fastened wide open so that if people urgently needed her services they could come in at once. The hut itself stood some distance away from the other dwellings in the plou and very close to the palisade and ditch which guarded the plou. Unknown to Ana, two of the wooden stakes of the palisade close to the hut had rotted away at their bases and so left a weak spot in this part of the defence of the plou. That night the deaconess had specially entrusted to her care Azenor, the young pregnant wife of a woodman who lived in the forest. For the coming birth, she was staying with Maria. The woman, small and plump, stood at the door of Maria's hut, her hands clasped beneath her enormous belly which curved right out with the weight of the child she was carrying.

"I can't see my feet now" she laughed. "Will my labour be tonight?"

"I don't think so" said Ana after she had examined her. "I am going to give you a sedative drink then you must lie down on the palliasse with Maria by your side and sleep soundly. No need to worry!" she gave her the drink then the two young women held each other for a few moments in a warm embrace.

"You are so kind" said Azenor." Daily I pray to our loving God that he will grant me very soon my dearest wish for you."

"What wish?"

"That, married, you should be as I – your belly big and round with child. Today I have felt this wish so strongly, Ana, and now I will pray to God again tonight especially for you!" She looked hard at Ana, who saw the beauty in her broad face, the high forehead, full lips, cheeks rosy with the outdoor life.

"Baptism comes first. Then who knows?"

Ana returned to her own hut. There was no reason

for her to stay awake. If need be Maria would summon her.

For a time she stood at the door of the hut looking out. All lights in the plou except hers had been extinguished. The pregnant woman was deep in sleep. The watchman by the gate dozed heavily at his post. There was no need for him to remain on the alert. It grew quieter and quieter until she knew that the whole plou was fast asleep. The night was almost silent with just a gentle breeze, a "hunter's wind", blowing from the plou to the dim forest. Over the trees, the huts, the whole land there reigned a great peace and serenity. All was secure.

She rested by the dying fire then, kneeling, said the words of the Lord's Prayer often. What was "temptation" to a young woman like herself? What temptations had assailed Gaius' wife as she looked at her burnt out fire or at Epona who in spite of her supplications had not saved her from death? As so often now, she wanted the ravine so much. The smell of the sea, of tackle, of Jahaan's boat. She wanted Norah. Only Norah understood. A strange desire for a man's body, a craving, too, to waddle around clumsily with a babe heavy in her womb. Norah called it the "tide". She thought it might happen again to her on the morrow. For the time being, she must master her feelings and prepare wholeheartedly for her baptism. Peace came to her. She knelt for a while at the deaconess' bronze cross. When she rose from her knees she suddenly felt overwhelmingly thirsty. She glanced about her and saw a small bowl of liquid standing by the embers. Assuming it was water she drank thirstily. The water had a peculiar, bittersweet taste as if a herb had been dissolved in it. But it did not matter: her thirst was relieved.

Ana's eyelids grew heavy and she made ready for slumber. In summer, modest young women in the plou, following custom stripped bare for sleep wearing only wimples round their heads. She removed all her clothing and put on Norah's woollen hat, smiling as she remembered that in its making every stitch had been accompanied by a prayer for her. She, too, said a prayer as she tied the strap tightly under her chin.

She lay down on the palliasse as she was, without covering herself with the blanket as the hut was very warm from the dying embers. She settled on her back with arms and legs outstretched for coolness and murmured her last prayer, "Dear Lord, I belong wholly to Thee!" She then fell into a very deep, dreamless sleep.

CHAPTER 6

Was it only a dream on her warm palliasse? A nightmare from which the awakening would be to another day of nursing the sick in the plou?

It was no fantasy. It was a reality of bodily discomfort, of mental anguish. Her kidnappers, silent and swift as cats, had carried the woman, very deep in slumber, through the fence gap to the forest. She had woken up only to find a blindfold over her eyes, her mouth gagged and her limbs spread-eagled on the back of a packhorse. Thongs on her wrists secured her hands to the front legs of the horse, her ankles were bound in similar fashion. A rope tightly tied round her middle held her down to the beast below her.

The horses, feet padded to muffle hoof beats, moved almost silently. She wore only the woollen cap given to her by Norah. In the sleeping plou no one had stirred, no dog had barked. The plou remained as quiet as the dead in the burial place.

Where were they going? She knew they changed direction often. Was this done to baffle pursuit or because they were following circuitous forest paths? Her captors whoever they might be gave her no inkling. All she knew was that there were several of them riding on horses ahead of her, to one of which her steed was tied; they spoke little then in whispers. Of one fact she was certain. They were not Sea Wolves!

Ana could not smell the sea about them, the odour of salt and boats.

The hours passed slowly but surely, with every mile covered so her hopes of rescue faded. The people in the plou would not know she had gone until morning and then they could not know where she was. No clues were left to tell them where to search. Worst of all was the awful realisation that Norah and Jahaan might never see her again. They would not know why she had left them as mysteriously as she had come into their lives. The plou young women would shrug their shoulders and say "A corrigan carried her off."

Why had they captured her? What was she to become? She learnt this soon enough at their first halt. They stopped in a moonlit glade and removed her blindfold. She saw her captors. Three short men with powerful arms and thighs wearing only cinctures. On their heads were leather helmets reinforced by metal and strapped under the chins with broad leather bands. Each carried a naked sword. Their faces were smeared with charcoal as camouflage to avoid detection. Their grinning lips appeared blood red against the dark cheeks, their eyes stared hard and with glee at their human booty.

They gathered round her. They checked her bindings, tightening a knot here, a loop there. One lifted her head. Something bright flashed by her eyes and she felt the icy touch of cold metal. A broad bronze band was passed round her neck! There was a click as the rivet was hammered home, pressing the close fitting ring hard into her neck. It was the slave collar she wore!

She wanted to protest but all that came from her throat was a choked gasp of despair. The men stood, enjoying her misery. She was now a helpless slave woman with all that it might imply for her!

There was more to come. Their leader stood very close to her. With his left hand he touched her slave collar. The fingers of his right hand slid down over her breasts until they reached her waist, a maiden's waist, flat and smooth. He stroked it briefly then raised both his palms high above her belly while his companions, their mouths gaping wide in dumb laughter, their tongues licking their lips lasciviously, pointed upwards to the moon then back to her belly. Her heart beat furiously, the blood coursed through her veins, she felt her cheeks growing hot and red as the significance of their gestures dawned upon her. As the moons came and went so her figure would inexorably change! Yes, Azenor's wishes would be amply fulfilled, her loving prayers answered sooner than she could have known! Her belly would soon be swelling outwards, as round and big as Azenor's! A baby would be growing in her womb. Proof of her slave master's virility! Her breasts, too, would enlarge with milk. Whether she wished it or not, she would suckle a slave!

What made it harder for Ana was the consciousness that her "woman's tide" was on her still, that almost intolerable longing to have a baby in her womb. As the leader beckoned to his men and they moved off once more on the via dolorosa, the tears began to flow from her eyes at her hopeless plight. Gone was the baptism for which she had so carefully prepared, gone too was the possibility of marriage with Jahaan, of carrying his child. No, her lot would be to bear slave children!

The metal collar was chilly round her neck but in contrast to its coldness, warmth came to her ears, the top of her head, the back of her neck. It was Norah's woollen cap, all that she now possessed of her former life in the plou. The warmth reminded her of what Norah had said that every stitch had been made with a prayer. Prayers of Norah for her. Prayers that she would always accept what was the will of God. The will of God? Was it His will that she should be a slave? Yes, she would accept wholeheartedly what Norah had said. It needed all her latent courage and devotion to the new faith of Kristos to accept what was inevitably coming to her. It needed, too, her love for Norah and Norah's love for her.

She said to herself, "Dear God, it was by your Will that I now wear the slave collar as token of my changed life. I will be obedient to my master. Cheerfully I will carry his slave children. It will be my new task to tell them the story of Kristos and I will help my fellow slaves."

This was the message that came from the comfort of her woollen cap, almost as if Norah herself were speaking to her. The stitches so redolent of Norah and her affection. Some great power outside her had entered her now to give her a lasting strength in all that could happen to her.

The tears began to dry on her cheeks. Her eyes grew bright with a strange joy. Above her appeared a patch of clear sky. Was it the beginning of a new day? The dawn of her first day as a slave woman?

They made another halt. For the first time the men relaxed; a flask of cervoise was produced. The man on the lead horse to which her packhorse was roped drank freely, the others preferred just to sip the powerful liquor. They smiled and pointed to her, then laughed, jerking their thumbs at the path ahead. The end of the journey for her was very near. Her heart beat fast again, she breathed deeply and quickly. Soon, very soon, they would chain her hands to the slave post in the market. Intending purchasers would come to examine her and she would feel rough hands on her body. Some man would choose her, she would become his property. And then? Her new life as a slave! "Dear Lord, give me strength!" she prayed. Her thoughts were confirmed when the two horsemen rode off, grinning, waving to the man with the lead rope. Their faces were cheerful. They were secure now from attack or rescue!

Left to himself, her solitary guard did not appear to be in a hurry. He drained the dregs of the cervoise, mounted – unsteadily – and they were off again. The pace became slow as the packhorse was both tired and obstinate.

There were now small thickets alongside the path. Ana, straining her neck to see behind them, noticed it. At first she thought it was a shadow but shadows are not usually a reddish-ginger colour and they don't move as she had seen it move! Intently, she watched it, her eyes eager to catch every movement of the animal, if it were an animal!

A dog was following them! The Irish wolfhound! Would there be men, too, or was the dog alone? Yet there were no voices, no sounds, no hopes that rescuers were anywhere behind. Only the soughing of the trees, the rustle of leaves, the creek of branches and the endless hoof beats. The wolfhound, a magnificent hunter, cautiously maintained its distance. Its sense of scent rather than sight told it that it was following Ana, yet it also perceived that there was a stranger with her from whom came alien smells and warnings of danger. It did not hurry but took advantage of every cover, slinking behind the thickets and avoiding open places – the paths – almost entirely. Often it halted, she knew, to read the message left by her body but some powerful instinct warned it that it must never be seen by the stranger in front of Ana, so there were very long intervals when she never saw it but knew that it was there.

It was enough hope for the helpless slave woman! It had latched onto its quarry! She knew the great stamina of the wolfhound and how it would follow a trail after its quarry hour after hour, through night and through day. It would never let her go. The dog carried on its game of hide and seek until the dawn was clearly in the sky. Until a second wolfhound appeared on a leash held in a Breton's hands. Then dark shapes, hunters in skins, crept in from the trees and shadowed the dogs. There was the blast of a trumpet, followed by a formidable barking. The wolfhounds raced at the horse, attacking the man from each side. A Breton, francisca in hand, ran up. Other horsemen galloped madly towards the kidnapper.

The slave raider, though drunk and alone, did not lack courage. With his sword he slashed at Ana's lead rope to free himself, then thrust at the first wolfhound. It slunk back, licking its wound. The francisca hissed through the air but glanced off the man's leather helmet. He turned to the other hound which had his leg in its huge jaws. It withdrew, his blood dripping from its teeth. He galloped off, lashing his steed.

"After him" bellowed Thomas. They were just too late. The horseman riding madly, slithered through the thickets and in seconds managed to evade the hot pursuit. They found only sporadic blood stains; the man had been badly wounded.

Ana's limbs were untied but her slave collar could not be removed without tools and she was compelled to wear it on the journey back. The men made for her a litter carried by two horses. The Irish wolfhound padded close alongside her. Its eyes were bright with affection for her. When they halted it would lick her dangling feet or hands or even her shoulders, bare above the horse blanket.

They entered the plou at sunrise. People had gathered anxiously to await their arrival and there were cheers when they saw Ana. Two persons who had been away all night had just returned. The deaconess was already at work in the hut where Azenor lay. Groans were heard as the young woman pushed the baby from her womb. Avel stood in the centre of the plou. His eyes were cold, his face impassive as he gazed at Ana. He saw the polished bronze slave collar shining brightly in contrast to her white and shapely shoulders. Though her eyes were tired she wore her collar with an air of pride and triumph rather than humiliation.

Ana's limbs were cramped and sore from the binding, but otherwise she was all right. The blacksmith eased out the rivets from the collar and it was removed from her neck. Thomas and the blacksmith examined the collar carefully but there was no proof of its origin. However, the blacksmith said that the collar was quite new. He measured her neck meticulously and said that it was so good a fit it almost looked as if the kidnappers knew her measurements beforehand!

Ana could tell them nothing from the few whispers she had heard from her captors.

Thomas told her about the rescue. Some hours after midnight, Azenor had very suddenly gone into labour and Maria had run to Ana's hut for help. When she found the bedclothes disarranged and the new gap in the fence she went at once to Thomas. It was clear to him from the footmarks and from her shift still lying in the hut that she must have been surprised, naked, and carried away forcibly. He had wakened the hunters, the Irish wolfhound had been sniffing round the hut and followed the spoor through the gap in the fence. They went after it, keeping it in view, but holding well back lest Ana's captors should kill her if they were disturbed. When the two horsemen had galloped off they began to close in.

Ana's wrists and ankles had been badly chafed but the deaconess applied one of her lotions and they quickly healed. She did not want to talk about her experiences. They had made too deep a mark on her for casual conversation. She yearned strongly for Norah to whom she would reveal everything. She insisted on keeping her slave collar and when she was alone and undisturbed would place it round her neck while she knelt and prayed for slaves.

Claudia thought it best for Ana not to return to the deaconess' hut for the time being, but instead she went to Martha's room – to Martha's bed. The dumb girl drew her closely to her own body and she slept soundly, clasped in loving arms. By the villa was a strong guard of Thomas's best and most trusted warriors.

Precautions were taken in the plou. The watch was strengthened and the gap in the fence repaired.

CHAPTER 7

Ana had come to no harm from her abduction but Claudia felt that she ought to have some time in the ravine before the rigorous preparation for her baptism began. The only person in the plou who knew the route over the marshes was Avel. He consented to accompany Ana and they set out very early on the long journey through the forests to get to the ravine within a day.

On the way they would break journey briefly to visit a swineherd who had been gored by a wild boar so that Ana could attend to his needs.

The rain ceased but there was a mist clinging to the forest skirts as they set out. They moved mostly in silence so that they should not be easily discovered if there were lawbreakers in the trees. Avel carried food and a knapsack with bags for the marsh crossing. It was better that any robbers should not know of their presence. Avel strode ahead of the young woman who reflected that it would be the first time they would be so many hours together alone. She wanted to understand him but could not talk since they had to walk in silence except for whispered instructions.

They found the swineherd cheerful except for the pain in his leg. Ana cleansed the wound with fresh water, packed it with comfrey leaves and clean linen and held her healing hands over him while Avel prayed for him. Then they were off again, this time on the path that would cross the old Roman road. Ana rejoiced to feel the sea wind on her cheeks but was surprised to find a mist drifting in from the sea.

"The mist doesn't matter" said Avel coolly. "I know the pathway very well. I think you ought to have a rest now on that big log as we'll have no time to rest when we cross the marsh."

She sat down on the log but he remained standing. Then she started talking to him. "You're from the South they tell me, Avel. Why did you come to this colder place?"

"You could say it was God's will. When I was a young child my mother dedicated me to the work of God whatever it might be. You know what my labours as a deacon are."

"Why don't you marry and thus live a fuller life?" She knew this question was almost impertinent but said it because she wanted to understand him more. What was it she saw in his eyes? Was it regret that he was not like other men? He repeated coldly "When I was young – a baby – my mother vowed me to the service of God. I repeated that vow when I was older. With us a vow is binding. I am as thirled to my vow as you would have been bound to slavery when they finally riveted the slave collar round your neck. Yet we have no time to discuss such matters. We are very near the Roman road and because it is sometimes haunted by thieves it is better to be as quiet as possible. The mists are coming down on the road and we shall have to keep a very sharp watch to prevent us being surprised by robbers."

CHAPTER 8

Their path now led uphill so that when they neared the Roman road they were well above it. They were concealed by dense, high bushes. For moments they stopped and looked down.

The mist suddenly thickened and blanketed the road so much that they could not see above thirty paces along it. An anxious expression came over Avel as he strained his eyes gazing into the near distance. He listened intently then clutched Ana's arm. "Hist!" he whispered. "I can hear people approaching."

Sounds muffled by the mist and trees came to their ears – the thud of hooves, the wheeze of harness. He thrust Ana down onto the ground behind a wide bush. What danger did he suspect? They peered through the leaves.

Gradually emerging from the mist a ragged column appeared. Spearmen, buskins thumping on the stony ground. A reek of tired limbs and sweat emanated from them. Two, white-faced, wore bloodied rags round their heads. Some led mules laden with booty.

The mist thickened still more and the foremost part of the column soon was out of sight. Then the commander appeared riding by himself. Well behind him were white, ghostly shapes moving one behind the other in single file, their hands stretched out in front as if in prayer. Each spectral figure glided along at the same pace as the one in front of it. Was it a religious procession? The commander was a sturdy man mounted on a shaggy pony, his long hair hanging below his helmet on which was an emblem – the double dolphin of Ys!

The strange figures now emerged from the mist. Ana gasped. They were not ghosts but a coffle of women. Their captors had secured each slave effectively by placing a long, forked pole on her shoulders and locking her head in by a crossbar round her neck. Her arms were then stretched out along the pole and bound there. This gave the semblance of prayer. They then lashed the far end of the pole to the waist of the slave in front. This arrangement ensured that each slave kept an exact distance from the one in front. They could not even whisper to each other but must walk in silence. Escape was virtually impossible.

The commander twisted round in his saddle and barked an order. The slaves, panting heavily, halted just in front of the bushes where Ana and Avel were hiding. The soldiers took out water gourds and quenched their thirst. Then they held the gourds to the gaping mouths of the fettered slaves, who lapped up the liquid eagerly.

The new slaves were sturdy young peasant women. They had plump bodies, breeding-ripe. Their breasts shining with sweat were round and high. The faces of some wore a sombre expression as if there was no hope for them. If they cried out for help now, who would hear them, who would help them against their guards? The last slave was different. She was a woman of striking beauty with dark hair and eyes. Her belly curved out with the weight of a baby she was carrying. It appeared that she had been captured apart from the rest. The raiders, except for the two wounded men who were speechless, appeared satisfied with their booty.

Afterwards, Ana was to learn of the misfortune which had befallen the women. The raiders were returning with the single capture, the pregnant woman, when their scouts reported that they had heard women on a lonely path in the forest, singing. The slavers followed their quarry to a rock pool. All these maidens, unconscious of danger, stripped naked and plunged, laughing, into the water. The men seized the bathers, bound them and fitted them with their yokes. Two rash but brave footpads had tried to seize this loot. They were cut to pieces but not before they had inflicted head wounds on two raiders.

A flood of emotions overwhelmed Ana. Sympathy for the women slaves, hatred for their captors. She had an almost irresistible desire to stand up and scream out her protests. She shook convulsively, her mouth opened wide, she clenched her fists. She had nearly pushed herself up when she felt Avel's palm on her mouth, his hand on her shoulders, preventing her from rising up lest she would be seen. She hated this restraint but knew he was right. If captured there would have been no rescue. She would have become a slave in Ys.

After a brief rest the commander shouted "On again! You'll soon be in Ys!" He cracked his whip. They fell into line and stumbled along. As the dark haired women came abreast of Ana she tripped and fell calling out words in a strange language. Unperceived by the guards she dropped a small object. The guards dragged her to her feet and the column passed on and was soon out of sight.

They got up and walked down the road. The object was a scrap of wood. On it drawn in charcoal was a fish.

Ana felt that the woman had left something of herself to them, though not knowing they were so close.

"What does that signify?"

"It's a symbol for Kristos used by early kristion. Perhaps she hoped that someone might find it and know that she, a Kristion, is a slave in Ys."

Ana shuddered. The memory of her own kidnapping was too recent for her to forget it. Her emotions welled up and found an outlet in her faith. She threw herself down on her knees and prayed. Tears streamed from her eyes.

When she rose up, Avel asked "Why did you pray?"

"I prayed because I am a woman and I felt for an instant that I was one of those being dragged into unwilling slavery. That is also why I wanted to cry out, rash though it would have been."

Avel said curtly "It's time we were on our way." They walked on. Ana could not understand his attitude to the slaves. In her view he had too little feeling. They walked fast and were soon on the ledge that overlooked the most perilous part of the marsh crossing. The great pools lay before them as placid, as smooth, as deadly as they always were. She smelt the reek from the marsh plants and saw the clusters of reeds that spelled out dangers. Marsh birds hovered overhead uttering their sinister warnings.

Avel stood long studying the leading marks. Though he had crossed the marsh before he was not as familiar with its hazards as Jahaan and he was responsible for another as well as his own life. He crossed himself, took off his robe and placed it in his waterproof knapsack. Then he beckoned to Ana. She understood. If she wore her clothing the water would drag both of them down. She had stripped with Norah once before for the marsh crossing. This time it was different. She felt a curious reluctance to bare herself before this man who stared at her more closely than she liked. Yet there was no alternative. Her life and his were at stake in these awful waters. He had promised Thomas he would bring her safely to the ravine and he must carry her naked body in the deepest parts, feeling with his bare feet for the rock where a single slip could mean death for them both.

Ana wavered. His cheeks reddened but he could not speak. Surely she realised what was necessary? Then, with even redder cheeks, she whispered "I'll put my shift in your bag." He turned his back and crossed himself twice while she removed her shift, tucked it into his bag, and tied the safety rope round her waist. Then she stepped into the water. Avel seized the rope round her with a firm grip. She could not protest. Her life was in his hands. Avel, holding her tightly to himself when necessary, trudged along cautiously without a word and so they reached the first resting place, the first rock.

They had to sit close together and Avel silently studied the leading marks for their next crossing. The second rock was the last stage on the crossing. Here Ana donned her shift and Avel his robes. She would have preferred that someone else had seen her body but she knew she must look on him with kindness and without suspicion. After all, the man had saved her from the hazards of the marsh.

Thank God it was all over! They stood on firm ground and the path to the hut lay before them. Ana trod on a thorn and cried out in pain, but sat down as

Avel pulled the thorn from her foot. As he rubbed her foot to ease the pain his teeth were chattering as if he had a fever.

There were fast running footsteps as Jahaan came into sight. He said to Avel "Will you not stay with us in the hut and rest?" Meantime he tossed Ana over his shoulder. Avel shook his head. "I must get back to the plou." He stepped into the marsh and they saw him leap from tuft to tuft until he disappeared out of sight. For Ana it was good to feel Jahaan's firm grasp on her and to know that there was security in the ravine.

Avel did not immediately return to the plou or to his own hut in the woods. Instead he chose to go to a nemet, a place of pagan sacrifices, of whose existence few people knew. It was in an open glade surrounded by almost impenetrable thickets. There were four ancient oaks and in three high hollows in the oaks stared out the empty eyes of skulls wind-bleached by long centuries. In a hollow in the fourth oak was a stone head narrow-eyed and with a huge nose and thick lips. On the reverse side of the head were two other faces the exact replicas of the one in front. The Triple Heads all had the same expression as they stared down at Avel.

There was a great stillness in the glade as if for countless years life and death had been frozen there. The moonlight barely penetrated the trees. Avel knelt for a long time before the three-headed God and when he finally rose by his side stood a shrouded figure grey and old as the oaks themselves. Fierce eyes glared out from under the deep hood.

"Why did you give us such bad advice, Avel? It was a perfect night for an abduction. A hunter's wind and we knew where to go but you never told us about the

Irish wolfhounds. Do you know what has happened to the man the dogs attacked? He is dying from a poisoned leg! You've lived with the Bretons, Avel. You must know that we can't afford to make mistakes where they are concerned. It's too dangerous!

"I did my best. The woman who was to be a slave drank the drugged liquid. She made no trouble. The man who led her was drunk and his comrades were fools to leave him to his own fate!"

"Don't call our men fools, Avel! Surely you realise that we rely on slaves for labour. We've got to have them either by capture or by breeding. The woman you recommended for abduction would have been good breeding stock, just the right kind of woman to bear many healthy children. However, we did get another coffle today and they are all in good health and will be useful in the future." He stared hard at Avel. "You'll really have to show us that you can make up your mind, especially in matters of faith. You cannot serve two masters. If you truly want to help our city and the Great Ones whom we worship you'll have to think and work more decisively. You're young. You're active. Perhaps you can be useful to us."

"What is it you want of me?"

"I have a plan in my mind. It'll need willingness and cunning on your part. I'll see you again at the next full moon and we'll talk over your future. I am patient, I can wait. Yet always remember that you cannot just play with our ideas, our faith, our people. However strange we may appear to others we have our own laws, our way of government and above all our religion. You, yes you, must decide what you want to do." He got up and turned away without another word and his ghostly shape vanished into the mists still clinging to the forest.

Avel did not go to the plou. Instead he went to his own lonely hut in the woods far away from human activity. There was little within the hut. Only the blackness of a dead fire and the spartan boards of the plank bed he chose for his couch when he meditated alone with his God. As he entered a frown appeared on his brow. It was the first time he had ever felt that the hut was hostile rather than friendly to him. Fasting three days and nights he sought to master the new temptation assailing him. When a raging thirst overcame him he gulped down copiously water from the spring and shrieking immersed his naked body in its icy waters to mortify his clamant flesh. In times past the spring indeed cured him of temptations. This night there was no respite for him in its chilly waves.

The night came. Often the night had been a wonderful time for him to struggle manfully against the sins of the flesh. Hours when the harsh severity of his couch had kept him awake so that he was like a soldier always on the alert. This night was sleepless also, but for other reasons. He longed so terribly that the flames aroused in him should die as quickly and decisively as the ashwood fire used to burn away so fast on his hearth. In his agony he found that his parched lips could no longer frame a prayer to God to help and comfort him. Instead in the dark it was a new and powerful demon who appeared floating on the calm waters of a deep pool and behind her were the evil mists that covered the marsh. He hadn't deliberately thrust himself into temptation. The Devil had beguiled him into thinking that he must hold her body tightly to save her from the dangers of the crossing. Yet now that the danger had gone and he had left her, the fleshly contact with her struck him with overwhelming force. His skin still trembled at the thought of how close her woman's body had been to him. He had felt her smooth, firm body under his hand, had seen her rosy nipples, erect with the chill, pointing upwards to the sky. The memory of this woman was strong. It gradually took entire control of him and assumed different forms. Sometimes he would see her rounded limbs, other times only her face would appear and hang over him. A beautiful, round face set in a halo of dark hair that covered her neck and shoulders. Her eyes would gaze at him, beguiling him, while her red lips shaped into inviting smiles. When he felt her gaze upon him his loins flamed into uncontrollable lust and serpents of desire writhed round his limbs as the Sirens had curled round the ship of Ulysses.

In moments of sheer exhaustion he cursed his own pious mother for vowing him to celibacy. He anathematised himself even more for making his own oath to live unmarried. In the grey of the morning he made attempts to say prayers that were familiar to him, appeals that had often helped him. To his utter dismay he found that his appeals to God had become empty formulae to him without meaning and powerless. His words now became savage protests against his destiny. Against the cruel blow of fate that had brought this Circe within his ken to inflict lasting misery on him. He even railed at Kristos himself.

On the third day of his ordeal the heat of his desire was fanned by a great jealousy. He saw Jahaan's hands as he bore the young woman on his shoulder. He perceived all too clearly the gratitude and tenderness – or was it love? – that appeared upon her face as she looked at Jahaan. When the fourth day came at last, the dawn saw his empurpled eyes, the blood-red sunrise heard his frantic cries.

"I can't endure this any longer. I must submit to the craving of my flesh for this woman who's ensnared me to her body with chains I cannot break. I cannot live any more unless I have this beautiful woman for my own, my slave, to enjoy. Let me be consumed for ever in Hell rather than suffer this deprivation on earth."

Avel looked up at the gloomy trees around him that were part of the great forest of Armorica. Within their depths there was the Three-Headed God. "Ye great gods, whom once I hated and despised! Your wonders are manifest in the skies, you ride on the storm or in the thunder which is your mighty voice. Aid me now and in the months to come. Help me with all your wisdom to weave a web so cunningly wrought that in due time I shall catch this lovely fly in its strong threads. Then I shall have my pleasure of this woman and make her forever mine. Let no man at his peril even touch her!"

"She shall be mine! She shall be mine!"

CHAPTER 9

In the weeks ahead Ana was to remember those days in the ravine before her baptism as the happiest times in her life. Norah devoted herself to caring for the young woman so that she forgot her abduction. She breathed sea air. She rested. Mind and body were refreshed. Above all, Norah told her what her baptism meant.

"It is the great act of faith for those who become Kristion" Norah said, as they sat by the stream. "You are re-born, enriched and glorified in those living waters in which they will plunge your body. When you take off your earthly garments the action is symbolic. Naked, you will be re-born just as a baby comes from it's mother's womb. Remember that Kristos was naked on his Cross. Oh, Ana, you will never forget this experience!"

"I long for you to be by my side Norah." Ana clasped Norah's hands in hers and drew them to her bosom.

"I cannot be with you in the water" Norah replied, "but I shall be near, holding the new garment which you will wear after the baptism and I will give you the meal of milk and honey. Your first food when the rite is completed. The whole congregation will be praying for you. One last thing I would say to you. If, when you enter the river you feel nervous, just repeat to yourself 'underneath are the everlasting arms'."

The following day they left for the journey over the

marsh. The crossing now no longer had horrors for Ana as Jahaan had carefully explained the system of secret pathways and leading marks he used. She repeated his instructions again and again until they were fixed in her memory and if need be she could find her own way over the marsh.

... ...

They were back at the plou. In a week's time she would be baptised. In seven days and nights, so eagerly counted by her, she would enter the holy waters in that quiet dell where alders bent low in benediction over the depths of the stream. Stone steps, never used otherwise, marked the site of baptism.

Peace had now come to Ana's mind and heart. Often, with a loving smile, she would think of all those who would be with her – Norah, Jahaan, Claudia – encouraging and loving her. There would be her fellow candidates for baptism, the "catechumens", Gaius and Susan a young bondwoman originally of pagan ancestors. She still wore her slave collar but would receive her freedom immediately after the baptism. The congregation of the plou would be there. Devout Bretons, whose faith was strong and who enriched their church and its ceremonies with love. She specially looked forward to seeing Maria, noted for her kindness to infants, and Azenor. She knew that in all phases of the ceremony they would be watching her, praying for her.

Gradually, hour by hour, Ana became absorbed in a world of ritual where every action, every thought was symbolic of the metamorphosis yet to come. Daily she bathed in the stream and knew that her bathe was a token of the mightier spiritual purification that would be hers. Every second day the catechumens knelt in the church while the priest recited prayers and the exorcisms that would cast out every vestige of Satan from their minds and bodies. Yes, Satan's power must be eroded until his claws relaxed their fiendish grip. Long, long afterwards she recollected that Thursday was an especially memorable day in their preparation. As she went up to the villa, she heard Guenole's voice, and as was the custom before baptism, he was questioning Norah and Jahaan about her life. He said "Speak now the full truth or forever hold your peace. Is the way of living of this young woman worthy of one who seeks to become a Kristion?"

"None better!" was the answer.

As Ana entered Norah smiled at her. "Come with me. I have a little gift for you". Once inside an inner room she placed her right hand affectionately on the young woman's shoulder. Her other hand held a bulky leather bag. She unlaced its thongs and out cascaded a cloth, white like foam from a mountain stream. Norah looked deep into Ana's eyes. "After your baptism you must be clothed with a fine garment, spotless and pure as you yourself will be. This dress was once my mother's and it was made from the finest linen they weave in Gaul. I've altered it so that it will fit you. It's yours forever. Just try it on now." The garment had an austere but wonderful glow about it. Ana touched it shyly. Tears welled up in her eyes.

"Try it" repeated Norah softly. "It's yours now." She removed her workaday shift and Norah slipped the new dress over her head. Chilly folds caressed her skin. The threads had the delicacy of the speedwell and it was spotless as the winter snows.

"How can I possibly take such a wonderful gift from you, Norah?"

"Take it Ana. I've no need for such dresses now. My next good covering will be the shroud you shall sew for me when I die. There's someone else should see you in it. Jahaan!"

He came in. He was dumb with surprise when he saw her. The dress had transformed Ana entirely. For him it was indeed the "Sigillum", the sign that God had accepted her. Her face was pale, her eyes shining. She was like the image of a woman saint that he had once seen. He felt a sharp pang. She had become remote from this world. His world. Would he lose her forever? At this wonderful moment for Ana he could not express his sad thoughts about her.

Ana was too shy to speak. Her gaze tried vainly to penetrate the shadow that had glided across his face. Then, impulsively, she grasped both his hands in hers and held them fast to her. "You, Jahaan, good and kindly man, saved my life for this purpose that I might fully become one of you, a Kristion. It will make me forever one with you, Jahaan. A Breton Kristion!" She held her hands upwards in prayer. "Oh my God, how I thank you for having led me to Norah and Jahaan."

Ana was smiling now and the joy on her face was as sweet as the rays of the western sun. How beautiful she looked in that robe from which her small pink toes peeped out. Her dark hair was smooth and shining. Knowledge of what she might mean to him was bursting in on Jahaan with the force of a spring freshet. It almost overwhelmed him.

Claudia had come in and indicated that they should

all say their Paternoster together. When they had said the prayer, Ana turned once more to Jahaan, clutching his hand in hers, feeling the calloused palm and the strength in his fingers. "My dear friend, on Sunday when the first cock crows, I shall be received into God's kingdom. It will be the most glorious day of my life." She turned her head away. She felt an almost unbearable longing to rest her head on his breast and say "I am yours!"

On Friday the period of fasting began for the catechumens. Guenole, like the plou priest who assisted him, believed in fasting, but Ana at first felt the gnawing sensation in her belly would never abate and lay hour long on the floor, seeking mastery over her too demanding flesh. The catechumens prayed in the church and received the final admonitions. The priest questioned them about the life of Kristos; the mystery of his death and resurrection. He gave them full instructions on how their limbs should be placed both in prayer and during the baptism itself. Also their posture when the final anointing – the consecrated chrism – was applied to their bodies. Three posts cut from oak had been set up about six feet from the congregational seats. Where they would stand the ground was raised slightly above the congregation so that the very last stages of the ritual would be clearly witnessed by all.

Saturday night at last! The setting sun traced fine patterns on the leaves and touched the converts with its soft rays. They wore only a single loose garment and walked barefoot to the place of baptism. Ana felt that this would be the apex of her life. She looked wistfully at those two devout men who would administer the baptism. They stood, heads bowed, waiting for the catechumens. Guenole, who had been invited to come from his own monastery to baptise them had set up an altar table by the stream and with him was the priest of the plou. There were seats for those who would watch and pray all night. Avel, whose duty it was to read from the Scriptures when required, stood ready behind a great oak, his eyes closed.

The river, broader at the point near the altar, was clearly visible to the congregation, so that every detail of the baptism would be revealed to them. At the bend further on, grey-white splashes denoted the rapids, but the river where the converts would undergo their immersion was calm. A white handrail marked the position of the steps leading down into water that was of suitable depth for baptism. Jahaan's crucifix had been brought from the ravine and suspended from a branch so that the catechumens in the water could gaze on the figure of Christ. It also meant that they would be looking at the East whence would appear the rising sun.

Darkness soon shrouded this outdoor baptistery. Resinwood torches set in cressets on the trees cast a sombre light on the dominicals and picked out the rounding of the pottery which held the oils for the two anointings. The small vessels contained the plain oil of the "catechumens!" The larger vases held the chrism, a mixture of oil and sweet balsam that had been already consecrated by the officiants ready for the last ritual. The torches were more numerous by the river and shone down on the steps. Guenole wore his long robes; the priest wore only a simple belted short tunic which left his powerful arms and thighs bare.

Ana stood between Gaius and Susan. Her body was tense, she trembled violently. Gaius alone seemed unmoved, sunk in his inner thoughts of his dead wife and child. Hours of prayer, hours of intense silent meditation followed, broken by interludes during which they rested to hear the Scripture readings. Avel during the readings never looked at Ana.

All through the night the river was the companion of their thoughts. It called to them in its dank voices and above the resonance of its rapids they could hear the trout splashing. Gradually some torches faded, becoming blackened skeletons. Those by the steps and the altar were renewed and shone more brightly. Ghostly wisps of night mist drifted by then vanished. The stars grew paler and a finger of white cloud broke the scintillating canopy of the heavens. Everything became beautiful to Ana's eyes and ears, especially the natural music emanating from the leaves as they moved in a timeless rhythm to the minute currents of the breeze. Sometimes there were brief pauses in their melody as if to allow the hearing time to absorb these Heavenly notes that came from Him above. Below the trees was a dark huddle of figures; the congregation. The catechumens stood like people carved in wood, swaying with fatigue and emotion. Guenole looked up at the sky. He said "The time is almost nigh when God shall speak to us."

They waited. In spite of the night chill Ana felt drops of sweat on her brow. Soon she must plunge into that river. Her body would undergo change. From a mere woman she would become a Kristion. There was no retreat now. The current of her life was carrying her along faster and faster. A clutch of hunger for an instant disturbed her body then vanished as tremors of more profound feelings thrilled through her.

"Pray!" said Guenole, raising his hands high.

A cock crew, three times. It was the divine signal. The deaconess, white-coiffed, came and stood close behind Ana and Susan. Her duty was to strip each woman when her turn came; Susan would be the last. Guenole and the priest led the three nearer to the banks of the river; the waters swirled silently beneath them, the upper stone step was a light patch against the dark green grass. In the east a nascent cloud was tinged with pink. Ana felt the young girl close to her. Susan was sobbing.

Every nerve in Ana's own body anticipated the coming spiritual event. Cold waters would lap limbs and body and she would bow her head in that ineffable purity of God that flowed to the sea. Naked as if from her mother's womb she would be cast deep into the river for only within its waters would she find the mercy that the God of the Kristion would grant her. She was not now on her own, she had never been. She belonged to God and to Him alone. Mutely she uttered a supplication to Him.

"O God, let these waters, the Seal of Thy Spirit, the Sigillum, cleanse me from all unworthy thoughts. Let Thy will not mine be done in my body. If it be Thy will after this baptism let them give me in marriage to Jahaan. Humbly, I will accept this noble man. For now I am downcast as a beggar who seeks her crust from others. My body soon to be naked, is the temple of Thy Holy Spirit. Do what you will with it." Tears trickled down her cheeks.

The plou priest now took up the vessels that contained the "oil of the catechumens" and stood by his fellow cleric. Guenole stepped in front of Gaius. He said loudly that all might hear, "Dost thou renounce

Satan and all his service and all his works? If so, say after me, 'I renounce thee, Satan!'"

Gaius, upright as a soldier, said in vibrant tones "Renuntio!" He threw off his tunic and stood naked before all. The holy man dipped his cupped hands into the oil and saying "Let all evil spirits depart from thee" rubbed the oil onto his chest and massive shoulders.

There was the patter of bare feet on the stone steps and a faint splashing. The three men were in the water. The congregation saw the powerful arms of Gaius held out on each side in the form of a cross, his sturdy head as he stood with legs apart, waiting. Words resounded above the clamour of the disturbed stream.

"Dost thou believe in God, the Father Almighty?" Then came the deep strong "Credo!" There was a sudden splash, a sigh from Gaius. Bubbles broke the calm surface of the waters. The head, streaming with water, rose again above the surface.

"Dost though believe in Kristos Jesus?" Again from a now wet mouth the answer "Credo."

More dipping in the waters, the question, the answer from once pagan lips "Credo!" The last immersion deep down in the blackness of the night river.

The stars were fading away. A blackbird called to its wandering mate. The night leaves were turning into distinct green shapes. There were tears on Susan's cheeks. Ana knew that all her unknown past existence was to be cancelled out by the power of God, making her a new woman. She was hardly aware that Norah stood not far off, a white garment on her arm, that Gaius, his white body streaming with water, had come up the steps and was being dried ready for the chrism. Nor in her spiritual exaltation was she even conscious of Avel nearby, his face three dark dots on a blur of white.

It was time for the baptism of the two females. The congregation was standing, their hands raised, their eyes eager to witness the supreme ceremony of the Kristion faith. The deaconess undressed Ana leaving her bare before all the people. She carefully tucked her hair into the white cap made by Norah. It fitted closely; she tied the strings tightly under her chin.

Guenole softly applied the oil of the catechumens to head and shoulders. The oil was soothing to her body. His voice was stern yet fatherly as he asked the initial question and she made the first responses.

Hands were leading her towards the steps and she was going down, down. The cold water spread slowly up her feet, her legs, her belly. She felt it lapping round her breasts. She gazed up at Jahaan's crucifix. Beyond it was the faint light of the new day glowing in the East. To her mind came the words "They are stretching out my arms firmly, Lord, so that they may be as yours were on the Cross. My eyes will be closed as yours were closed in the death that came before the resurrection. I give my body, naked, to the whip strokes of these waters as your bare back, chained, received the soldiers' cruel lashes. I know that underneath are the everlasting arms!" Black, moving waters embraced her limbs, their message keen as sword blades. She stood motionless in the dark water, her hands now raised high about her head to Heaven. She was ready now to make that supreme act of submission, to give herself wholly to Him; she was helpless. She felt the touches that were so tender yet firm. Guenole's hand was on her head, his other hand clasping her arm, the priest was holding her other arm with both hands. She felt a downward pressure soft yet irresistible. She bent her head in full surrender and said the words that were now burnt deep into her being. "Renuntio!" "Credo!" and again "Credo!" In her ecstasy she could have cried aloud but rendered out her emotion in deep, sustained breaths. Thrice they asked the questions; thrice she made the responses that were the affirmation of faith, thrice she underwent the immersion as she bent her knees and her bowed head and shoulders were plunged deep beneath the water. The hands no longer were on her head or arm after she had said the last "Credo!" The first part of her baptism was over.

She remained in the water to be with Susan during her baptism. The deaconess briskly stripped the young slave of all save her gleaming slave collar and they led her down the steps. Susan made the correct responses and was thrice immersed, her slim white body quivering. She came up spluttering and gasping for air. The two young women climbed the steps together and were dried. Ana felt she was now one of a mighty congregation throughout the world to which the plou itself belonged.

The last part of the rite had come. The three catechumens took their places by the oak posts allotted to them. There was no place in that holy ritual for false modesty. Ana, naked, stood by her own oak post, her hands stretched upwards above her head. She looked into Guenole's saintly eyes as he applied the holy chrism to her head and body. Eyes that held the purity of God within them.

Ana was conscious with an intense happiness of the presence of Jahaan so near to her. Through her tears of fulfilment and joy she saw him as never before. His great hands were raised in prayer. Was it also the tinge of a burgeoning tenderness that she read in his eyes that gazed so reverently at that anointed, sanctified body, at her belly's roundness, the curves of her thighs and her breasts glistening all over with sacred oil and shining in the torchlight? There was the sweet smell of balsam in her nostrils. She murmured as she looked at him. "Kristos, how great is thy love to me, to Jahaan, to Norah, to all the world!"

So came the benison of the white shift, the last token of baptism put on her by Norah's gentle hands. The three newly baptised walked to the altar. Many others stood around, their hands raised in prayer. The chalice was placed before Ana; her lips touched it. A flame ran through her, burning, consuming. It was followed by a feeling of unutterable peace. She rose from her knees. She was one of the Kristion!

The three rested under the awakening sky. Susan knelt and the blacksmith removed her slave collar. She was now a free woman. The converts sipped eagerly of the milk and honey given to them by Norah. People clustered round them. Everywhere there was an atmosphere of contentment and peace. Broad bands of sunlight were spreading across the forest. Leaves rustled as the breeze fingered them. From the plou came signs of life. Women chattering, a wisp of smoke from a fire, a horse whinnying.

Beyond all these was a far distant sound of hoof beats. As they came near, those listening knew that they were those of a horse ridden at great speed. They came still nearer. The rider cried to the watchman and at once a column of fire shot up from the beacon. Voices shouted again and again "The Bagaudae! The Bagaudae!"

Now the horseman was in sight, galloping to the plou in a sauve-qui-peut. His beast was white with lather, its eyes pools of fire. He shouted at Thomas without dismounting. "It's the Bagaudae! A party well armed, some on horseback! Get ready at once! If my horse will take it I'll warn the other plou."

All the people except one were clustering round Thomas. Women were screaming, children crying, men shouting for weapons. Guenole did not hurry to leave the place of baptism. He gathered up the vessels, the chalice, the paten, then knelt in prayer. He rose and carrying his baskets came into the plou. People made way for him and he took his place by Thomas. When Ana looked at his face she thought of a great granite rock by the sea. It was strong and had weathered many storms.

Thomas held up his hand. At once the hubbub ceased. They listened as he explained the situation and what they must do. A band of Bagaudae were coming and would soon arrive at the plou. They all knew who the Bagaudae were; banditti whose aim was to attack defenceless settlements, burn houses, snatch what loot they could and drag women and children away into slavery.

"They'll rape us!" shouted a distraught young woman. "What can we do against such monsters?"

"You can do a great deal!" said Thomas coolly. "The plou will be defended by such men as are capable of bearing arms. Mothers with children and unmarried women will not stay in the plou but will go to a safe hiding place that is unknown to any attackers. There you will find food, water and blankets for your comfort. There will be armed guards with you but you must stay there until we send a messenger to tell you when it is once more safe to return to the plou. Your guide is ready to lead you there." He turned away from them to the waiting men. Some already had weapons in their hands, all were stern faced, prepared for the grim task ahead of them.

"You are Bretons! You are warriors! You face tough enemies who would snatch from you your harvest, your homes, your wives and children! You will fight hard both inside and outside the plou. You will conquer them and drive them away. Get your weapons and defend the plou with all your vigour and strength!"

Women were clinging to their men. None were screaming now but many were weeping. Gaius was kissing his little daughter. In his hand was a great broad-bladed spear. Claudia said to Ana "You go with the women and children and nurse the sick or infirm." She embraced her.

"And you, Claudia?"

"I will stay here with the deaconess. We may have to tend the wounded."

Ana left her to join the women who were already lining up behind their guide, the charcoal burner. They moved off. Once she turned to wave back at Claudia. Then the plou was out of sight and they were trudging into the forest. Four older male Bretons accompanied them. They would defend the entrance to the hiding place in the unlikely possibility of any enemy wandering that way.

The women carried or led the smaller children and struggled hard when they had to pass through the dense thickets. All was silent. When at last, weary, they arrived at the mouth of the strange pit, unknown to them all except Ana, they shuddered at this dark hole and wondered what lay beneath. Yet Ana unhesitatingly swung herself down the ladder. The women followed. Their guards were cheerful. "Don't you see that this is the safest place in the whole forest? Down with all of you and we'll close it up firmly. Outside they'll camouflage the entrance slab with branches and leaves. Don't worry."

The women and children scrambled down the ladder and moved into the first chamber. It had been changed. The image of Epona had gone and all was clean. The inner passageway had blankets and benches and the women made themselves as comfortable as they could. They heard the scraping sound as the stone slab above the pit was pulled into position by the men outside and the rustle of branches as the camouflage was placed over everything above. The footsteps died away. They were sealed in, cut off from the world above.

Down there it was very quiet. Mothers talked in soft voices and even the young babies were subdued. They were secure. They had food and water for several days but still feared to disturb the silence of their hiding place. Yet it was hard just to sit there and wait. The oldest women sat back and told their beads. Ana tended ailing infants and had not much time to brood. Snail-like the hours dragged by. Most women were too anxious to eat or drink. All they could do was to wait, their ears alert for sounds above. Was that someone on top of the slab? The brushwood was being pushed aside. Then three taps, followed by two more! The signal! The slab was prised away and their guards stared up into the eyes of the charcoal burner.

"Thanks be to God and the saints! We've driven them

off! They're fleeing through the woods, our horsemen in hot pursuit! Thomas told me to run as fast as I could to free you now that the result of the battle is known!"

Pell-mell they rushed through the tunnel and swarmed up the ladder. They ran back to the plou. In the west the sun was sinking into a shroud of blood-red clouds and the acrid tang of burning wood insulted their nostrils. Columns of smoke and flame shot upwards, wounding the peace of the evening.

The first dead! The man lay face down as if he were asleep but there was a spear thrust through his ribs. Another, whose torn helmet lay by his side, his skull crushed by the francisca. The dead hands still clawed at the earth as if they would grasp it even in death. Fierce looking men the Bagaudae, but none with a wound in his back. They had died in a hand to hand struggle and fallen where they had stood. Among the mists of the coming night grey shadows waited – the wolves.

The Bretons had paid their price for the victory. Battle scarred warriors were carrying back on litters the twisted bodies of men who had held off the first onslaught of the raiders while defence was rallied. By the gates of the plou the struggle had been at its fiercest. The Bagaudae riders had tried to force their steeds over the palisade stakes. Horses lay eviscerated, men crushed beneath. The ditch was choked with corpses. One of the raiders had fired two huts and an adjacent haystack and the flames were spreading to everything in their path. The smoke veiled the villa and the swordsmith's shop. Everywhere women were shouting for their men.

Ana heeded none of these things. She was running, running towards the cross that towered up immutably in the centre of the plou. Towards the thing of white and red that lay beneath. Where two men knelt. Thomas and Guenole. It was Claudia! Someone whispered "It was a spear thrust from behind!" Guenole held the viaticum in blood-flecked hands. Behind them knelt Martha and Maria, weeping. Ana threw herself down and clasped Claudia in her arms to ease the agony. She tried to grasp the last message for her etched in those pain-crazed eyes. A faint smile was on the proud lips. She bent low to hear the words.

"I shan't see Burdigala or the vineyards again but all will be well for you." The eyes moved wildly; they were glazing in the moment of the separation of the spirit from the torn body. She spoke so low that only Ana could hear. "*Quis separabit?*" – who shall separate us from the love of God?" "You're from the future! I see you in Britannia – far from here! You'll wed Jahaan – An" – the last syllable was cut off abruptly.

The eyes closed. She spoke only one word more – "Thomas" – before she died. Guenole said quietly "We've lost the best woman we had."

The women clustered round. They mourned her; the sound of their keening was as the moaning of the sea before the storm breaks. A great ocean of loneliness laved Ana in its bitter waters. Even Norah's hand on her shoulders could not lessen her grief and despair.

Ana sat by herself in the guest house. It was growing dark. Her thoughts were not focused on the world outside, on the plou where men and boys were toiling to repair the houses, where women prepared the evening meal. She was recalling all that had happened in the last few weeks especially from the time of the alarm to the moment when they had laid Claudia in the grave next to her child's. The Bretons had faced disaster with the stubborn will inherent in their natures. After the initial shock – besides Claudia eight had been killed and three died later from their wounds – they had set to work.

Ana herself had washed Claudia's body and arranged the fine hair round the face that bore an expression of wonderful peace. During this rite the priest and the monks had sung psalms and prayers for her and for all the dead. Then the procession to the church. Youths carried the shrouded dead and there was a pure simplicity in the Kristion ceremonial that uplifted her heart. Alone now, she heard again in her mind the monks chanting *"Jehova pastor meus est non possum egere* – the Lord is my shepherd, I shall not want ..." Then Guenole had given them an address to remind his people of the shortness of life – but also to tell them that death was nothing more than a gateway to a greater world than this life of sorrow.

There had been the heavy smell of incense as they walked to the gravesides, bearing the dead. Then the last words *"Ego sum resurrectio et vita* ... I am the resurrection and the life; he that believeth in me, though he were dead yet shall he live." She saw again the ashes – they were grey like the gloom around her now – that they scattered, heard the patter of the sods of earth, falling. The last farewells. The torches were extinguished, people, exhausted, slept. On the morrow they must awaken to recreate their own lives, rebuild the plou and get used to the gaps in their ranks.

During the time that followed Ana fell into a mood that was strange for her. She felt that she was waiting for some event to happen but did not know what it would be. Her days were filled with work. There were the wounded to care for, women to console, sick children to be healed. In the evenings other matters obtruded themselves, thoughts of her own future. She had become a Kristion, but what would be her life in the years that lay ahead?

Four young women had already been spoken for in marriage. One of them, Susan, was to be given to Gaius. She was eagerly awaiting union with him as she spoke the same tongue as he did. It was the duty of every nubile girl to marry and thus provide children. Once Ana had accidentally overheard two women gossip while they beat out their blankets on stones by the stream. One said, laughing, "What of that fair wench? She's old enough and strong enough! Time we saw her carrying a child!" The other laughed. "Oh, they'll give her to Jahaan all right! He needs a woman down there in the ravine to broil his fish and bear his children. She's a bit of a vixen but he's tough enough to tame her."

Nothing had been said as yet to Ana of marriage. If indeed Jahaan wed the fair girl there was no man else whom she would wish to be her husband. She had no desire to take a vow of chastity like the deaconess and live like a nun, the only alternative to marriage. No, she knew that she wished to marry and bear children. What had stung her like an adder about the women's idle gossip was the implication that Jahaan might marry another woman. For after the death of Claudia she had suddenly found that Jahaan was becoming much more part of her innermost life. Or perhaps her perception had been there months before but she had not really understood it fully until those casual remarks had awakened her to the yearning she had for a closer fusion with him, a deeper friendship possibly? With him she felt that she wanted to share her thoughts, her anxieties, her hopes. With him, as with Claudia, her unknown past would never be a burden to her.

In her doubts and perplexities, Ana unconsciously sought solace in Norah who had constantly remained calm in the presence of hardship and danger. Once, when they were talking of returning to the ravine now that Claudia had gone, Norah said "We are wholly together now, you and I. What you have to endure I will endure, if you must suffer, I too will suffer in the same measure. If you have sad thoughts, I will likewise have sad thoughts." Ana had always been close to Norah. Now a flower of still deeper affection was growing between them and except for her own work, Ana hardly ever left Norah's side. At night it was a comforting delight for her to see Norah's face in the glow from the fire or the rushlights, waiting for her. The bond between them was as strong as the bond of kinship. Norah even began to use the term "my daughter" to her and she could sleep soundly in Norah's arms.

One evening which they had devoted to the shared tasks of spinning or carding wool, Norah began to chat again about mating; the child growing in the womb, the gentle joys of suckling. It seemed to Ana that there might be some purpose behind this talk. She saw very little of Jahaan in the weeks after the raid even though he lived in the guest house. Indeed, sometimes he worked long days in the woods and even slept there. He was cutting down suitable timber which he brought back to the plou and used skilfully to repair the roofs and walls of the huts damaged by the Bagaudae.

Jahaan seemed to be as reticent as he had been when

Ana first knew him. Quietly he had eaten with them that evening and was about to return to the smithy to sharpen some tools when Norah said gently "Jahaan, isn't it time you thought of wedding? We lost six unwed men in the battle and we need children for the plou. Surely there's some maiden who would be a good wife to you?" Jahaan flushed but said nothing. Norah knew him far too well than to press him to discuss so intimate a subject. He muttered something about being so busy and returned at once to the forge.

Ana was glad that she had been sitting in the darkest part of the room. Her face had gone very white and putting down her carding comb she said abruptly "I'm weary, I must retire early." She went to her palliasse but could not help a sigh escaping from her. Norah sat for a while, pondering, over the dying fire. From the palliasse came the sound of breathing but occasionally a rustle told her that the sleeper was restive. She pattered over to Ana's bedside.

It was a warm night. Ana, her arms outstretched, lay on her back. The blanket did not cover her entirely and Norah saw the full young bosom, the rounding of the shoulders and the third breast set in the four moles that made up a cross. A deep sigh came from the sleeper's lips. Norah looked more closely. The face was flushed and there were traces of tears on the smooth, round cheeks. "You may bear God's cross on your body – it's His will that you should do so – but you shall not bear a cross of pain, of unnecessary longing, in your heart. God does not want you to suffer in that way."

"I would give my life for you. You shall be wed! You shall be the mother of my grandchild! How can I stop those tears? I know! We'll go back to the ravine! There, alone with Jahaan, you shall know serenity again. We won't hurry matters but the future is going to be bright for you – even happier for all of us when I dandle your first baby on my knee." Her eyes twinkled. Silently she laughed in her own way that bore the wisdom of countless centuries of womenfolk of her tribe. In a few days they went back to the ravine. There, in the little hut, Ana had no more feelings of loneliness. She was contented in her work with Norah. Above all she shared fully in Jahaan's life and work. She astonished him by the dexterity with which she could weave baskets and at her quickness in mastering the heavy oars when they went out fishing, though sometimes she feathered badly, but he always smiled at her mistakes.

The supreme moments of their life together were when she assisted him in building a new curragh. Like many true crofters whose lives are wedded both to land and sea, Jahaan was an expert boat builder. For months he had collected the woods that together made up the frame. Hazelwood strakes, ash members, pliable yet strong and hard oak seats. On them when they were fitted together must be placed the ox hides that formed the skin hull of this craft. He taught her the hard but essential task of sewing the joins in the damp ox hides. They had to be very well sewn for their lives depended on their boat. When all was ready the two of them completed the boat.

During all this work, Ana had to be often in contact with Jahaan. His hands would touch hers as she held one part of the woodwork against another or as they tugged and tugged to pull the skin hull taut. Twice she had to hold him tightly round the waist to give him purchase as he made the last firm adjustment of a frame within the boat. With the perception of a sensitive woman, she found that his body responded warmly to her firm touch and she was glad at what she found. The time of full ripeness and understanding came in the last moments when the boat was finished. Tired, she was standing up very straight to ease her aching back and stretched her arms high in the air. He came up quietly behind her. She was conscious of his heart beating furiously, of the warmth in the man's body, of the strong limbs against hers. He laid his hands very gently round her waist. She knew from the touch that he had never caressed a woman before in that chaste life of his. Yet his touch was so considerate to her and through his hard fingertips flowed a fire of tenderness and affection to her. She could do nothing, say nothing, only stand there, swaying back against him, feeling him support her, wishing nothing save to be there always by the boat, their joint creation, and the blue sea beyond. "You're such a good man" she whispered.

He came round and faced her, looking into the depths of her eyes. "You'll be my wife, Ana? I've often dreamt of the time when you shall be always by my side – together with our children."

She looked down at the rock ledge. There he had found her, there she had declared that he must always trust her when she told him she knew nothing of her past life. There, rode on her new painter the boat that they had created together. She smiled. "Yes, I'll marry you, Jahaan. I've always wanted you to be my husband."

They were wed in the outdoor church in the plou. Afterwards, Ana went alone to the burial place and knelt by Claudia's headstone. "So it has been, Claudia, as you foresaw with your Second Sight. I'm wed to Jahaan, a good man. Shall I ever know that future in which once I lived, that you told me about in your dying moments?"

The stone was silent.

AD 495

PART 2

THE CITY BY THE SEA

CHAPTER 10

It was one of those days towards the end of summer when the sun was showing signs that it had given of its full power and was now on the decline. Though the morning had been heavy and the air warm, in the afternoon a chill crept in from the sea and touched the cliffs near Ys with damp, searching fingers. The temple high above the city began to cast cold, grey shadows which lingered on the houses below where the priests dwelt. Lower down in the city in a building larger than the rest, a sharper shadow rested on a woman who stood in her room absorbed in her preparations.

Dahut, Princess of Ys, was some thirty years of age but her incomparable body showed no signs that her first youth had gone. She had bathed herself with great care and now, anointed with fine unguents, stood in front of the great bronze mirror on the wall. She gazed hard into the shining metal eager to see every graceful movement of her limbs and body, from the voluptuous swaying of her hips to the dainty steps of her small feet. She set her hands high above her head and clasped them together while she admired her full breasts. She saw a slender waist and the smooth stomach of a woman who had borne no children. On her white thighs there was no crease nor did her proud face bear a single wrinkle.

The clepsydra, drop by drop, oozed out its measure of water, marking the passage of time.

When she was satisfied with her appearance she began to dress. At every movement she paused to see how well her garments suited her. Her hair, whose brilliant sheen was displayed beneath a veil of red satin gave a touch of flame to her ivory cheeks. As she shook her small round head, golden earrings shaped like tiny dolphins swayed and glittered from her ears. She sat down in the carved oak chair and fingered an ornament, a great gold breast pin, whose dagger point thrust inwards as if to pierce the heart above which it lay.

Yet Dahut, now virtual ruler of the city of Ys, during the indisposition of her father, King Gradlon, had nothing to fear from the city she governed. She knew neither threats nor menaces. Gradlon's daughter inherited the respect in which Gradlon, once ruler of the kingdom of Cornouaille, had been held.

Set deep in the wall of her room was a stone carving. It was the image of a demon, squat in body and with an enormous face whose massive, protruding eyes followed her all round the chamber. The gaping lips, crammed with huge teeth, expressed sensuality and lust. For a long time she gazed at this symbol then said "If you truly represent the demons whom I adore then let Evil rule over Good. Let me have the power to choose Evil for myself. Let me enjoy forever the wickedness of all sensual delights of the flesh."

Dahut looked through her window and saw Gradlon seated on the colonnade. His hair waved unsteadily in the breeze. He was old now but once he had been renowned as a famous warrior who had led his armies to battles and success. He was chatting to a grey haired harper who fingered his strings with a skill that came from many years of devotion to his art. Gradlon's head swayed a little in time to the rhythms that the harper was plucking out. His hands, too, were uncertain in their movements until a vigorous champing came from the nearby stables when his eyes grew bright and he smiled. A horse's head appeared over the half-door, the beast gave a loud whinnying. The groom hurried up. "When you have fed my horse saddle him, for I would ride through the city down to the sea. Meantime I shall quaff a goblet of cervoise to warm me."

As Dahut watched a sneer appeared on her lips and her eyes grew hard. "A King in name but who would know him for such? All he cares for are his horse and his drink. As if to ride a horse made him King. He's so proud of that horse; he values its well-being as if it were his own life. Also, he has a hankering after the Kristion despite the ban on their living in Ys. I truly believe that if I were not the real ruler we should see hordes of priests swarming like black flies through our streets. That shall never be while I hold the reins of power!"

Dahut stamped her foot and immediately a slave appeared. He wore only a leather apron on which was gold-tooled the double dolphins of Ys. The heavy bronze collar riveted round his neck that denoted his servile condition likewise bore the same emblem. "Has the man been brought here?"

"The guards conveyed him secretly into the palace as you asked and have put him in the small lower room where he awaits your pleasure."

"He has the sign manual?"

"They would not have admitted him to this part of the city without it."

Dahut followed her slave to a staircase. Like most of the larger houses in Ys, the great hall of Gradlon was built on several levels. She went down a flight of stone steps some of which bore cracks in their surfaces. At the bottom was a thick oak door which she opened with a large key. The slave looked enquiringly at her. Two guards had suddenly appeared. She spoke sharply to them. "You may leave me alone with this man. I've no fear of strange men." She entered the room. It was lit by candles and contained another dragon sculpture similar to the one in her own room. The monster stared insolently with its terrible eyes at an individual clad in a long woollen cloak with a cowl. Dahut went up and partly pulled back the cowl to reveal a thin, pale face, gaunt cheeks and eyes red and tense.

"So you're the man? A shaven head? A priest of the Kristion? And yet you dare to come into Ys? You must have very strong motives for risking the hostility of our people. We've only allowed one of them in recently – not you." She moved into the darkness so that her face and expression were concealed.

"Why did your guards bring me here and then lock me up as if I were a criminal?"

"I give orders to the guards! Those were my orders and mine alone. They arrested you for your own safety. Don't you realise what would have happened to you if you had been caught wandering around the city in that outlandish garb?"

"I had your sign manual. I trusted in that. I showed it to the soldier at the postern gate. He recognised it, then immediately called the watch and had me brought to this room. I don't understand why I, as a man of peace, am treated thus."

"It's not for you to ask questions. Let me see the evidence."

From his long sleeve a muscular hand protruded which she gazed at with some care for it held a ring with a bronze bezil on which were incised two interlocking dolphins. Over them was further engraved into the metal the letter D followed by two minute lines or scratches. "Hm!" said Dahut. "That's my sign manual and you may keep it as long as you are useful to me. Yet I must point out that this ring is not given to you on behalf of the city of Ys but only as pledge of my personal protection. If I choose to withdraw that protection you would be simply another stranger – an alien – and no one would lift a finger to save you if you got into trouble. You know our city law? If a stranger stays here after sunset he shall be put to death unless he has my sign manual and my signature written on a tablet to show to the guards. This permission is rarely granted."

The man shuddered. "Your laws are harsh and cruel it seems."

"It is our law. It is the way we are governed and you'll have to obey us. Now you've got to earn that ring and safe conduct. What do you want to do for me?"

"What I have to speak about is for your ears only. You have guards at the door. Surely, they may hear our words and talk about them."

Dahut laughed, a long laugh that grated on the nerves of her listener.

"Do you think that I've any wish to betray you? As for my servants, look!" She jerked open the door and dragged one of the waiting guards into the room. The slave did not resist this rough handling. She pulled apart the man's lips. The stranger recoiled back in horror. The tongue had been cut away. The man left. She closed the door on him. They were alone again.

"No one talks about my private life. These men are dumb but I assure you that like everyone else in Ys they won't speak about me. They serve me faithfully like all people in Ys. Also, you can speak freely in this room." She spoke with a slight emphasis on the word "this" – "no sounds at all carry to other parts of the building." Something chilly had begun to pervade the room. The air was dank and close. It was very quiet.

"I must know as soon as can be what you intend to do and whether you'll do it more efficiently than before. You bungled an attempt to capture one of the young Breton women whom you suggested could be a slave here. I don't like bunglers!"

The man moved uneasily at her words. "What is it that you want? Another slave? After the Bagaudae attack the Bretons guard their plou more assiduously than ever. They still don't know that the abduction was attempted by your men but they're not taking any chances!"

"I'm not interested in slave women though we need

them in Ys to breed children for us. We lose so many offspring through the marsh fever. However, do you know a Breton who sometimes comes here? He is the only Breton to visit us apart from Guenole, the monk, whom we invite here as a water diviner. I have glimpsed this man once in our market place. He's a young man, very strong and tall." She paused for a moment and drew a deep breath. "I would like him for one of my bodyguards, tongue or no tongue. We could teach him our martial arts and train him well to defend me. I need men like that – bold and courageous men whose loyalty to me would be unquestioning. Men who, when the time comes, would give their lives for me."

There was a peculiar intonation in Dahut's voice. Her speech had begun to slur, her eyes flashed and her body swayed from side to side. Her hearer still could not fully see her features beneath a veil but became uneasy at the way she talked and the marked emphasis she placed on certain words. His feet shifted beneath his long robe. The air in the room grew damp.

"You would have a Breton, a Kristion, a stranger to you as a member of your bodyguard? Surely that's dangerous?"

"We're not at war with the Bretons now. To us they're only a potential hazard. Of course we capture slaves but chiefly at a distance and by raids. If we had this man here we could ensure his loyalty by various means which would make him yield. If he refused to take an oath of loyalty there are strong chains and other means to compel the most unruly to submit."

Her listener was silent for a long time and Dahut did not hurry him. His lips tensed and he breathed hard. In a sombre voice he said "I know the man you mean and I know where he lives. He stays in the plou occasionally. He lives in a hut some way off. He's married. There's also an old woman with him and his wife."

"Then all we have to do is to send a strong party of men to surround his hut and capture him."

"That's practically impossible. His hiding place is remote and very inaccessible. The only route to it leads through a dangerous marsh which could swallow up a whole army. You would throw away the lives of your men if they attempted to cross it."

Dahut stamped her foot impatiently. "I must have this man! How can we capture him?"

"There is another way. You have noted that he comes here sometimes to sell fish. He stays only briefly in Ys."

"Naturally. He must know our law about leaving before sunset."

"When he comes here you could seize him."

"How shall we know when that will be? Sometimes many weeks elapse before he appears again. Once he was away for over four months. When he came he stayed only an hour and went away again. He comes by boat."

"I will watch his movements and when I find out on what day he intends to come to Ys to sell fish I will come here and forewarn you."

"You say the man's married. What of his wife?"

"A comely woman." His words were sharp. "Sometimes she goes out in the boat with him but she has not yet been to Ys."

"You've no liking for this man?"

"I hate him. I wish he were dead."

"How you Kristion love each other! You're a Kristion, a Breton, yet you would betray a fellow Kristion as lightly as I crush this woodlouse beneath my foot." She thrust savagely down on the grey shape. It became a squashed blur. "You don't have only a motive of dislike for a man to throw him to the wolves like that? You've some other deeper motive for your enmity. A woman? It's for some woman that you would be a traitor to your own people? I tell you, Avel, that we don't like traitors. Traitors are only good when they are dead. You'd better tell me the truth before we go any further."

The candles flickered in their sconces. Dahut came closer and stared hard into the man's eyes. "Answer me at once! What's your real motive? Yes, it's a woman. The man's wife! I know it!"

"You wouldn't, you couldn't know the hell on earth that I have been through these last few months!" his voice erupted with such fury that he almost choked on the words. "I wanted her for my own but he took her, used her body, enjoyed the limbs that I should have enjoyed. In the name of your gods help me as I will help you!" Sweat poured down his livid cheeks.

Dahut appeared unmoved by this outburst. "I think we can leave this woman alone for the time being. Let us talk about this man, her husband, first. The plan is that as soon as you know definitely that he is coming on a boat trip here you will alert us."

"I won't fail you. The time of day will depend on the weather and the tides and it must be before the winter storms break." Dahut had begun to breathe deeply. Her lips were pressed convulsively together, her hand forced against her breast pin. A scarlet drop quivered on her finger tips. "Once he gets here he'll never leave Ys, alive or dead. But what reward do you want for this betrayal? Silver, gold?"

"I would like to live in Ys and become one of its citizens."

"After getting this man to me?"

"I doubt whether he would ever know that I had any connection with his abduction, if your men hold their tongues. Besides, I have another reason which so far has remained a secret. I have been to the nemet, the sacred grove, and I would worship the ancient gods in your temple up there."

"You're satisfied with just that? No, you want another greater reward?" The woman's eyes were piercing.

"If this woman comes here" said Avel, "I ask that she shall be allotted to me as my personal body slave. I know you don't acknowledge the marriage rite of the Kristion, therefore it would be within your power to grant her to me."

"You seem to know a great deal about Ys and its customs." Dahut spoke in the slow voice she used when she was deeply interested in some subject. "Very well, provided you get the man here to Ys it shall be as you wish. Once here in Ys, we shall capture them. I foresee one possible unpleasant consequence which you have not anticipated. If the Bretons discover that the man, and perhaps his wife too, are missing they may think that we have kidnapped them and there would be trouble, serious trouble, between them and us."

"It's very unlikely that this would occur. The old woman who lives with them would report them as missing. Nothing more, for she could not know what had happened to them. She might even think that there had been a boat accident at sea and both had been drowned. Or it might be surmised that he had left your city and then just vanished into the woods or on the sea. After all, you cannot be responsible for the welfare of strangers once they have left your gates."

"You've a subtle imagination good at playing with possibilities. Have you forgotten that Guenole comes here with his hazel rods?"

"Guenole will know nothing about the man's visit to you and indeed he may not visit you on the day that you capture the fisherman."

"All right, we'll take the risk then." Dahut unlocked the door. "These men will escort you back to the postern and see you out of the gate. Keep your shaven head always covered by your cowl and take great care when you come back here. Do what you have to do and the gods be fortunate to you!" Avel hid his face and head once more in the hood and left the building, accompanied by the guards. They followed a solitary path that led to a small postern. Dahut looked out from her own window and saw him enter the gate of the small tower. Then he disappeared from her sight.

Dahut stood for a few moments by a little torso in stone of a goddess. The expression on the goddess's face was serious and dignified. For an instant a deep longing and a great sadness came into Dahut's eyes. "Yes, I can think of you when I am in the sea – only there – but here on the land my life must be hard and ruthless and I can have no time for your compassion." Dahut passed on to the great hall of the palace where she was accustomed to meet the important people of the city. Today her council or curia was waiting for her. She smiled graciously when she entered. When they assembled it was less to give her advice than to endorse the decisions already made by her, the ruler of Ys. Yet she was wise enough always to give them the impression that it was their wisdom in the curia that really governed Ys. For Ys did have grave problems. On that particular day there was an atmosphere of despondency among those attending. At one side and close to her sat the vergobret or chief man in the council. It was a tribute to an ancient tradition that they had chosen to give the old Gaulish title to him. Next sat the captain of the guard, an able man, who combined courage with a keen mind. He had the difficult task of keeping order in Ys. Just now he looked alertly round him at the other councillors with whom he had just concluded a discussion. Gradlon sat huddled apart from them.

The vergobret bowed low to the princess and opened the proceedings at once. Their task, he declared, was to discuss the difficulties facing Ys. He said "We live in apparent isolation from the world outside our city but we have come to realise that the Franks and the Bretons, who are close to us, dominate much of the lands nearby. Our own internal difficulties are considerable. We have small fields and the yield from them in the past few years has grown less and less. Our poorer people have barely enough grain to keep them alive. Will the spectre of starvation soon be stalking our streets? Moreover, we have recently begun to suffer from a shortage of water and our springs flow sluggishly."

A yellow faced man interposed. "The health of our children is appalling! Many die like flies from the marsh fever. Look what has happened to Ys! She is like a worn out pillar that is ready to fall. There are streets where grass grows and where no footfall is heard for they are empty of life." He sank back in his chair. Waves of shivering seized the man.

"It is very true" said the captain in his strong, clear

voice. "I can still summon a hundred stout fellows with weapons but for how long? We've no boats even to meet possible attacks by the Sea Wolves and as for the Bretons, they have good cornfields, they are healthy and their women are excellent at bearing many offspring."

The air in the room had become heavy with gloom. Then the vergobret's secretary spoke. He was a dwarf of a man. "Isn't there an answer to our problems in expansion? Shouldn't we get right out of our city boundaries and farm the lands further away? We could set up settlements in the woods and plant our crops there. We need men and women. Let us carry out slave raids."

The captain, his face red with anger, jumped to his feet. "Are you to become solely a city of slave raiders? Doesn't the curia understand how hard it is to get slaves now? The Bretons? We can't raid their plous. They're as dangerous as Irish wolfhounds and we should bring a fearful vengeance on this city. Go further afield? Raid merchant convoys? We've tried it and little comes of it. A few slave wenches, maybe, and a heavy price. Wounds or death. We dare not rouse the Bretons or there'd be serious trouble. No, we must be cautious. Our seclusion so far has protected us but we can't go far afield. If we want slaves we must breed them here in Ys."

There was uproar in the curia. Voices, excited and bitter, clashed with other voices. It was clear that the captain had not won over the curia. Dahut sat quietly by, a barely perceptible smile on her face. Then a new voice was heard, young, clear and powerful. It was the new priest at the temple who in time would succeed the old priest, now bowed down by years. "If you look long round Ys, you will not lose hope. Some houses are empty, but your temple is worthy of your great city and its building stands firm thanks to the devotion of our mason who has worked so hard to repair it. Daily, up at your temple I see evidence of a great human affection for the gods. The humiliores, though lacking food, always bring us flowers and sometimes morsels from their scanty nourishment to present as oblations to the Three-Headed Ones. Yet the gods are still angry with us. They thirst for blood, they demand still greater sacrifices. I know why. They are incensed by their foe, the Kristos god who is there in the forests of the Bretons. Yes, our gods must have sacrifices!" He paused for breath. He was making some impression on the curia.

The secretary peered at the priest. "What other sacrifices do the gods want?"

"Our ancestors long ago gave bodies of large animals to them. Epona demands from us her appropriate sacrifice – a horse!"

"A horse! You'd kill a good horse!" Gradlon exploded into action. Foam crested his lips as he jumped to his feet as agilely as a younger man. His huge fists were clenched, he towered over the curia, threatening. The rafters above rang as he bellowed "If any scoundrel lays hands on my horse he shall know cold steel through his guts! There'll be no more talk of killing steeds in my own hall while I can still ride." The captain got up and gently placed his hand on the old man's arm. "There's no question of your horse or of any other. I'm sure that our priest would not want to kill good animals that we need for the defence of our city."

Gradlon's eyes lost their fire. He sat down, breathing heavily. The discussions went on in the curia in a calmer frame of mind.

Dahut now spoke crisply as one who would draw matters swiftly to a close. "I think that the curia has expressed matters well, we will meet again soon to discuss peaceful ways of acquiring a little more land. As for breeding I know that there are fertile women slaves as well as free women who should be with child, who are not doing their duty. I shall rectify this situation. In conclusion I have a suggestion also to make about the humiliores." She had the attention of all of them. "We must let the humiliores – the poorer folk – in our city know that their rulers do think of their welfare. Have we still stocks of rye, vergobret?"

"We have good stocks of rye grain left over from previous harvests in our public warehouse. Why do you ask?"

"Let us make a gesture of generosity and goodwill at the autumn festival. We must select a number of the more needy people and each of them in the market place shall receive some loaves of rye bread together with cervoise in plenty. Let them eat and drink and be merry before the onset of winter with its darkness. And let each also receive a small sack of rye grain for the winter so that their bellies shall not be empty. But guard the seed corn with your lives for it is vital for our next harvests!"

The curia unanimously approved the proposal. They also assented to the suggestion, already mooted among them, that Guenole, renowned as a water diviner, should be invited to visit Ys to seek the necessary springs of water. Only the priest disagreed. "I don't like shaven-headed Kristion meddling with our water."

"The man knows his work" said the vergobret sternly, "and if he can help us let him come and go in peace."

"I'll ensure the man comes to no harm" said the captain, "provided he bears your sign manual and your signature."

"That will be so" said Dahut, "the secretary will prepare the needful written permission."

Outside, the harper had begun to play a melancholy air while Gradlon alone listened. As the curia left, they paused on the terrace outside to look towards the sea while they discussed the banquet in the house of a wealthy citizen to which they had all been invited. The sea was now bright from the reflection of the sun on it but one object only stood out very clearly in contrast. The dark shape of the cross that still towered up from the disused church of the Kristion.

CHAPTER 11

Dahut had insidiously gained for herself the position of ruler of Ys once held by her father and she was determined to keep that position. A shrewd woman of energy and willpower she showed these qualities when she met the poorer people.

On the day after the curia Dahut went down on foot to the lower part of the city. Then her subjects crowded round to air their grievances. One woman complained that her house was very damp. Indeed some houses were actually below sea level and only a low wall kept the waters back. "The slaves repairing the wall shall be kept on this task until it is finished" said Dahut. "Your homes must be protected." A group of women came up and threw themselves at her feet crying out "Have pity on us for the love of the gods! Give us food for our children. They die for lack of nourishment. Give us food!" Dahut had the Secretary take their names and pledged that food should be supplied to them. Constantly she gave assurance to these sufferers that their hopes would be fulfilled and they went away remembering her gracious smile and certain that their princess thought always of them.

When she came to the Square of Justice hard by Execution Place her smile left her lips and her face became that of a stern magistrate. She sat in the great wooden chair with the mighty Sword of Justice held upright before her. She disposed of the cases carefully and rapidly. First was a pair who had stolen grain from the public stores. They were sentenced to be hanged. Last was a woman slave, heavily chained. From her neck a bloodstained knife dangled down. It was the corpus delicti for she had been taken red-handed stabbing her master.

"Mercy! Give me mercy!" screamed the woman. Dahut listened attentively to the evidence then said gravely "There can be no pardon for you. Tonight they will take you to the place of execution. They will chain you to a stake with faggots below your feet. Fire shall be set to the wood and you shall be burnt alive and so expiate your terrible crime."

When she left the Square she was accompanied by a retinue. Her guards; the chainsmith, the Secretary. The two slavemasters, one for the men slaves and one for the women slaves.

She strolled onto the harbour area. This was relatively uninhabited except for the public slaves of Ys who lived there. Male slaves who had committed serious crime often received a double punishment. They were castrated to stop them having children and to render them docile. Their second punishment was severe; they were placed in the chain gang. The iron collar of each slave was fastened to a long chain which held the gang together. Naked, they stumbled along, backs tingling from the lash of the overseer and dragging heavy stones to rebuild both the outer and inner sea walls. Some, immersed all day up to their necks, had the hardest task. They guided the stones as they fell down into the water. The sea accepted the stones with a lazy splash. They vanished out of sight. Outwardly, the sea walls appeared adequate protection for the harbour.

Dahut inspected their sleeping quarters. To prevent any escape the guards put each slave on the plank floor. Two guards squatted astride his belly while others stretched out his limbs then fettered his hands and feet to ring-bolts set in two beams on the floor. In the morning the slave was again fettered by his neck ring to the long gang chain before his feet and hands were freed. Dahut noticed a loose ring-bolt and ordered the chainsmith to repair it at once.

Dahut now visited the women slaves in their work hut. Six were spinning thread to feed the upright looms, others were weaving or washing and dyeing the woven fabrics, others squatting over querns were grinding corn. Two were tending the fire for the cooking. Except for their slave collars they were bare. Dahut examined their bodies closely and spoke to each one. She asked them about their health and food. They had only one complaint; their sleeping hut was so stuffy that they found it hard to sleep. They thought it was because the doors were tightly closed.

One young woman slave came up to Dahut, knelt down and held out her arms. "Here are my hands and feet! Chain them if you will to prevent escape but for the love of the gods let us have fresh air at night through an open doorway!" Dahut said only "I will consider your request, Ridna."

Her next visit was to the sleeping hut of the women slaves. It was a sturdy building, long and narrow. Many years before it had been a boathouse and therefore was close to the harbour though separated from it by a gentle slope. The slaves found this an advantage for they could bathe in the harbour. Its double doors, fast locked, were very broad. To facilitate handling of the boats the hut had been built sloping down fairly steeply to the harbour.

With Dahut were the slavemaster for the women, the chainsmith and the officer in charge of her guards. There was an elderly slave woman who slept in this hut and with the second slavemaster was responsible for the women slaves. The slavemaster unlocked the door.

Dahut entered. She sniffed the air and her nostrils wrinkled in disgust but she made no comment. She inspected the hut meticulously. On the floor, as in the male slaves' hut, two strong beams ran from end to end of the hut with a space of seven feet between them in which were arranged at right angles to the beams twenty five palliasses with a small round log at the head of each for a pillow. As the floor sloped upwards away from the harbour each slave slept a little above the palliasse of her neighbour. Two slaves slept side by side at the door. Ridna was in the highest position furthest away from the door. Dahut pressed the palliasses to see how thick they were. She scrutinized the pile of blankets that were not in use.

"Do the women sleep naked?" Dahut asked the elderly woman slave. "Yes" she replied. Dahut turned to the assistant slavemaster. "This place is very stuffy. It is important that we keep our slaves healthy. They cannot be fit if they breathe this bad air. Can't you keep the door open all night so that the slaves can breathe the pure sea breezes?"

"If I did that they would escape" said the man, a look of deep anxiety coming into his eyes. "I'm responsible for their security."

"You are" said Dahut, "but you are responsible also for seeing that their bodies are healthy. There is another matter too. I have not yet seen any pregnancies. We need children urgently to replace those dying from the marsh fever."

She beckoned to the chainsmith and the slavemaster. Her words were curt. "These are my orders for this hut. Carry them out at once before darkness falls! As in the men slaves' hut you will set two ring-bolts wide apart in the beam at the head of each palliasse. You will do the same in the other beam at the foot of the palliasse. You will also provide chains of different sizes for the slaves' wrists and ankles. As each slave comes back to sleep spreadeagle her on her own palliasse then shackle her hands and feet firmly to the ring bolts." She looked hard at the assistant slavemaster. "This will effectively prevent escape. You can now leave the doors open all night. Ridna begged to be chained, so let her be the first to know what it means to be fettered. See that her shackles are tight fitting! Her ankles and wrists are small!

She smiled. "It will be a delightful surprise for them when they enjoy the fresh sea breezes. These maidens will also have another pleasant surprise!" She turned to the young officer. "When all are chained choose your most suitable men and bring them here. Allot a woman slave to each guard. She will then get herself with child by him, an infant to be born next year. A child for Ys! Take Ridna for yourself!"

She beckoned to the elderly woman slave. "There will be no promiscuity! No brutality! A lamp must be kept burning so that each slave woman can see clearly the male whose offspring she will bear. These women are not common harlots but slaves of Ys under my control. Their children will be lawfully begotten. Their babies are vital for our survival as a city." She raised her clenched fists to the sky above. "May the gods help us! May the slaves have healthy children!" She spoke to the captain. "You will set a guard on the door. If any man not designated by you for this work enters this hut castrate him!"

She turned away and left the hut. Accompanied now only by three discreet guards and a young girl attendant she went to a part of the coast where there were no houses. It was not visited by the city folk as they respected the privacy of their ruler in going there. The seas washed the shore but rocks broke the force of the waves. The girl stripped her mistress and laughing and splashing Dahut entered the sea until she was above waist level when she halted and laved her hands in the clear waters. She raised her hands very high above her head and extended them outwards to the distant horizon in a great invocation to the Sea-god who ruled those waves.

"See my body! It is beautiful! It longs to feel the touch of the god on it! You are my lover, my only real lover. When will you be the only master I ever had?" Her voice trembled. "Won't you dare to use me as if I were a slave woman? Come and take your Beloved! The Lovely One of Ys!" The only answer was the sound of surf gently breaking on the sea defences of Ys.

CHAPTER 12

The banquet was a great success. There was good food and excellent wine. It finished at midnight when Dahut and the guests strolled through the city. On the way they looked at Execution Square. It was dark but a spot of light suddenly appeared and quickly grew into flames that shot up and engulfed a woman chained to a stake. "So perish all evil-doers in Ys" said the princess solemnly.

She led them close to the sleeping hut of the women slaves. A lamp glowed inside. An elderly curia member saw the open door and asked "Why are there lights on? Surely the slaves don't work at night?"

"The slave women work hard at night making men and women for Ys" replied Dahut dryly. Next summer we shall see the results of their toil."

Dahut returned to the palace. Gradlon was asleep and she went to her own room, stripped off her clothing and looked at herself in the mirror. There was a red glow in her eyes like the flames curling round the limbs of the erring slave woman. She spoke to her reflection softly yet with intensity. "My body is good even if I cannot satisfy its cravings. It burns as hotly as the fire consuming the woman criminal. What does my body say often to me? 'I must have this man for myself'. He'll be the finest lover of them all when I've tamed him! When I've subdued him to my will and he's known the embraces of chains for a time he'll accept my caresses. My kisses, my hands, my thighs, my breasts will enchant him. Body, do your magic work on him as you have laid spells on so many other men! I'm young, I can enjoy men, the warmth of their skins, their hair entwined in the fetters of my hair and the touch of their strong hands. Yet first I must seduce you from the path of what fools call virtue. Ye gods, let him be mine for there is none in Ys that can evoke such passion in me as you, the fisherman, Jahaan. When I first saw you, your voice was sweeter to me than any other voice. I can only be content when at last you are by my side."

She clothed herself in the coarse woollen garment worn by the women of the humiliores when they went about their errands. It was dark in colour with a hood which she gathered round her face so that she would not be recognised. She went down the steps and into the narrow street. She looked up and down. No one was about and it was dark with a hint of rain to come.

Only in one house was there a light showing. The house was as fast closed against all intruders as the thoughts of its owner. Within, alone, lived the lawyer Malek. Dahut knew him well. He was a man of gigantic stature, the strongest man in Ys. He had created a group of volunteers, expert swordsmen, who might help in need to defend the city. He had studied ancient laws both in Ys and elsewhere and knew much about them. Just now he was poring over a passage in the Latin text of a manuscript.

"A woman accused of causing death by witchcraft must undergo the Trial by Water known as 'Swimming'. Near a place where there is deep water a stake should be set up surrounded by dry faggots. The accused witch is then taken to the place of Trial, stripped naked and prepared for her Swimming in the traditional manner. Her right thumb is bound to the left great toe and the left thumb is bound to the right great toe. A long rope is then tied round the woman's waist and she is placed in the water with two judges, one on each side of her. They are assisted by two helpers, one of whom stands at the head and the other at the feet of the prisoner. The rope is used to control her Swimming for she is never permitted to be free. Being bound firmly she cannot help herself but is forced to obey the pull of the rope on her waist. Sometimes the rope is used to jerk her upwards, sometimes it holds her down under the water. Her swimming reveals whether she be innocent or guilty. An innocent woman's buttocks may show above the surface but her head will be under the water and no matter how hard she tries she cannot breathe for her mouth and nose remain there where she is forced to stay for five minutes. The water, being pure, has accepted her for she too is pure. Most innocent women do not hold their breath and so perish. The guilty woman displays her Swimming differently. She floats because the water has rejected her, the impure thing. Sometimes a guilty woman, knowing that she faces a prolonged death by fire rather than drowning, calls for mercy and makes frantic efforts to sink her mouth beneath the water. It is to no avail for the judges holding the rope pull firmly upwards and compel her to breathe. She breathes only for seconds but that is enough. She hears the fatal word 'Guilty'. Bound as she is they hurry her to the stake, chain her and brand her on her breasts. The faggots are lit and she is burnt alive for that is her punishment for fatal witchcraft."

Malek pondered over the manuscript. He was sure it was a law of Ys that had not been used for years.

His thoughts turned away to a woman of Ys whom some called a witch but many people respected for her palm reading and knowledge of simples. He had met her casually. Malek was a powerful swimmer and one day, when he was swimming in shallow water, he noticed a woman floating on her back. Her legs and arms were stretched out like the limbs of a starfish, her back was hollowed and her belly flat. Only the tips of her slender fingers moved gently as if caressing the waters. She floated superbly and with ease and appeared to be enjoying the experience. Yet to his surprise Malek heard her voice crying to him, "Help me! Help me!" With quick strokes he swam towards her. She explained. "My thighs, as you can see, are large and round and aid me to float very well, too well, for I cannot bring my legs down to the bottom. Just now I was conscious of the current. It was dragging me further and further out." He put his arms under her armpits and jerked her up. As she was still nervous of floating right out to sea he arranged to bathe with her regularly and help her over her fears of the waters. She loved to feel his strong arms on her shoulders. So began their acquaintance, almost always during bathes, for they seldom met in the city.

Malek hadn't much to do with women. He almost shunned them and perhaps some called him a misogynist. Yet this woman awakened feelings in him that he didn't understand. Was it because she was attractive or was different somehow? Or was it because she was a witch? Certainly her knowledge of herbs was wide. Yet in her knowledge of people he found her a little innocent. She had too easily forgiven and forgotten those who had threatened to beat her, not understanding that those threats had their seeds in a deeper element of mob violence.

The woman's name was Gwendaline....

Dahut walked up the lane that skirted the outer part of the city, her unshod feet making no sound as she read the way she must go through her sensitive soles. The lane climbed steeply until it came to a place where there were only bushes. A pinpoint of light showed up. It grew until it was a faint glow from a hut made from branches capped by reeds. A woman was within chanting. Dahut knocked thrice on the hut entrance.

"Who comes so late to see me?" came a gentle but firm voice.

"It is I, Dahut. Open, for I would consult you! I am alone."

The door hurdle was scraped back slowly and Dahut entered. The witch immediately replaced the hurdle and tied it fast against intruders. "Stay where you are by the door without moving" ordered the witch. "You mustn't disturb the circle."

The hut was warm and so filled with smoke from a fire that at first Dahut could not clearly make out the objects within until her eyes had grown accustomed to the obscurity. The only furniture was a neat palliasse and the main feature was a circle, some five feet in diameter, which had been scratched deeply into the earthen floor. At four points on this circle were flickering rushlights. By one was a clean linen cloth and a bowl of spring water, by another a wooden cup of salt, a curiously engraved sword marked a third point and a disk of polished copper on which triangles were marked together with stars and the crescent moon rested at the fourth. From an incense burner yellow trails eddied upwards. There was a strong smell of rosin.

Bunches of many kinds of herbs hung in the nets from the ceiling and the air was filled with strange odours from these plants.

The witch looked hard at the newcomer from eyes in whose depths was embodied wisdom and love. She was much younger than Dahut and a beautiful woman. Indeed, unconscious envy mixed with hatred for her loveliness was aroused in the depths of Dahut's mind. The face opposite Dahut was a perfect oval. The fine hair was cut short so that it appeared like a close fitting silken cap. Her hands were long and slender, the tapering fingers betokening great sensitivity as well as strength of purpose. The feet were small, with delicate but sinewy toes. Like the hands they were sunburnt from exposure. She wore only one garment, a clean woollen shift.

Her hands rested on a shelf of rock on which lay a dead frog, a dried up bat and a glass jar which glowed a dull red from some liquid within. By the palliasse an adder was coiled. It had raised its head when Dahut entered but lay down again.

"Whatever brings you here past midnight must wait! I've just cast the circle and cannot be interrupted so you'll have to go through the rites with me first." She picked up the sword and faced towards the east.

"Ye lords of the watchtowers of the rising sun! I do summon and call you! Witness my ritual! Guard my circle!" She waved her sword in the shape of the star then kissed the pommel fervently and repeated each invocation at the points of the circle. She stripped off her shift. Dahut stripped likewise. Gwendaline's slim body was displayed in its virginal perfection. The finely moulded breasts, thrusting themselves outwards provocatively. She gripped Dahut's hands and they moved together round the circle, making incantations to the night and moon, the earth, water, air and fire. The witch appealed to the powers of the Sword, the Queens of Heaven and Hell. She invoked the Horned One that her rites should work her will. At last she cried out repeatedly "Listen to the words of the Great One, the Earth Mother."

She stood still, panting for breath. For a few seconds she had lost all sense of time and place. Then she saw Dahut looking at her with longing in her eyes.

"You didn't come here only to dance with me the sacred rites. Nor is it a visit for me to read your palm as if you were an amorous cottager. No, you've something more important on your mind. What is it?" She fingered her amulets. The viper stirred. "Before we begin have you not heard the rumours about me that stalk some streets? Foul tongues whisper that I have evil powers and no good will come to Ys while I live here. A few would strip my torso bare and scourge me, then drive me forth with execrations. Even the young priest could poison their minds but he at least knows well that the gods I invoke are older and mightier than his Teutates and you know that as well, for you came to me before to learn something of the rites. What is it that tonight so urgently you seek from the arcane mysteries that I can unfold to you?"

"I would seek two things" said Dahut. Her voice was tremulous. "I want great power over a certain young man for whom I've felt the desire that expands my breasts and inflames the loins. Often, before, I felt lust for the youths whom I used for my satisfaction then flung aside. For this young man I have felt a much more powerful urge. It consumes me like those flames that burn away the twigs." The witch was watching intently every expression on her face.

"Is this man a stranger to you? A low fellow – one of the humiliores? Not one of your station?" Her voice became deeper. "Is he beloved already by another woman? You want to take him from her?"

Dahut's cheeks went as scarlet as did her neck and naked breasts that swelled visibly with emotion. A drop of blood stained her bitten lips. "Does it matter who he is? He'll soon be in Ys, as a prisoner in my power and I want him for my own, body and soul! I want something more from you as well. I wish to see your crystal ball and divine from it what my life and his will be in years to come. I want also to find out what will happen to Ys, my city, in the future." The witch gave a deep sigh and shook her head in sadness rather than denial.

"Your body has the natural magic of a beautiful woman. Your power lies within it. You've no need of a love potion to win a man. Still, if you really desire to see the future I will guide you. Yet remember when finally we look into the ball that the future of all life is death. The grass withers, the flowers lose their beauty and pass away. The young girl, dancing so joyfully in the sunshine will be carried past on a bier to her grave that soon is overgrown and all the world's rosemary won't bring her back to remembrance."

She paused for a long minute and looked with a sad expression at Dahut. "You must believe me when I say that the Second Sight is a curse to those who have it. Often I've seen the Banshee washing the death clothes of young children or the garments of women in their travail, doomed to death. After this warning do you still persist? You want to see the future of yourself, of this man and of the city of Ys?"

"I do" said Dahut, tossing her head defiantly. "Then squat down yonder!" ordered Gwendaline. Dahut obeyed.

The witch took a large glass ball that was stoppered in its base. From a phial she dropped a crystal into the ball, added drops from the jar of ruby liquid then filled it with water from her spring. She smoored the fire with turves and put out all the lights except one that was struggling towards its death. On the embers she cast a handful of incense. Heavy pungent fumes filled the air; they mounted to Dahut's head and filled her with exhilaration. Nothing could be seen in the hut except the red glow from the viper's eyes.

"I must cut off your earthly sight entirely." Gwendaline poured drops of a lotion onto a white cloth with which she closely bandaged Dahut's eyes. "We must remain in total darkness without speaking until the revelation is vouchsafed to us at the proper time."

How long Dahut sat there in the darkness she did not know. The bandage was slipped away so deftly that it was off before she realised its absence and looked at the crystal ball. It now held a greenish-blue liquid which whirled round incessantly. Abruptly the liquid ceased to rotate and became quite still. Dahut had become no longer conscious of the witch or of her own identity. She felt detached from this earth, floating in another world which was living in the clouds of incense that now descended and encircled the ball. Within the ball the colour of the liquid changed almost imperceptibly from green to yellow and then began to burn with an intensely bright orange glow in which vivid streaks of red appeared which were momentarily chased away by a blackness. The orange glow returned and remained steady. Indistinct shapes writhed and wriggled within the glow. They coalesced and became a reddish brown mass which then assumed the shape of a monstrous dragon. It's vast mouth was wide open and the serried ranks of massive teeth dripped torrents of blood. In these crimson cascades were hundreds of twisted human faces with mouths gaping, frozen into a voiceless, unimaginable horror.

The image changed. A naked man was galloping bareback on a stallion and lashing it furiously with his whip while he clung to its wild mane; he was riding away from the dragon. A nude woman ran up, her eyes wide with terror. She clutched desperately at the mane of the horse but fell and then became one of a multitude of skeletons. An old harper, his face drawn by sadness, sat by a stormy sea whose waves threatened to engulf him while he played. He became a skeleton but his bones diminished until they were no more than tiny, bleached fragments.

The next picture that came into the ball was different. Men in strange sombre clothing were digging the earth with spades. A bell rang whereupon they stopped work and knelt down on the soil, their hands together in prayer. A golden cross appeared, floating above their close-cropped heads.

The last picture was of the sea near the coast. The sea was calm and on its surface projected a woman's hands tied by the thumbs to her great toes. They gently danced up and down in the waves in a steady but brief rhythm. Then their movements ceased. The sky above became like blood.

The image faded right away. The crystal ball assumed once more its dull greenish-blue hue. The smoke had gone from the hut. The witch, white-faced, staggered to her feet and lit the rushlights then sank back on her heels as if the effort had been too much for her. Her face and breasts were glistening so much with sweat that she might have been bathing. Dahut was frowning.

"What am I supposed to understand from your limnings of the future? You have shown me dragons and dead men's bones, harpers, shaven heads, toes and thumbs, nothing that makes any sense! What do these images mean to the living? I've learnt nothing either of the man for whom I yearn or of the city of Ys. Can't you interpret these images even further?"

The witch shook her head repeatedly. She swayed backwards and forwards on her haunches as if she were in great pain. "This night my power was indeed very great. So too was my agony of mind and heart. I've witnessed more human anguish and death than ever before. My body and soul are totally stunned by this weird vision. You really want me to give you the portents of all that you have witnessed? The gods reveal their presence always in mysteries; the future is unfolded in riddles. You asked me to give you a foresight into the years far distant. It was your will not mine that made the magic liquids spell out events yet to come. I cannot tell you whether they relate to next year, a century or a millennium hence. I am only the humble channel through which the message has flowed to you. All that I can tell you is that you cannot alter destiny. It is fixed for you, for me, for all of us. Immutable as the rock on which

Ys is built."

Dahut's eyes were stern as she looked at the witch. The viper stared back at this strange woman. Its reptile orbs were filled not with hostility but understanding. "You're a witch who has spells and crystal gazing and can scry the future for others. Can you foretell what will happen to you?"

The witch did not answer at once so intent was she in peering at the crystal ball and when she spoke it was to herself. "Strange! Even when I'm not scrying the liquid inside shakes as if from some vibration. Yet when I go outside to see if there is any reason for it all is calm and peaceful!" She turned back to Dahut.

"Should I be any happier if I knew how the woof of my life was woven? All that I know is that I shall die in the faith of my gods. My body I give to earth and water whence it came but my soul shall live forever more with the Blessed Ones. I do not fear death for beyond it lies Avalon on the isle of the Fortunate, where there is freedom from hunger, cruelty or the terror that can come in the night."

Oblivious to all else Gwendaline crouched down over the ashes, her head buried in her arms. She had forgotten all about her visitor. Dahut rose up in silence and donned her cloak. She went to the door and untied the hurdle that had closed the entrance. She dropped a purse heavy with silver on the threshold and left.

Gwendaline did not stir. She herself had become almost like a dark shadow. The shadow of a woman to whom had been given a revelation too great to bear, a revelation of her own fate and that of others. A woman huddled over the embers of a dying fire, while far beyond her hut, the city of Ys slumbered on.

CHAPTER 13

Spring or summer, autumn or winter, Koneg, the old priest of the temple of Ys, would always leave his house before sunrise. He would shut the door of the home where he had so long dwelt and for a few moments stand looking around him while he gathered his strength and his thoughts for yet another day. Though his was only a humble dwelling it was the highest house in Ys for it was built right up against the great cliff on top of which was the temple. His nearest neighbours were superiores, wealthy people who had retained their riches through all the vicissitudes that had befallen the city and through its decline. They were considered to be men of position and power who lived in relative comfort almost entirely free from the marsh fever. Their cellars never lacked wine, their storehouses were full, he had little to do with them.

Koneg's glance did not linger on their houses. Almost at once he would look at the cliff that towered above him. Its precipitous sides were nearly free from herbage. Stark and bare they soared right up to the overhang that shot outwards in a magnificent curve that was poised over the houses themselves. The beauty of this cliff was the first object that greeted him in the mornings. His temple was built partly on top of the overhang and partly behind it. Its columns looked down on Ys sleeping below as an eagle gazes down from its eyrie. After this delightful pause, so refreshing to his eyes and to his body, he would turn away and follow patiently step by step the winding zigzag path that led up the cliff and so to the temple itself. As the long years had passed he found that he had to pause more often for breath at every bend in the path. When he was forced to do this he would smile, for it gave him another opportunity to gaze at the tranquil city below as it shone with dew and was beautiful as a bride awaiting her wedding day. Beyond the broken sea walls and the ruinous harbour was always her bridegroom, the sea. Sometimes it was a deep blue clad in long shawls of white surf, sometimes a sullen grey, and even occasionally mirror still. The sea was always there, waiting. He loved Ys and his only regret was that her waters were no longer speckled by sails as they had been when he was a very small boy. No foreign traders now chaffered on her desolate quays, no sailors bawled out crapulously in argot from their craft. He knew that there was misery and squalor in the lower city but in the dawn such defects were not revealed to his eyes.

Slow as his climb was and weary as he might be with his advancing years, Koneg knew that he would always reach the summit, the temple where his duty lay. Long before he had reached it he could make out the shapes of the Holy Heads, the Triple Ones carved finely in stone as weathered as his own wind-seared cheeks. He would raise his withered hands to them, the first of many invocations that he would make during the day. When at last he gained the temple steps he would pause, panting, leaning on his great blackthorn staff and with the fingertips of his thin hands he would touch the masonry reverently. Even the spring flowers, gentle interlopers that had crept into crevices to cover the nakedness of the stone with shades of red or mauve felt the love in those fingers. For with Ys itself, the temple and its flowers had become the most beloved things in his life. Whether the temple gleamed, glistening in the autumn rains or was dry-parched in high summer, he was devoted to it and to its worship. When sunset came to finish his day, the blocks of stone would glow like precious jewels and he felt power come into his enfeebled body from those mighty columns that would stand proudly there forever.

When he passed on into the temple precincts themselves he smiled thankfully in his joy for there lay the offerings. A loaf of coarse bread, a jug of sour wine, even just a few grains of wheat. All reminders that others worshipped the gods and gave much to them. When he prayed he pleaded with the Great Ones that they would be generous to those who sacrificed from their own meagre food and drink.

Beyond the temple lay the sacred oak trees. Koneg always walked there and stood near to the trees. He closed his fading eyes the better to feel the texture of the ancient bark beneath his sensitive palms. He knew every crack in their bark. Every branch as it grew had been welcomed by him. They were old but they would outlast him.

In the past people had come to him for advice about the best time to sow or reap their crops and whether there would be storms at sea or heavy rains. He would stand all night gazing up at the clouds and feeling the wind on his cheeks. He had an uncanny prescience in interpreting the language of these natural forces partly by some weird instinct, partly from the experience that comes to those close to the earth and near to the gods.

The farmer and the hunter grew to rely on the accuracy with which he could predict the weather.

There was a rocky platform projecting from part of the temple over the cliff brow and here he always waited the rising of the sun. As he stood there it was his daily habit to thank the gods for their mercies to him. They had granted him a long life, the temple and the love of plants and rocks. They had given him Ys.

The city even at that early hour told him its story for he would see the first signs of activity. The stable-man leading out Gradlon's fiery horse for exercise. Thin pencils of smoke rising from the holes in the roofs of the small dwellings where the humiliores lived. He knew that they would chat together in their old half-Gaulish tongue, using words that were unknown elsewhere because they had been forgotten. Ys too had been almost forgotten by the world outside it. Once it had been known as a strong city with a formidable army but now no provincial governor with haughty retinue ever bothered about it. No *agens in rebus*, sniffing for taxes unpaid had ever risked his neck within its walls. In their turn the people of Ys had wished only to live remote and undisturbed behind their fortifications. Very rarely did strangers come to it now. He knew of only one young Breton who ventured there to sell a creel of fish, a basket, or a wood carving.

Koneg frowned. Neither their thick walls nor their isolation had saved them from more dangerous foes. There had been the marsh fever that struck so viciously in the summer and sapped the will of all affected by it. People had often come to the temple and asked him for advice about the illness but he could do little for them save to ask the gods to take this scourge from them. Another even darker shadow had affected Ys. It had come so suddenly that he himself had not really recovered from the past shock. He would like to forget it but it would come creeping into his thoughts like a serpent through the grass. He was much younger when it happened, the violence that had erupted one summer in the sordid, fever-infested quarters of the city. Violence like a canker with abominable crimes had destroyed the good name of Ys.

Once a stranger merchant had been foully murdered even while he stayed at the xenodochion – the guest house – of the city. Koneg had seen the blood-stained corpse lying, forsaken, in the tiny lane. Yes, from that moment on, the people had grown unstable and they had now a dangerous and wanton woman who had replaced the sturdy Gradlon as their real ruler.

In these later days, Koneg himself saw little of the city for his infirmities prevented him from walking down there. He lived in an isolation of his own given up to thoughts about life and death. Only the younger priest who would in time take his place ever descended into the city. He himself knew that a time might come when he would be too weak even to climb the cliff path to the temple. It was his dearest wish that he would die in the temple itself, to die where he had lived so fully with all that he cherished around him.

The clink of a heavy scutching hammer broke in on his thoughts. He looked up and saw a young man occupied in cutting a broken temple coping. A glow came over his aged features at the sight. He went over and placed his hands on the mason's back feeling the great muscles.

"You work very hard, Caradec. I'm always up with the first light but you're always here before me. I believe you even toil in the night because once I saw a faint glow – perhaps it was your lamp – here in the temple. I have seen you so late, trudging, weary, hungry, back to your little house down there among the humiliores where you dwell quite alone. It is not good for you to live thus. Surely it's time you got yourself a woman slave? A clean woman, comely and healthy, who would look after your fire and share your bed. Whose womb would give you sturdy sons the images of yourself. Children who would perpetuate the love of the gods that you show so much in your work for the temple and how much you have repaired it. No other man could have worked so hard!"

The man looked away from Koneg. He yawned, straightened his back and stood up. His shoulders were so powerful and broad that they looked as if they belonged to an Atlas who could uphold the world on them. His limbs, too, are cast in the same mould as the temple itself, thought Koneg; strong, enduring, and above all else, reliable. While he dusted his mason's tunic down Koneg was able to observe Caradec's hands. They were huge, ingrained with grime and covered with countless scratches that told of his dual work with stone and wood. Yet he stood as light on his feet as a pugilist. Every movement was controlled, smooth, sinewy.

"I want no slave wench in my bed or squalling brats at her breast! This temple is my wife, my child, my life. Nothing else matters to me now." He pointed with one finger to the walls of the temple, to the columns standing out so clearly against the sky. "These hands of mine have come to be faithful servants to me. With their help I am making sure that the temple of Ys shall become known in the whole world! That's my work, day and night! The memory of man is feeble but in the long centuries ahead they will learn what this temple really means. They will never forget either this temple or the city that lies below it."

How grave his face had become over the years, thought Koneg. Even when he smiles his lips grow tense. Caradec hardly ever laughed and never went drinking with other men in the wine shops where the cervoise flowed so freely. He spent all his days at the temple rarely coming down except to eat and sleep in his house. Yet to Koneg he seemed contented with his life and happy in his work. He also preferred to toil alone. That suited him and he could do two men's work so strong and capable was he.

"Caradec, you've always been a good foster son to me. May the gods reward you richly for all your care of me! I've never forgotten how often you helped me especially when I became less robust. Even when you left my house and started your own life in your own dwelling close to the old prison, you came daily or more often to enquire about my health, to bring me foods that I liked and to repair the walls of my own house which were getting cracks in them. Ah! those walls, and their fissures not only in my dwelling but even in the homes of the superiores! It almost seems as if this populace of Ys, grown so wicked and cruel in outlook to the lives of other people, has been punished by this strange weakening of their own dwellings."

The mouth of the man opposite him had a faint smile on it but the eyes were stern. The priest went on, "I believe that a great change must come to Ys.

Instinctively I feel that strangers will arrive whose very presence will destroy our evil customs and drastically alter human life here. What that change will be I don't really know or when it will be. You, Caradec, will live to see it, not I."

The mason nodded in an absent-minded fashion. He was part of the temple and had little to do or interest him in the city below. Yet despite his apparent aloofness from Ys he had good friends there who respected him for his work, and from them he knew very well what was going on, whether in the narrow streets or in the debates in the curia.

The old man was in no hurry to leave. He went on, almost as if he were speaking to himself but his words were for his hearer.

"Daily I thank the gods that when I depart from this world I leave you behind me. You are a worthy descendant of mine although you were not sprung from my loins since I never wed. This sunrise Caradec I reached seventy and five years. It is a span of life greater than that of most men. Tranquilly I can look back on my life. Yet the time has come when I must tell you the truth about my health." He paused, breathing deeply. "I have a good medical knowledge and it tells me that I have serious physical weaknesses. My heart is feebler, my pulse slower. At night my heart throbs sometimes and strikes me like a hammer. I will not last more than a few weeks or perhaps months at the most then I will go. The young priest will succeed me. He is an active man. He needs more experience and lacks understanding but he will step into my shoes. As for the building work on the temple and the repairs there; that will be quite safe in your capable hands."

A shadow passed over the impassive features of the mason at these words but he remained silent.

"When I know that I must leave this world I think of the person in it who is most dear to me – you. Frequently I recall the circumstances of your birth and your life about which I first spoke to you years ago. There was your father, a Breton, of whom you've no need to feel ashamed. You're proud, aren't you, that you wear the dress of his occupation? He, like yourself, was skilled both as mason and carpenter." He sighed and his face paled for an instant. "No man mourned his sudden death more than I did or was more shocked by it. Some said he died in a fall from scaffolding, others that foul hands pushed him and his fellow workers to their doom. I was young then but I believed that it was my duty to care for you, an orphaned baby. Indeed it was part of my faith. Sadly, your mother died in her travail and I took you, an infant, into my home, fed you, clothed you, fostered you and gave you what learning I had. I also taught you Breton the mother tongue of your father and mother. You grew up an intelligent and strong boy." Caradec's hard eyes softened as he gazed at Koneg yet he said nothing.

"When the time was ripe and you could understand, I confided in you the secret of your origin and birth though none in Ys except myself knew the mystery. They always assumed that I had adopted a motherless child from my own people. Then I did something that was perhaps strange for a man of my own religion. Your father was a Kristion. Perhaps because of that they murdered him and his fellow workers as well as the Kristion priest. It was an outburst of savagery that good men in Ys would like to forget. It's hard Caradec, to be tolerant of another faith if you love your own." He looked around the temple, at its stones, its altar and the sacrifices by the altar steps.

"I pondered over your future in the long watches of the night that I held up here. It so happened that lying by the dead body of your father I had found a manuscript which bore a resemblance to a portion of a manuscript that I also discovered in the abandoned church of the Kristion. It was in Latin, a language which I knew tolerably well, and it told of the life of Kristos. I had taught you Latin but I hesitated a long while before I gave you the manuscript to read. Was I unfaithful to my own beliefs to let you have knowledge of another religion? After all you were acquainted from an early age with the worship of the Three-Headed Ones. You had sacrificed here as piously as any folk who climb up to the temple. You read the manuscript and it made no difference. You went on sacrificing up here and you became the mason of the temple using your skill to ensure its permanence."

Koneg was wheezing now, struggling for breath and gasping from time to time. The sun was rising fully over Ys.

"I'm already weary. I must go down back to my house at once for I feel that knocking in my breast that could be the premonitory summons for those who must die. I must rest for a long time."

Caradec knelt down before him making a deep obeisance. He watched anxiously as Koneg slowly and painfully descended the steps of the path. His gaze followed the priest as far as it could until he could no longer see his bowed shoulders or hear his feet on the rocky path. Then he stood motionless for some moments looking cautiously around him. There was no one in sight either on the pathway or further down and he knew that the young priest was away in the city.

There was no smile on his face. He gathered up his tools and placed them in a canvas bag which he hung round his shoulders then went to a place just to the side of the temple where it was suspended over the giddy heights. The exposure was very great but Caradec was as surefooted as a hill goat and had no mountain fear. Cautiously he slowly edged his way round the cliff face and into a thick patch of scrub which seemed to grow from the very verge of the precipice. There was a bunch of grey almost dead foliage in its centre. He inserted his hand into it and touched what was concealed by the leaves. It was a small trap door unseen by prying eyes and unknown to any who went to the temple except himself. With a jerk of his crowbar on the ring-bolt he wrenched up the trap. A circular hole yawned before him. Steps were cut into the stones which lined its sides. He clambered down and once inside closed the trap with its pad of foliage right above him so that no one would know where he was. A chink in the wood above emitted a splinter of light and by this glimmer he lit a candle from his touchwood using his flint and steel.

The candlelight showed up a low tunnel leading away from the hole. On hands and knees he writhed his way along this tunnel until it ended in a chamber that abutted on one side onto the solid rock face of the cliff brow. The roof of this chamber was actually the very base of the temple above and was upheld by a row of slender stone pillars. Over the years some had developed fissures under the tremendous pressures from the structure above them and appeared as if they would collapse under the strain. One had even broken entirely and lay shattered on the floor. Had the weight of the temple been taken solely by the pillars it would have fallen long ago. However, the roof had been skilfully shored up by balks of wood, mostly rough-hewn logs which formed an entire forest both the width and the length of the chamber. It was clear that the wood shores took the whole weight of that which was above them so that the stone pillars played now no part at all in upholding the temple. All depended on the wood shores. Between the shores was a great quantity of bone-dry branches packed closely in piles round the bases of the shores. Rivulets of molten resin had been poured over all the branches and had set hard in glittering, frozen cataracts. In the candlelight they gleamed like fresh spilled blood.

Caradec would not advance among these inflammable substances with a naked candle flame. Instead he lit a lantern fitted with a horn window and blew out his candle. He spoke to himself as he moved, in a harsh whisper, though no one in the temple above could have heard him.

"My God, how many years have I given to this chamber in toil and pain! When darkness fell on Ys it was the signal for my secret work and I would steal into the wood with my axe and cut down trees suitable for these shores, trimming rapidly the projecting branches. Night after night, while the city slept, I would carry back my booty, dragging such of the timbers that were too heavy to bear on my shoulders. If anyone had seen me they would have thought that I was a giant corrigan bent on his deadly work. Yet no one was abroad in the night during all those years to witness Caradec's labours of Hercules and to tell the tale." He paused and looked around at the shores. The tiny lamp barely outlined the lines on his anguished face.

"Always, always I must erase all traces of my forest work, covering over my tracks as much as a man could and cleaning the temple floors from tell-tale mud and footprints. Then I would lower the balks into the chamber through a small aperture I had constructed in the floor of the temple almost by their sacred altar itself. When I had enough wood I set to work in the chamber. I cut and fitted the shores and hammered the wedges into position with back breaking toil and care until I felt I could loosen the stone pillars themselves! It was very dangerous work; one wrong miscalculation and I could have been crushed like a fly! Then, of course, I had to work in the temple during the day no matter how exhausted I was. I had to give the impression that I was the mason of their temple. Yet it's nearly over now. It's all right and I will make one more check!"

He moved round every part of the chamber groping his way between the massive timbers. He inspected the stone pillars first, tapping them cautiously with a light hammer. Dust motes floated down from above. Then he turned his attention to the wooden shores. He hit them with slow blows carefully working out the weight of each stroke and listening intently to the creaks emitted by the wood. He read these messages with furrowed brow and looked hard at the wedges. When he had finished all the shores he took up a jar of oil and moved to the centre where was placed a small bundle of twigs. He soaked each twig with great care so that drops of oil hung trembling on each parched branch. "This will be the firing point for the ignition right here in the centre."

His voice was hoarse with the dust and his efforts. "Everything is ready now. I've fully undermined the temple by the altar so that only the timber shores carry the main weight on their wooden backs. If all goes well and I've made no mistakes it should happen. There are enough breezes here for a strong draught of air to feed the flames! When I fire the brushwood the main timbers will be set alight and burn through. Then most of the temple, thrusting outwards, will collapse and fall right down clear of the cliff. Ys is below, a long way below. They'll have a great surprise when their precious house of the gods comes tumbling down on them."

By this time Caradec was standing near the largest wooden shore, right in the centre. On it hung a wooden cross rudely made by bringing two straight branches together. The bark had been stripped away, the wood was white in the lantern-light. Close by rested a manuscript flecked by oil marks and grimy from contact with work stained hands. He took it up and held his lantern close to the words. The suspended cross quivered gently in the current of air from holes in the floor of the chamber.

"Thus I first learnt about you, Kristos, and from these soiled pages! Learnt to love you and at the same time to despise and hate with a burning anger the heathen gods and their images made by the hands of men. Figures of stone before which the deluded or ignorant grovel for they know not better! Yours, only yours, Kristos is the one true faith. From this battered vellum I learnt by heart the Ten Commandments. What do they say? 'Thou shalt not kill! Thou shalt not murder!'. You, the people of Ys, bear blood guilt on your hands. It was you who basely slew my father and my mother whose womb had scarcely time enough to thrust me into this world before she died from your brutal handling! My God! They were so pitiless to the weak and helpless! Let them be shown not one grain of mercy!"

He knelt down on his discoloured and worn knees before the wooden cross and raised his huge, calloused hands so firmly clenched together. In the lamplight his face was scarlet.

"Help me. Oh help me, God, to whom all Kristion pray! Help me now! Make bare thy mighty arm! Thou knowest the life I have lived here. Unaided, unknown, in this accursed heathen city without a friend of my own faith to whom I might turn. I've tried to live according to Thy will and have struggled with evil! Year after year like a mole under the earth I've worked in darkness until my sinews ached and my body was worn out. By this work and in this manner let me avenge the deaths of my father and mother at the bloody hands of the wicked heathen of Ys. Let me be the humble instrument to carry out Thy awful vengeance on this foul city where the very stones cry out against the savage deaths that so many have died unjustly!"

His voice softened, his taut features relaxed. "Yes, so long have I toiled until the hour is ripe to strike the fatal blow. Yet of Thy great mercy grant me patience to wait a little longer. Let me in peace wait without fretting until Koneg, the old priest, has died. He could not be one of Thy servants and this temple which he cherished so long is a damned thing together with the city below. It must be blotted out from the face of the earth but don't let Koneg witness its annihilation! Let his weary eyes be forever closed before the searing mounting flames of my hatred and your vengeance leap up and the infamous Three-Headed Ones shall be blasted outwards to fall in the dust of a dying city!"

CHAPTER 14

Down in the ravine it was autumn weather. The sea was gentle, the days fine and sunny. Avel was enjoying their hospitality for a day and night. Though gaunt from his ascetic life he was more relaxed than he had been for months. Once when he was alone with Ana his hands trembled. She attributed this tremor to fasting.

Jahaan had planned to row to Ys with Ana the following day. There he hoped to sell some fish and a wooden bowl which he had carved with fish symbols. Avel smiled when Jahaan showed him this handiwork and said "Isn't the double dolphin the emblem of their city?" He helped Jahaan prepare the curragh for the journey.

The four of them, Jahaan, Ana, Norah and Avel had chatted over past events. They spoke about the Bagaudae raid and the effect it had on all of them. They talked of Ana's marriage and the life she was now leading. She had only one regret. She was not yet with child. Jahaan praised his young wife for the many ways in which she was helping him, from making fine nets to handling an oar. What Ana did not discuss in Avel's presence were the joys and peace that she had found in marriage. The three of them, Norah, Jahaan and Ana, had come back almost at once to the hut after the wedding. It was so quiet there. At nights Norah prepared the bed for the three of them. No longer did Ana sleep only with Norah for the palliasse had now been made to take three persons. So she slept in the middle with Norah on her left and Jahaan on her right. They always said a prayer together before they bedded down in their comfort and happiness.

Avel left in the late afternoon. They had pressed him to stay another night with them but he had refused. Their gaze followed his spectral figure over the misty marshes as he strode with haste and quickly vanished from their sight.

Jahaan and Ana went back together to the hut. The two talked about Ys and what they might find there. As Jahaan spoke Ana felt a great longing to see this city so remote from her and to probe its mystery. What had enabled it to survive for centuries? She wanted so much to know what Jahaan knew, to experience what he would experience in Ys, to have the same thoughts as he would have. It might be her last opportunity for Norah had warned her that once she was with child it would be impossible for her to go to Ys.

Norah felt tired. The night before she had a nightmare in which armed warriors, the sea and stone houses were all mixed up. Would the sea tomorrow be too much for the new curragh? Jahaan reassured her. "You worry too much Norah" he said. "The craft has a good ox hide skin and has been properly built." He repeated their plans for the morrow. They would go to Ys, spend three hours there, sell the fish and the bowl and return before sunset. Norah still looked reluctant as they sorted over the gear for the boat and their provisions for the day. She insisted that Ana should leave her silver cross in the hut. "You might lose it at sea" she said.

When they finally pulled away in the morning Jahaan

shouted "Farewell!" in his deep voice and Norah, her hair blown about by the breeze called "Be back before sunset!" Jahaan laughed. "I hope we bring something back from Ys."

Then they were off at last, Ana bent to the oar in a rhythm that matched Jahaan's careful, effortless strokes. Feathering the blade exactly as he had taught her, breathing deeply at every stroke. A good partner for a fisherman!

The curragh was a well found craft moving easily, its soft skin giving slightly as it met the force of the waves. There was no need for them to hurry and while they rowed along Ana had time to think of the changes that had come to her after her wedding. Their rowing in unison was a mirror of the inward harmony that was growing between them. After their marriage she had learnt much. Jahaan had been a reticent person but now she was able to listen to the doubts which he expressed about life and the fears which could seize him. She had learnt to understand the dark moments of melancholy that came over him when he thought back to Claudia's death, for he, too, missed that wonderful woman.

Ana was still puzzled by the subtle fascination that Ys had for Jahaan but remembered that she was very ignorant of this city so remote from other communities. Jahaan's emotions were very deep and perhaps he found it difficult to reveal them to her. He had not even spoken to her of his father's death. She had only learnt of it through Norah. Certainly they had no need to sell fish in Ys. They did not require money or goods. She felt that it was not her place to question the urge that drove him at rare intervals to go to the city where his father had died. Yet when he had said that he was making another journey there and wanted her to accompany him she felt joy come over her at the thought that he relied on her ability to row and share with him the toil of coping with the seas. Secretly, however, she was feeling a keen curiosity about the city and a mounting excitement to be there as a free woman. If there was a hidden fear that she could be enslaved in Ys springing from her past abduction it never came to the surface.

At first they spoke little to each other. The constant talking of the waves against the hull, the regular beat of the oars lulled them into silence. Mist began to drift up from the distant horizon, its purple folds concealing the cliffs. It was coming from the direction of Ys.

"Must we turn back if the mist thickens?"

"It won't be necessary. It will pass as the sun rises. But we'll delay here for a while until it clears. Meantime we'll have some food."

He sat, oars lightly resting on the water. She broke the rye bread and said Grace. The mist lasted longer than Jahaan would have wished. Granite cliffs suddenly loomed up. The swell had grown calmer. "It's clearing, we must get on our way for we're late already. You'll soon see Ys." They rowed on and there appeared in the distance a break in the cliffs. It was a broad ravine which penetrated deeply into the land. As they drew nearer they could see a narrow neck of land right in the middle of the ravine on which was built the city of Ys. The city sloped steeply upwards towards the cliffs beyond.

The cliffs that were the shoulders of this neck of land were linked to the ravine sides only by a slender bridge that soared out in a graceful arch from a gatehouse. The Bridgegate, Jahaan said it was called.

It appeared to be the only opening in the high walls that encircled the city. Within these walls huddled the dwellings grey, brown and white. The lowest dwellings were so far down that they appeared to be floating in the sea itself. Distant on the summit of the rocky bluff gleamed white columns. It was the temple well away from the city yet from its high position the dominant building. Ana stared intently at this evidence of pagan faith and at the strange looking houses. She could feel already the mystery and the attraction of Ys.

"It's very beautiful, Jahaan. To me the city appears like a necklace clinging to the neck of land on which it is built."

The curragh swayed uneasily as some hidden current coming from the land seized it. Jahaan held the boat fast against this alien intrusion. He sighed. "You're seeing it at its best, Ana, from a distance, but for those who live there all their lives it must seem akin to a poison circlet held tightly round their necks. Just look closely at the right hand side of the ravine and you will see a feather of mist creeping up silently. That is the vapour that in summer is the harbinger of the marsh fever here. Above it all is the heathen temple, apart from the people, yet poised over that bluff like a hawk about to stoop for its prey."

... ...

While Jahaan and Ana were approaching Ys two persons were talking together by a lane in a higher part of the city. They were alone and it was very quiet. Gwendaline looked closely at Malek's face, at his fine hair and powerful arms. Malek spoke first.

"What will you do today, Gwendaline, since it is a feast day? They say there will be dancing and the poorer people are to have a feast in the presence of our rulers. It will be a fine sight."

She sighed and gazed up at the blue sky. High up in the sky a single shearwater was winging its way out to sea. It would soon leave Ys far behind.

"Often, in these past few days, I have envied the freedom of such birds. They can leave Ys when they want to and abandon its squalid streets. I feel claustrophobic here as if I had to live my life in a prison. How wonderful just to wander far away beneath those hills yonder. The hills which embrace the great forests where the trees are clad in coats of fresh green. Where I might lie alone in some leafy bower and hear nothing but the sweet voices of the birds instead of the bitter wrangles of our cramped lanes. There I could satisfy a yearning which has grown so strong in my heart. To be closer to the gods I cherish even if I can only achieve this aim through my death." She sighed and smiled ruefully.

"I don't know how far you believe such things but I do have the Second Sight and a feeling is coming over me that for me this day in my life will be a day I shall never forget. A day when I shall really know my fate."

She smiled again and her cheeks flushed with thoughts that had come to her, unspoken warm desires. "I suppose it will be just another day. Since there will be many people in the market place I shall go there and read palms and perhaps sell my herbs. Yet I have not asked what you will be doing today?"

"You will not see me at all" said Malek. "I shall go down to the harbour where I shall be training my troop of swordsmen. Now, I regret that I have work to do. I must not linger with you though I would like to stay." He shifted his feet uneasily. He was always busy. "I am sorry that I have to leave you. Perhaps we shall meet again in the evening." "How stiffly he spoke" she thought. "His words don't reveal what he is. Is it because he's a lawyer and they keep close guard on their lips?"

The time was coming when they must separate. They had only a few more moments together. She put her hands tightly round his upper arms feeling the immense strength of his arm muscles and the warmth of his blood coursing through his body. She wanted to be longer with him but could not somehow express her feelings in words, only in that simple gesture of departure used by the people of Ys. As she broke away from Malek and went down the lane there were tears in her eyes.

"I believe I love this man" she whispered. "I feel he understands me though he says little. I think that if I were in danger he would protect me."

Malek stood for a few minutes in deep thought gazing at her slim figure until it disappeared from his sight. The blood was pounding through his veins and he trembled with an unwonted excitement. He went back to his house and polished his sword until it gleamed like silver, glad that the work took him away from those strange feelings that were a consequence of meeting Gwendaline. He still had time to spare so he took out the old manuscript about the Trial by Water of witches and conned it once more. He read it carefully, memorising every word.

CHAPTER 15

They rowed on until Ana saw the low sea wall and the little dwellings huddled behind it. Then a small tower on whose apex was a cross. "The church of the Kristion, now abandoned" said Jahaan. He steered the curragh straight at the cliffs and they glided into a narrow creek concealed by high rock walls. There was a ledge with a projecting rock spike. To this he made fast the painter. It was an ideal hiding place for his craft or for themselves.

"I always leave her here as it is unknown to the people of Ys. We'll go on foot and carry our fish to the market place." They climbed the cliffs by a path almost overgrown then walked to the ravine and the bridge. The bridge was narrow and its planks could easily be removed, making it a formidable obstacle against besiegers. The watch at the other end, the Bridgegate, grinned at Jahaan with no malice on their faces though they stared lecherously at Ana.

On they walked through winding streets and narrow lanes into the market place. There was little trade. In twos or threes, people drifted in to glance idly at all that was there or more often simply to stare greedily at the tiny amount of food that was on display. They hardly bought anything. Idle and unkempt, they glanced around with looks either apathetic or wild. They stared at Ana, a stranger, with a curiously studied indifference as if she were a mere shadow. Few children were there and those feeble and shrunken. In muted voices people gabbled in their peculiar tongue. Sometimes it was almost impossible to make out the meaning of some old Gaulish words they occasionally used.

Jahaan was used to the inhabitants and set out his wares on the pavement. They waited a long time there for custom seemed very poor. A shrewish woman attracted apparently by the silvery bodies of the fish paused by them but more to goggle at Ana than the fish. There were unspoken questions lurking in her suspicious eyes but with a bare word of greeting to Jahaan the woman moved away. Two men came into the market place carrying banners which they hung up at the far end opposite to Jahaan and Ana to whom they paid no attention. Since time was passing they decided to leave the market place and were about to gather up their unsold wares when two women appeared. Ana thought that they could not really be from Ys itself as they spoke a language volubly that was neither Breton, Latin nor Gaulish though its sounds were pleasant enough. One glanced at the banner bearers with a look that betokened an underlying dislike of Ys or the people. They came to the waiting pair to examine both fish and the wooden bowl. They chatted and looked with a friendly interest at Ana, the stranger. Ana noticed how greatly they differed from each other in appearance.

The first, older woman was a harlot slave and she wore a bronze collar from which depended the two long metal interlocking dolphins, the badge of Ys. So that males always knew she was of harlot status, the chainsmith who fitted her collar had cunningly made each dolphin so it hung down, its mouth enamelled a bright red, touching the scarlet painted nipple of each breast. She could never move her dolphins away for the chainsmith had linked them to a metal band encircling her upper body and riveted behind her smooth back. The woman seemed unembarrassed by her conspicuous ornament. Perhaps she did not even notice it.

She was a swarthy woman with dark hair in long curls and eyes that flashed brightly as she spoke. Above her breech clout, her torso was bare and on her arms she wore bangles of silver. After looking at the fish she lolled against the nearby wall, her scarlet smeared lips uttering maledictions, bitter as aloes, against two roughs who had sidled up, their lustful looks directed at her and her companion.

Ana was surprised when she looked at the other woman. She was the last woman slave in the coffle taken to Ys by the slave raiders! She likewise wore only a breech clout and underneath her polished slave collar, the two dolphins grinned lasciviously from her bosom. She was fair skinned with finely chiselled features. On her shoulder was the mark of a brand. It was clear that she would soon bear a child. Her eyes were sad, her mouth silent as she gazed at the strangers.

The other woman, the whore, had no difficulty in communicating. She knew Jahaan from his previous visits and jabbered away in a speech that was a mixture of a crabbed argot Latin with Breton and Gaulish thrown in. When she was at a loss for words she resorted to expressive gestures.

"Poor Greek wretch! She was brought to Massilia where I came into this dismal world. She was sold into slavery then captured by slave raiders from Ys. They dragged her to this gloomy city far from the sunny South. Curses, a thousand execrations, be on their miserable heads! Theodora's a Kristion of the Greek persuasion though that doesn't matter does it? God have mercy on her! Life's so hard for women slaves. You have to work all day and then at night all they can think of is to get you with child. She'll have to bear this child and others for these rascals! Brats who'll die from the marsh fever before they're weaned! God help us all, I say!" Her lips curled in contempt as she glanced at some men coming into the market place. "Thank God I don't bear and never will! All I've got is my body. I'm just a machine!"

"You two are close friends in a strange land" said Ana gently. The woman understood the pointed hand, the expression on Ana's face rather than the Breton words. Her face softened. "We share the same hovel. We warm each other at nights on the same bed of straw. She's got some cloth. It's only a little but she'd like to barter it for the fish and the wooden bowl if you're willing. It'll cheer her up to know that a Kristion hand has made the bowl. I've not got much of a faith but I can still befriend her." The barter was soon concluded, the fish and bowl exchanged for the cloth.

The harlot said "Follow us but at a distance. Theodora will show your wife the church of the Kristion. It's forbidden for us to use it. Look at the church but not too closely. We may be followed and watched." This part of the conversation had been carried on in furtive whispers that no passer-by could follow. They left the market place walking well behind the two Greek slaves. To reach the church they had to cross an open stretch of ground, bare and dismal. On this, two great beams had been erected vertically and across these at the top was a massive horizontal beam. Two black shadows dangled helplessly from it. Suddenly a gust of wind caught them; there was a clinking of chains and the two things swayed hither and thither in fettered obedience to the breezes. At this sight Ana felt her belly grow taut with fear but she went on gazing because she wanted to conceal and master her horror at the spectacle.

The two shadows were human beings suspended by their necks! They had been long dead for the flesh had shrivelled on their bones, the eyes had rotted in the bony sockets, and there were gaping holes in their skulls. The bony necks wore slave collars. The breeze grew stronger, blowing in gusts and the skeletons under its influence suddenly seemed possessed of some macabre life. They swayed more vigorously then like puppets on a string bounced up and down until in their diabolical gyrations it seemed as if the man were dancing with the woman and kissing her cheeks.

A man of Ys who had just come up gazed in morbid fascination at the criminals and laughed. "They've deserved it" he cried. "That's our justice to thieves in Ys! There's another couple over there hanging, too. And there's the ashes of a fire with which they burnt a woman slave, a murderess."

His words were interrupted by the rushing noise of a great flock of birds, black wings darkened the sky and hovered over the dead couple suspended in degradation. The ravens alighted on the crossbar and croaked defiance to the human beings standing by. Something alarmed them and they soared up wheeling over Ys and uttering, as birds of ill-omen, their grim warnings. Ana shuddered but knew it was better not to show her feelings while in Ys.

Beyond the Place of Execution and its gibbets rose up the church of the Kristion where the Greeks in the shadows waited for them. The small church had long since been abandoned. The roof was in ruins and swallows, calling out their strange cries, circled in and out of the moss clad arches. Rushes grew by the nave and grass was thick on the steps to the altar. It would be only a few years before the church would die which was perhaps why the heathen of Ys didn't bother to pull it down. Yet in the tower still hung the bell intact and enriched by a fine green patina.

The most remarkable feature of the church was in a shallow niche at the tower summit. It was the tiny statue of a woman angel whose right hand was clasped to her waist while her left was held out and sloping downwards as if she were granting a blessing to the city. Beneath her short cut hair her face was exquisitely carved out of stone, the sad eyes downcast in prayer. The weather had spared this statue completely. The swallows always avoided the holy figure.

They said farewell to their new acquaintances. Their way back to the market place led them close to the dilapidated quayside and the decrepit remains of the old harbour. The rotting skeleton of a long dead boat lay in the shallows, sole evidence that Ys had ever had any link with the sea. They heard the overseer bawling as he urged the slaves repairing the sea wall, the crack of his whip on naked backs. Beyond all sounded the gentle murmur of the waves as they thrust day and night at the base of the low walls that alone protected Ys from the waters.

Ana and Jahaan had wanted to leave Ys early. By now it was impossible for them to do so. The market place and every lane in its neighbourhood were crammed with crowds of excited people laughing and talking to each other in boisterous voices. There was no way out. Their route to the Bridgegate was completely blocked off. It was clear that some festival was to take place for on the walls of the market place now hung more highly coloured banners and two chairs had been draped in fine wool. Every minute the crowd was growing more dense and mingled with them were men, helmets faced with iron, and on whose bulky hips swung long swords. Their task seemed to be to control the throngs of people.

Ana was surrounded by men. The only woman close by was Gwendaline and they were the only women near a group of people separate from all others and standing by a long table on which were loaves of bread. Ana was so close to the bread she could almost have touched it. The stunted bare legs of the children showed in the rents of their ragged tunics. Some were naked. Their huge eyes burned with a weird fire in sunken sockets. The women, pallid faced, stood listlessly by their offspring. Their lacklustre eyes and gaunt features contrasted with the bright flags and air of festivity. The eyes of this group were hardly ever turned away from watching the table. Even in their apathy they were waiting for something to happen.

The sun was now already beginning to sink in the heavens above though it had not yet gone below the top of the temple. Jahaan managed to get near a guard and told him that he wanted urgently to leave the city.

There was a sneer on the man's face. He waved his huge thumb at the crowd. "I know you by sight but you're still a stranger indeed if you don't know what today means to us. It's the day when every man and woman that loves the gods enjoys for a few brief hours life to the full before the winter clouds are on us. It is a time for merrymaking and getting drunk. You can't go until you've seen the fun. The curia and Dahut have ordained a feast for those who need it and some humiliores will receive gifts of bread and cervoise. After the gathering has broken up, you can certainly leave. Only these things can leave the city now. I've never before seen all the rats of Ys desert us."

Close to the houses was advancing an enormous column of brown bodied animals. The rats, moving head to tail, had no fear of the human beings but moved slowly and deliberately, their sleek fur brushing the walls of the houses and even the legs of people trying to avoid them. As if directed by an invisible general, the long thin line passed right through the market place without halting and into the lanes nearby. Thence they marched to the Bridgegate where the guard wisely made no attempt to interfere with them. The strange brown snake appeared on the bridge itself. The formidable army was crossing the ravine and leaving Ys. Without haste or hesitation they moved along a pathway and at last vanished in the surrounding woods. They left behind a foul stench and excreta. A momentary chill came over the chattering crowd.

Amusements had not been forgotten. After the rats had gone, two dancing chits clad in brief cinctures appeared. Small papped creatures, looking like painted dolls, they waggled buttocks and bellies lewdly while a piper played a tune to keep them in time. Their movements excited bursts of coarse laughter from the men. Then a juggler came. Unerring, he displayed his art to the avid eyes of the crowd and won their applause. He ceased when a guard blew three notes on his trumpet. The guards forced an opening in the crowd. The rulers of Ys were coming to preside over the feast.

First came the vergobret and his secretary, conspicuous in his embroidered coat. Other members of the curia, then Gradlon and last Dahut. She looked all round the crowd. A flush came to her cheeks when she perceived Ana and Jahaan and how tightly they were hemmed in by the crowds. She wrote on a wax tablet which she handed to the captain of the guards. He spoke to an officer. The man wormed his way through the people and vanished. Gradlon and Dahut took their seats.

Ana had been nervous at the passing of the rats. Now a fear of some greater evil as yet unknown struck at her heart and mind.

"Can't we get away somehow – now?" she whispered.

"You see how difficult it is. We're trapped here. When the bread's been given out we'll have to make a dash for it and slip away unnoticed."

The trumpet once more gave out its brazen message. The vergobret cried out in a powerful voice.

"Hear me well, ye men and women of the most ancient city of Ys! On this joyful day we have ordained a gift for its indigent citizens. On yonder tables stand loaves of bread, well baked from the finest rye flour. There is ample for those who need it. This shall be our ceremonial. When the lady Dahut raises her hands up to the heavens, the baker shall allocate loaves. The feasting shall commence. The vessels of cervoise shall never be empty. They shall be filled and filled again until all have drunk to repletion."

The attention of all had been wholly given to the words of the vergobret. All, that is, except Gwendaline. Unconscious of the crowd and the event taking place she was entirely absorbed in reading the palm of a small thin man, both indifferent to where they were.

Dahut, gathering her robes around her, now stood up. The buzz of talk subsided. She looked hard at all there but more especially at Jahaan and the woman with him unable to flee from her and she smiled. In her eyes envy, hatred and desire were mingled. Yet when she spoke it was without hesitation and her voice rang out boldly.

"Men and women of Ys, whom your great city cherishes and to whom we wish a long life! Heartily enjoy the food that comes from our city granaries, the fine rye bread. Feast, feast on this great day before the storms and darkness of winter are upon us! Warm your hearts, be merry with cervoise! When you have finished and are replete, you shall carry back to your dwellings sacks of grain for the cold months yet to come and you shall no longer be hungry!"

So saying, she paused for a moment then raised her fine arms high above her head as if making an oblation to the gods. Without a moment's hesitation the famished people rushed in a body to seat themselves at the benches by the table and clawed at the loaves, tearing the bread to pieces and stuffing them into their mouths until their cheeks swelled out. They were as fast in these actions as starving dogs wolfing a meal. Quickly they disposed of the food until they were full then with mouths still crammed with bread bellowed loudly for more. Women slaves, swaying under the weight of heavy baskets on their wide hips, brought loaves. Others bore pitchers of cervoise on their heads. These were quickly emptied and refilled. Even young children gulped at sops of bread soaked in cervoise. The feasters' faces grew round and flushed, their eyes bright. Shadows stretched out fingers that grew longer as time passed. Ana grew more weary and anxious as they awaited the outcome of this orgy. Gradlon, accompanied by the vergobret and the curia, left the market place. Dahut remained a while, standing and smiling all round at her people. Ana felt a coldness in that smile. The eyes and the open lips that smiled so reminded her of the deadly serpent that Thomas had killed.

CHAPTER 16

Unheeded by onlookers, under the table crouched a black cat. An emaciated animal that frantically devoured bread scraps that fell from the feasters. It moved its head uneasily as if fearful of the tumult above. Then it crept cautiously into the market place where there was a tiny space left free. The spectators laughed uproariously at its antics. Oblivious to them it jumped in the air, its head swaying aimlessly from side to side, its eyes ablaze. Its body was more twisted than those of the dancers. Dahut looked, unmoving, at the cat. There was no emotion in her cold eyes.

Next to Ana was a rough looking man on whose body ran a red scar. He had watched the feast with saliva drooling from his lips. "Ha! Ha!" he gloated. "The cat's drunk with too much cervoise! So they will all be intoxicated. A fitting state for feasters!" His pitiless eyes stared, gimlet-sharp, at the cat.

Suddenly it ran full speed at a pillar and beat its head against the unyielding stone. Thrice it did this in a frenzy of self-destruction, staggering more and more from the impact. The last time there was a horrible crunch. The creature fell down lifeless, its skull broken. Blood gushed from ears and mouth and the soil of Ys lapped it up eagerly.

With the strange death of the cat unease spread through the watchers. It were as if a demon of death had come amongst them. "The cat's gone mad!" muttered the man. The words died in his throat as all eyes were now intent on watching the feasters.

One of them clutching a chunk of bread staggered up onto his feet. He stretched his hands with the bread in them upwards pointing to the skies above. His eyes rolled uncontrollably in their sockets. Then screaming he ran swiftly from the table and battered his shaggy head against the column above the body of the dead animal in a suicidal fury.

"Seize that man! Bind him in chains lest he do a mischief!" cried Dahut, turning away and leaving the market place. The guards struggled through the crowd and tried to hold the madman but he tore himself away with supernatural strength and speed shrieking in a peculiar high pitched voice "I see the heavenly lights of the gods! They're wonderful red and green and the brightest gold! The buildings all round are aflame with colour! They're mine forever!"

The other eaters en masse surged, yelling, from the tables. Some uttered inhuman cries and beat their heads on the walls. Others ran swifter than hounds bellowing that their skulls had become liquid fire. They would kindle the whole city. A few climbed to the steepest house roofs and flapping their arms as if they were wings, threw themselves down. The streets below were littered with broken or lifeless bodies. Everywhere resounded the yells of men, the agonised cries of women, the wailing of children. The guards were almost helpless. They tried in vain to secure the most violent madmen or pick up the dying. The crowd shrank away from contact with these horrible spectres. Night was approaching. People would have escaped but they were too tightly packed into the market place.

A dark haired man shouted in a voice so loud it could be heard above the tumult. "Close all the exits from the market place! Let no one leave until the guilty woman who has bewitched those people has been captured! There is the wicked one! There she cowers! The woman who has driven so many to madness by her spells!" His long finger pointed at Gwendaline huddled in a corner, tears streaming down her cheeks.

"That's the woman!" shouted another man. "She was at the baker's when he ground the grain and baked the bread. I saw her!"

"I saw you!" shrieked a gaunt chit. "You spread your hands over the loaves and muttered incantations so that the bread, poisoned, should make mad all who ate it!"

"She's made them mad! She's made them mad! The cry was taken up and repeated by scores of terrified voices.

"She's guilty! Seize her, she must die! She's earned the penalty of death!"

"See those awful bodies broken by her magic! Away with her lest she casts any more spells on us!"

An avalanche of men bore down on her. She was trapped, forced hard against the wall. No guards were in sight and Dahut had long gone. The shouts grew louder. They were closing in on the victim. Fear clung to her assailants' eyes but they struggled to get near. The cries changed. "Punish her!" the dark man shouted. "Give her the punishment due to a wicked witch!"

Her hands shook like aspen leaves, only a rattle came from her throat.

Then they were right on her. Some gripped her, others bound her hands behind her back. They pulled her away towards the harbour. Ana and Jahaan unable to flee were borne along with the mob. With every step as they dragged her along came the cries "punish her!" With every step hands clutched at her shift, her hair, her shoulders, her face. Claw fingers slashed at her like famished beasts rending terrified prey. With every movement her passage was marked by fragments of torn cloth floating away in the air. Now came a new shout.

"Burn her! Burn her!"

As the mob moved there came the crack of branches torn off trees. Some men snatched up scrap timbers. The wood was waved in the air by triumphant hands. Others seized ropes, chains rattled!

The western sky was troubled, the clouds red in colour, the tide coming in, its waters swirling against the harbour walls. The day was fading.

They had almost reached the harbour when their pace abruptly slackened. The front ranks halted as suddenly as a horse pulled up by its rider. A score or more of armed men stood right in their way. Each man wore a cincture and a leather helmet on which was engraved the double dolphin of Ys. On the left arm was a round shield. The right hand held a long sword, highly polished. It was clear that this troop knew how to use swords. A gigantic man was in front. Their leader, Malek.

The mob hesitated for a moment, wavered then stopped still.

"What is the reason for this stampede?" Malek said with a tinge of sarcasm.

"We're going to burn the witch! She cast spells upon the bread!" said the dark man.

"We'll talk about it first" said Malek with cool pugnacity. "Let me have a quiet word with you, their leader." He pointed to a dark man then to a place where they could talk out of earshot of Gwendaline.

He spoke calmly. His face was impassive but he was thinking fast and furiously. He knew that the mob were out to burn her. What could he do? Escape with her? Impossible with the mob clogging the lanes. Fight his way out with her? He had twenty warriors who would fight to the death but he was facing hundreds, many with concealed weapons. No, it wouldn't save her from the stake.

The guards? Supposed to keep order! Probably pursuing the madmen. Coarse laughter came to his ears. Men were piling faggots round a tall post at the harbour waiting for its victim. He looked at Gwendaline. Her hands were tied behind her back, her breasts bare. From one shoulder drops of blood fell. Her gaze held a mute appeal.

There was only one way he could save her from burning and he'd regret it all his days! As dusk approached he saw the serried ranks of cruel faces, the lustful eyes, waiting to see her in flames. He heard the murmur of impatient voices. They wouldn't wait much longer.

Malek spoke. "What will you do with this woman?"

"What do we do to a witch? We'll strip her, tie her, put her in the water!" A plump wench, she'll float. She'll show us she's guilty! Then we'll chain her. She is a witch but she won't wriggle out of our fetters." Malek looked the man full in the eyes. "I warn you that if she is executed it must be done in full accordance with the law. I am a lawyer, I am trusted by Dahut and know what I am talking about. The Princess does not like people who act outside the law. You do not know how to Swim a witch. I do, and the responsibility must be mine, not yours. I know exactly how to prepare a woman's body for her Swimming and to carry out the Swimming to prove her guilty or innocent! My men know this as well and will obey me. All you have to do is to watch. Do not approach close – not to men carrying swords!" He jerked his pointed thumb at his companions – "or you'll have no guts left! Give us time! No more bawling at the wench! No more mob violence! I'll Swim her in a legal manner!"

For a short time the two antagonists glared at each other. Then the dark man said "All right, I give in. I'll bring her over to you. Do your job and we'll watch silently. But don't let us wait too long! You won't let her escape by using her magic?" "Of course not! But I warn you you'll get a sword in your belly if you come near!"

"If she floats?"

"That will prove her guilty and you may burn her." The other grinned. "We'll do that job well! It will be a rare sight! All right, you can have her for her Swimming."

... ...

They brought Gwendaline to him. Her hands were tied. She smiled with relief that she was away from the mob and Malek was in charge of her. She had thought he would untie her but he whispered "I must leave them tied. I must not give them the impression that you are to be set at liberty yet. Endure a little longer and everything will be all right." He left her and went to speak to his men who were a little way off leaving two of them to look after her. She felt so grateful to him, the man who had once saved her life when she was floating, the brave warrior who had rescued her from the mob. He returned, unsmiling.

"I want to get right out of Ys" she gasped, "away from this mob, into the woods." He paled. Malek was a brave man but at this point he was tongue-tied. He could not tell her the truth about the binding of her limbs, of what he planned to do during the Swimming. He loved this woman but he would have to drown her to save her from burning!

He knew that she was in a state of euphoria after her rescue from the mob. Better to keep her feeling happy as long as possible while his men secretly prepared the cord to secure her. Just now he must lie to her. "My men are getting ready to prepare you for your escape now from the mob. We'll join them. They are all ready to look after you."

For a brief moment she experienced again that longing to go to the woods with Malek and see their beauty once more. Then a strange feeling came to her, which she had never known before. There was a warm sinking sensation in the pit of her belly and her breasts swelled outwards with her strong desires for a man. For this man!

"Come" said Malek. "They are waiting."

As they approached the little group of men who stood in a circle he untied her wrists. She swung her arms round and round, smiling and enjoying this freedom of her limbs. The circle opened as she came to them then closed up round her and Malek.

... ...

If Gwendaline had really hoped that she would soon make a getaway from Ys she had been swiftly disillusioned. She was lying, naked, on her back with a man squatting on her belly and gripping her shoulders to hold her down. A dozen pairs of strong hands grasped her legs and arms. She felt her thumbs and toes being tied with cord, other hands tied cord to her wrists and ankles and there was a long rope round her waist. Unresisting in her womanly weakness she shed tears while they completed their task and firmly bound her right great toe to her left thumb and her left great toe to her right thumb and to make doubly sure she could not escape tied her ankles to her wrists.

The men worked in silence. She felt that they had no ill-will towards her but it was hard to be tied so firmly and still not know what was to happen to her. Malek's voice was hoarse, his face pale. In his expression she read only her doom.

"You're prepared for your Swimming now!"

"Swimming?" How could she, a weak woman, with limbs tied and unversed in the strokes, try to swim where a strong man could not keep himself up? Malek went on "You are to undergo the Trial by Water. We shall place you in the sea. If your face remains above the water you will be adjudged guilty and that awaits you." He pointed to the pyre where men waited with torches ready to kindle the faggots. "They will burn you alive. It will be a terrible death. If, on the other hand, you sink beneath the water you will be deemed innocent."

She shuddered. The fear of the fiery death was upon her. Malek knelt beside her and put his mouth close to her ear so that even his own men could not hear the words. "Don't be afraid Gwendaline, you will not burn. I will make sure that you only know the quick drowning by water not death by fire. It's all I can do for you." His voice shook, there were tears in his eyes. "There's no escape!"

Then came to Gwendaline thoughts which made her forget the cords cutting into her great toes and the crowd waiting for her death. She believed in her gods and their power. They had ordained everything that had happened to her today. It was their will that had sent her to that fateful market place, that the mob should capture her, that she should be bound for her Swimming. Even when her lungs gasped out the last breath they would only be obeying the divine behests. After her death they would unfold the Great Mystery to her as she stood before them clad in purity and knowing a boundless love.

"Then let death be! To the good man or woman no harm can happen!" she whispered to herself as much as to Malek.

They carried her to the harbour's edge. They laid her down on the stone footing above the waters. No guards had appeared to halt the proceedings. The western sky was still troubled, the clouds bright red. She was surrounded by the men of Ys filled with the lust to burn her, only held back by Malek's men, swords loosed, ready. She spoke. The voice was not loud but it reached the uttermost part of the crowd. "I, Gwendaline, am an upright woman! I am no worker of evil! I have done no harm to the people of Ys! Untie me and let me go in peace!"

The voice was so piercing that for an instant everyone in the crowd became silent, listening to her. There was flame in her eyes as she gazed up at the sky above, at the pitiless faces, at the sea. She was no slave wench meekly submissive to a mob, condemned, and bared for Swimming and the Fire. Her voice had no trace of fear. The words burnt like molten iron. "You! You scum of the earth! You who'd push an innocent woman to death! Let me tell you one thing before I go! I may die but first you must hear the truth from these lips! Cursed, cursed be forever this Ys and cursed be its ferocious people who've done so many unspeakable evils! Those who slay the guiltless! May the hands that seized me wither to dust, may your children perish in your sight so that none shall be left! The judgment of the Great Goddess is that you shall be wiped forever from the face of the earth and your city totally forgotten!"

One of the mob cried, trembling, "She's said enough! Let the water judge if she be guilty! A mouthful of salt water will stop that tongue from uttering its curses on us!"

"Away with her!" someone else shouted. "Fill her belly with salt water!"

Malek and four of his men carried her down the steps and waded into the deeper water. His other men formed a tight cordon round the top of the steps and stood, hands resting on their pommels. The two men in the water on each side of her grasped the rope round her waist to control her Swimming. Their work could not be seen. Malek's face was pale. He spoke but his words were only heard by her.

The Swimming began. Her head sank, then her white lips appeared, quivering above the surface. The struggle for life was brief. Then all movement ceased except for bubbles that came to the surface. She had gone to the Isle of the Blessed. To her Avalon. Her Swimming had lasted five minutes. At no time had even her face been seen.

"She's innocent!" cried a woman bystander.

Slowly, like sleep walkers, with averted eyes and pausing on each stone step, Malek and his men carried their burden up to the harbour's edge and laid it down on the paving stones. The crowd, with staring eyeballs and muted lips, gazed in a weird stillness at this victim of their fury. Not a word, not a whisper now escaped from their gaping mouths. The white body and rounded limbs still glistened like marble from the immersion. Ribbons of sea wrack were intertwined in her hair as if the sea had sought from its own bosom to give her a wreath worthy of her noble life. The eyes gazed fixedly upwards, the face bore an expression of peace. The lips had only a gentle, forgiving smile to those who gazed on them.

Now she was dead, shame overcame decent men. One said "We have slain a blameless woman. She had lived years in Ys. Many knew her. She did not do any harm. The gods will exact a fearful punishment for this deed. I for one wish I had never been present to see this." He turned away as if he could not bear to see the corpse.

"You're a fool" said the dark man, breathing deeply. "Gwendaline, an evil woman was tried properly for her crime by being Swum. I'd be glad to do the same to any other witches who crossed my path! Be heartily glad that we've rid the city of her. No more wicked spells cast over us! No more poor wretches writhing in agony from food that she poisoned by her magic. It is the end!"

"It is the end!" cried a terrible voice. A tall man clad

in a goatskin apron towered over them. In his huge right hand Guenole held a cross, in the left a wooden oval and tablet with the sign manual of the double dolphin. Two slender rods were thrust through his girdle.

His eyes turned to fire as he looked from the dead woman to the men and back again. Instinctively they recoiled from this apparition. He held high up the dolphin symbol so that all might see it. "Your rulers invited me to come here to your city of Ys. I came in peace under their full protection and that of the God whom I serve. I hoped that by the mercy of God which He gives to all men who repent of their sins, Ys would get to know of His salvation. It was God's Will that I, his humble follower, should walk round Ys to discover the springs of water which you desperately need. God gave that water to you. It was His purpose that these wands, guided by Divine hands, should show the watchers among you where the waters at last would gush out. Yes, I've done my work and His and then what do I find? I find murderers, cowards, taking away the life of a human being."

"She – she was a witch" stuttered the dark man, white faced and eyes unable to meet Guenole's gaze. "She – she had poisoned the bread by casting a spell over it."

"She was a woman" said Guenole with a terrible slowness and emphasis which sowed fear in the hearts of his listeners. "Her body was the image of God, given to her as the temple of her spirit by her Maker. Without proper trial before your magistrates" – he was speaking rapidly now – "without due examination, in a moment of rage and fear – for none of you was man enough to stand up and say 'no' – you snatched the breath of life from her as you've done to so many others."

They looked like wild animals caught in a snare with the hunter's spear poised over them. They could not escape. They were nailed to the spot by his fury. "Everyone of you, man, woman and child living here has incurred the wrath of Almighty God! I tell you that for your awful sins He will come to mete out a fearful judgement on this wicked city." He looked at the sea so calm – where the woman had died. "You, too, shall die by water!"

Two men in burnished helmets, on which was engraved the dolphin and armed with long swords had forced their way through the onlookers. Guenole stared them full in the face. When their eyes met his gaze they flinched and slunk away. He walked away, alone, to the Bridgegate. No man dared to say a word to him or went after him.

CHAPTER 17

Ana and Jahaan, caught in the crowd, had been unwilling witnesses of the Trial by Water. Guenole had not seen them.

It was growing darker and a cold wind gusted through their clothing. Jahaan tried by quiet words to allay her doubts though Ana showed no fear. "We must get out of the city at once! I've never seen the people of Ys in so dreadful a mood. Perhaps after Guenole's words they won't touch us. We must get to the Bridgegate as fast as we can."

They hurried through a maze of lanes taking the shortest route to the Bridgegate. The streets were nearly empty and they were already in the lane that was the last stretch between themselves and freedom when the opening out of the lane ahead of them was blocked by a file of guards who stood, spears raised for action, at one end. A voice roared, "Halt at once as you value your lives!" Jahaan swung on his heel. He looked back. The way they had come was also black with soldiers. They were trapped.

The commanding officer shouted again. "Stay where you are without moving!" He came right up to them and held up a tablet on which was engraved the double dolphin. There were letters on the reverse side. "You're Jahaan, the Breton fisherman?" "Yes, that's my name." He felt a sinking feeling in the pit of his stomach. He had only a knife in his belt. Even if he were alone, he couldn't rush them. There were too many of them.

"You have a woman with you. Who is she? We've not seen her before in Ys."

"The woman is named Ana, she's my wife. Why do you detain us? We're on the way to the Bridgegate to leave the city and return to my home. I've sold my fish. I've no wish to stay here any longer. Let us pass." He spoke boldly but his heart was torn by worry more for Ana than for himself. For answer the officer pointed up at the temple to the west. The golden disc of the sun had long sunk behind its columns. All was growing dark in Ys. "You've been here before, Jahaan. Surely you know our laws! Any stranger found in Ys after sunset without a special authorisation from Dahut and the curia, properly signed, shall be put to death. You have no such authorisation. I could have both of you executed if I had been ordered to do so."

"We've committed no crime. We tried to get out well in time but were blocked by the crowds round the market place. Let us go! Surely you can excuse our error? You've no right to hold us." Ana had gone pale but kept very calm. The guards had come in closer and were holding their spears levelled at them. She could see their grimy cheeks, smell the reek of sweat and leather, see the threat in their bloodshot eyes. The commander's teeth gleamed. His voice was harsh.

"I don't argue with captives. My instructions are not to put you to death but to detain you in prison at the pleasure of Dahut. See, this is the sign manual for your arrest, your name and that of the woman are both on it and it is signed by Dahut. You'll come to no harm if you and this woman obey me but don't try to escape. Come, man, it's better to submit!" The word "escape" had already entered Jahaan's mind but he knew it was impossible; there was no hope for them now.

"Kneel down facing that wall and put your hands behind your backs!" They obeyed and at once felt the cord tied round their wrists. They were helpless now, prisoners of Ys! Then they stood up and were frog-marched away from the Bridgegate. Few people were abroad at that hour to look at the couple as they stumbled along through lanes that bore cracks across them. Once they nearly fell into a cavity that yawned by the way but were yanked to their feet by their captors.

The old prison of Ys was in a district now almost uninhabited and close to the city walls. Opposite was a small house in which the mason, Caradec, lived. He was just about to sit down and eat, for he had worked a long time up at the temple, when he heard the measured tramp of feet. "It must be guards" he thought, "but why are they abroad at this hour?" His window was closed by a thick wooden shutter that had a small eyehole cut in it, through which he could observe, without himself being noticed, what was happening outside. He looked closely at the party of guards. They had two prisoners. He knew the man, Jahaan, but there was a young woman quite unknown to him.

The prisoners were marched right up to the prison which had a vestibule at the front for the reception of prisoners. The jailer was called and appeared with a pile of chains. The man, Jahaan, was dealt with first presumably because he was considered the most dangerous. Jahaan was unbound then stripped. The jailer put on him a tiny breech clout, the sole clothing allowed to prisoners, as it meant they would be easily recognised in Ys. Then fetters were fastened on both hands and feet and he was held firmly while they dealt with the woman. Ana also was clad in a breech clout, which left her torso bare, but she made no protest. The jailer could not tell whence she came but he could see that she was a comely young woman. Her small hands and feet were bound in heavy chains and the jailer led her off into the prison.

There was the clink of chains from a cell near the street. The jailer growled a farewell to the soldiers and the men marched off.

The mason stood for a long time gazing at the prison. He was thinking about many things and it may have been force of habit that made him turn two or three times to his tools neatly hung on his wall from wooden pegs. His brow was furrowed as he pondered on the strange pair who were now in the prison so near to him. Then he smiled and sat down to his simple meal with the air of a man who has solved a problem.

After the death of Gwendaline the spectators had hurried away from the harbour. One man alone lingered by the harbour's edge. Malek. Then he returned to the body of Gwendaline and sat by it so rigid in thought that he might have been a statue. He had untied the great toes and thumbs and straightened her arms and legs. Hour after hour went by and still he maintained his watch until all lights were long extinguished in the harbour dwellings. It was midnight. He rose and tied her wrists to the sides of her body by the long rope that was still round her waist. He lifted her up and bearing her over one shoulder trudged to a part of the seashore where there were no inhabitants. It was the place where he had once helped the floating woman to put her feet back on the ground.

The sea had become quite calm and the tide was on the ebb. He gazed at it for a long while then stripped and said in a low voice, looking at the face of the dead woman, "As the sea brought about your death, let it now be your tranquil grave where you may rest in peace." Carrying the body in both arms he waded out until the water was almost up to his shoulders. Then, standing behind her, he gripped her under the armpits and began to swim out on his back, towing Gwendaline and using vigorous strokes with his muscular legs. Aided by the tide, he swam further out until the land was barely visible. At this point he had reached a large ledge of rock, just above the water's surface. Here he rested for a few moments while he looked around for a heavy stone shaped like a dumbbell. He tied cord tightly round its neck and secured it to Gwendaline's ankles. Standing on the rock, he said "Rest in peace, dear one." He released the body which, weighted by the stone, sank down into the depths.

He turned away from the rock and swam onwards towards the horizon, not looking back to the land. Hour after hour he swam with his powerful strokes always towards the horizon. Thus it was that he never saw behind him, moving fast with no ripple in the smooth water, a triangular fin.

There was no sound, no cry for help.

CHAPTER 18

Day after day rain was falling in Armorica. Grey clouds had drifted over forest and field, sea and river and released their deluges. The streams overflowed, the rivers ran brown with silt and the trees dripped ceaselessly.

The Breton fishermen, heedless of the weather and eager to use the calmer seas that came with the rain, rowed out with nets and lines and came back with their silvery prey. The rocks on the seashore were bright with the anointing from above and on the sea itself spray and raindrops contended in an unending battle. The winds were westerly and blew over wave and foam.

In the plou of the Bretons the sheep, stolid and tough as their masters, huddled for comfort beneath the massive trees. The farmers themselves went out daily in the lulls to inspect stock and drag in wood for their fires. The boles of the great oaks glistened with a beauty all of their own but the birds when they sang did so in muted tones.

Within the huts of the Bretons, people were far too busy to heed the downpours. Women sat spinning or weaving and told tales of the past. Young men were occupied too. Some sharpened spears, others ground iron sword blades. The hub of activity was the blacksmith's workshop. Here they prepared ploughshares and made bits for their steeds. Here also the swordsmith plied his craft. The forge roared and spluttered as the men toiled at the bellows. Even boys helped at some tasks. On their eager faces would come a glow of pride as they watched the swordsmith at his highly skilled work, that of making a pattern-welded sword. They were absorbed in watching the careful, measured hammering, the heating and cooling, oft repeated, the superb tempering of a sword that might be needed in a desperate struggle for life.

Save for Martha, Thomas was alone in the villa. Every day he would walk to Claudia's grave and kneel to pray, often remaining there a long time in supplication to God. He was essentially a man of action, not given to brooding, and his prayers were almost all appeals to God that He would protect his own people, the Kristion. His devotions would end with a plea to God that He would give him wisdom in the new ordeals that lay ahead of the Bretons.

Often, but mainly in the evenings, he had meetings in secret with messengers who came to him with news. A charcoal burner, a woodman from far away in the forest, a swineherd from a distant coppice, a fisherman from the bay. From all of them he would glean information about many matters but especially on those topics which bore on the security of the plou. He was determined that the Bagaudae should never surprise them again and also that they must remain ready for any Saxon attacks. He expected his messengers to report the movements of any strangers in their localities, no matter how innocent the man or woman might appear to be. He knew who the important men were among the Franks and what their attitude was towards the Bretons. It was his own plou that interested him the most.

One evening when it was twilight he had a visitor, Norah. She was soaked to the skin and green weed clung to her clothing. Her teeth chattered wildly and only after she had taken a stoup of hot wine and was drying by a blazing fire was she able to speak. Then her voice was firm and clear.

"When it happened I would have liked to have come to you at once but I was not sure. I kept on hoping that all would be well. Then the rain came and when I tried to cross the marsh I found that it was behaving in an abnormal way because of the flooding from the rain. I wanted to follow our usual path across but the marsh water had become too deep for me and I was nearly drowned. There was nothing for it but to go back to our hut and just wait. I had plenty of food. It was the waiting that was so horrible. Often, hourly, I would go to the marsh and see if the flood water had gone down. Always I found it impassable. I prayed to God that He would answer my prayers and help me to leave the ravine and come to you." She wiped away moisture from below her eyes. It was not just raindrops.

"This morning quite early He answered my prayers. When I went to the marsh at first light I found that the waters had burst one of the banks and had flowed away, carrying mud with it. The marsh was still dangerous and the ledges slippery but I somehow managed to cross it, sometimes floating on my back or even paddling like a dog. Thank God, I've got to you at last!" Steam rose up from her clothing. She gasped for breath and there was a great sadness in her eyes.

"I will tell you fully how it all happened. Jahaan had planned to go to Ys in his curragh with Ana. As it occurred, Avel was staying with us the day before. He helped Jahaan to prepare the boat for the journey but he left us in the late afternoon in a great hurry to get back to his work here."

"I've not seen Avel" said Thomas, "but I suppose he's living in his hermit's hut in the woods. The rain would keep him from coming abroad. But what's troubling you?"

"Jahaan and Ana never returned from their trip. They are both missing."

"Missing? Impossible! Jahaan's an excellent boatman and we've had no storms that his boat couldn't cope with!"

"They're missing! A few nights before they left I had one of those dreams that is a premonition. A dream of armed warriors and of the sea. Jahaan laughed at me when I told him. They set out rather late, but the weather was good. I gave them food to take with them." She sobbed for a while then went on. "I'm not really a person to sit around all day moping and anyway I'd plenty of work to do. I tidied the hut, made the bed and prepared some food for them to eat when they came back. I chopped wood, got water from the spring. It was a fine day, little wind and only a smooth ground swell on the sea. Yet I'd got to go down to the harbour and look for them. I know it was foolish but I must have done it at least six or more times that day. I couldn't rest, I was so uneasy. Evening came on. The shadows lengthened and I stayed down by the harbour, looking always towards the sea. No curragh appeared, gliding into the harbour. I knew what my duty was. I fetched the lanterns, lit the candles and hung them up on the Leading Marks; it's not a thing we would do unless it were really necessary for they might attract an enemy though he would have to be almost on the cliffs before he saw those lights. They're only useful to a man like Jahaan who knows the coast like the palm of his hand. I had used them only once before and never when Jahaan went to Ys. He almost always returned in daylight. I waited there until it was full night and stared and stared into the blackness until my eyes could only just make out the warnings left by the waves as they dashed in foam on the rocks. I shouted and shouted. My voice might have been the shrieks of the benighted seagulls. No curragh appeared, no friendly hail came from the sea. I stayed there all night keeping my vigil then went back to the hut where the empty bed stared at me in silent reproach as if longing for its occupants to return to it. I rested a couple of hours then went back to the harbour. No sign of them. I saw a solitary fishing boat but something told me it was not Jahaan's and it was not from the direction of Ys. Night after night I lit the Leading Lights. In the day I watched for them but did not see them any more. I had to come to you for help."

"What was the condition of the curragh?" asked Thomas.

"It was in excellent shape. It was new and Jahaan had re-greased the hull. No boat was better found."

"Was he ever so late before in coming back from Ys?"

"Never. I've tried to imagine all possible situations. Was he carried out to sea? He's too good a sailor for that. Something wrong with the curragh? Had he put into some cove to repair it? He'd surely be back by now!" She sighed.

"By day, in the rain, while I longed for the marsh

waters to subside I went down to the sea and waited for them. My heart was filled with anguish, my eyes bleary with straining to see them through rain and sea mist. I've a feeling that they're still alive but why don't they come back? There are severe westerly winds now. They make me fear for their safety. Soon its not going to be good weather for small boats even for a seaman like Jahaan. When I hear the wind howling about my dwelling I could shriek out in dread, "My God, can't you reveal to me where your two servants are?"

Thomas had sat quietly, listening carefully to her. Inwardly he was considering all the possibilities. He did not think that Jahaan had gone to Ys and vanished on the way back. He dismissed that conjecture, knowing Jahaan's skill as a boatman. Then the two must have gone to Ys and for some reason stayed there. But why? He felt it was his duty as chief of the plou to find out exactly what had happened to them. It would take time but find out he must. There was another minor matter. Avel had disappeared. This was not so remarkable an occurrence as the sub-deacon was accustomed to be absent for long periods. It could only be inconvenient for the plou if he missed duties in the church but sometimes the man needed to live the life of a hermit. Everyone accepted that. Or he could have been visiting the community of monks that Guenole had established.

However, what he did say to Norah was, "Don't lose hope. Be patient as much as you can. There may be some perfectly good reason why they're away so long. You want to go back to the ravine again so that you can wait for them in their home. I'll send Martha and another strong young woman with you so that they can help you and bear you company. You can show them the way over the marsh.

Norah went back to the ravine with her two young companions. The day after, a fisherman who was very observant came to Thomas and told him that he had once seen a boat with two persons in it, one of whom was a woman and it was passing along the cliffs very close to Ys. He was almost certain that it was Jahaan's boat. It was approaching Ys.

"Keep a silent tongue in your head. There's something very nasty about this matter and I mean to investigate it."

When the man had gone, Thomas fell into deep reflection. He already knew what had happened in Ys from the report given to him by Guenole when the monk had returned from his water divining. Yet since Guenole had not seen either Jahaan or Ana he thought there was a possibility that they might have left Ys quite early. What was to be done? They must wait a little longer and hope that Jahaan and Ana would return either in the curragh or some other way but once more he saw Norah's eyes with the deep despair in them and heard her last words to him, "Why did I let them go to that awful city?"

In his little oratory in the woods Guenole sat alone. For days he had fasted with all the rigour that was part of his nature and had endured long nights spent in vigils during which he took no heed at all of the inclement weather. Often, in those midnight hours when the showers drove in gleaming spears across the ghostly forms of the trees, he would kneel until the dawn telling his beads, reciting Ave Marias and Paternosters. Rarely, stiff and cramped, he would rise to his feet and go to the door hole of the hut and look out.

Over the canopy of the wet branches soared the clouds that carried the tempest. He would gaze up at them and say in a voice sturdy as the stones in the forest, "Is this Thy sign at last, O Lord, my God? Thou hast promised a sign for thy servant, Guenole, who has prayed all night before Thee. He has beseeched Thee to teach him the patience he needs but Thou knowest his heart is human and he longs passionately to witness the manifestation of Thy irresistible power in a great miracle. Forgive me, Lord, for I am a sinful man. Forgive the sins of the Kristion in this land of Armorica, this realm of the sea."

There were great tears glistening on his sunken cheeks.

"Thy name, Thou knowest full well, is reviled in the city of Ys. I'm only a poor servant of Thine but I did Thy will. I went to that heathen city at Thy bidding. A city whose gods are demons. You granted my hands the wondrous power of Thy spirit to use the hazel rods so that, unbidden by me, they quivered, they touched the appointed places. Waters gushed forth, the waters that run deep beneath the earth. Yet, though Thou didst this miracle for them, their hearts are as hardened against Thee as those of Egypt were hardened against the Lord God of Israel. They despise and hate Thy minister and Thy church in Ys stands in ruins and will soon fall and be forgotten. How long, how long, O my God, wilt Thou allow this people of Ys to live in their terrible wickedness and abominations? How long wilt Thou allow them to despise Thee? How long? How long?"

CHAPTER 19

Caradec sat alone in the house of the priest Koneg. It was chilly and he was cloaked in a sheepskin soaked by rain. The sheepskin clung to his brawny figure but the man did not notice it. Nor did he heed the rain drumming on the roof tiles or the wind gusts that shrieked as they stormed at the temple perched on the cliff top.

He was as silent and unmoving as the carved figure of the Three-Headed One that dominated the room so familiar to him from boyhood. On a bier rested a body under a linen covering. After a long while he rose and slowly drew back the sheet to look on the form of the old priest. He bent down over the dead man and gazed at the features. Over his stern face came a look of great tenderness.

"I've seen dead people in Ys. Slave women stricken down in the agony of travail. Men with the terror of death in their eyes. The empty look of infants seized by the marsh fever when they were barely out of the womb. Yet your face, Koneg, has an expression of great tranquillity on it as if you knew that you had fully lived all your days. As if you had done everything that you wanted to do for your temple and for me, your foster child. Or was it because you died in your sleep, deep in a dream of the blessed realm to which you go?" He sighed.

"I've lost you who were as a father to me. No more shall I be able to talk with you while you rest on the way up to the temple in which you had spent your life. No, that's all gone. You cared for me and loved me as if I were your own son. During your life I would never have pained you with thoughts alien to you. Yet now that you have gone do not think the worse of me for what I have to do. It was by your own life that you taught me the hardest lesson which I had to learn. A man must serve his gods and obey their will even unto death. I, too, must die soon for what I believe is the only right way for me. My death is bound up with the deed I soon must do."

The man's features were distorted by the agony of his soul.

"I realise now how hard it is to live without you. My life was so much part of yours that now I feel it has no longer any worth. The temple up yonder was your life not mine. I welcome death because living without you is impossible."

He looked at all the objects in the room. For him it was a last look at earthly things that would soon perish. Things that were associated in his mind with Koneg. His face had gone calmer again. He knelt in supplication to his God for the acceptance of Koneg's death. Then he rose up again and stood looking down at the bier.

"Rest in peace, Koneg, rest in eternal peace! When you died, up at your temple, I composed your features and closed your eyes. Do not in these last few moments together think of me as an ungrateful son. My hands have prepared your grave. I've used all my mason's skill to shape the stone that shall be set by your head. On it, I cut your name. When men and women in years to come pass by they will see that stone and learn who you were. But how will they tell you were once a priest of a temple that you loved more than your own life? Let me tell you now a secret that only I know. Your grave I've made near the hidden graves of two Kristion. A man and a woman. I have carved the fish symbol on stones for them. I buried those stones by their skeletons. You will lie close to those you befriended, though they were of another faith." With his lips he touched the icy hands then gently replaced the cover. His face had gone stern and hard again.

There was a knock at the door. Four men with hesitation written on their faces stood there. It was the young priest and three burly men with ropes in their hands.

"Are you ready, Caradec? We didn't want to disturb you if you wish to stay longer with him but there's a lull in the rain. Perhaps it would be better if we did it now."

"I'm ready."

They fastened ropes to the bier. With care they walked through the mud-splashed streets. They passed through a postern gate to the open space outside the city where the people of Ys buried their dead. There were many graves. Before them yawned an oblong pit which Caradec had himself wrested from the soil. Into it, the three sextons lowered the corpse and the priest said a brief valediction.

Caradec said "I'll fill in the grave myself", and the three other men departed. The priest lingered for a moment after they had gone. "Now this is over, I should like to talk with you about your work up at the temple. I shall be in charge now and there are certain alterations I want made to the building."

"There'll be changes to the temple, I'm sure" said

Caradec as he took up his spade. The priest departed and left him to his work. He was quite alone in that desert of the dead. He knelt down and with the tips of his fingers touched the hillock beneath which, now unknown to the people of Ys, lay the bones of the man who had begotten him and by it the smaller skeleton of the woman who had given birth to him. He liked the long grass which grew so freely near their graves. It reminded him of family love and of his parents. He made the sign of the cross then turned to Koneg's grave into which he shovelled earth and stones, spreading over all a layer of sharp pebbles and stones to deter prowling foxes. When he had finished, he set up the headstone and tapped it firmly with his mallet into the ground. All was now in order.

"It'll last much longer than I will." He sprinkled dried rosemary all round the three graves and the damp air was permeated by the fragrance of the plant. Caradec stood for a few moments, bowed his head low, then went his way.

In his eyes was sadness but when he gained the postern gate he never looked back. His attention was suddenly given to the great cliff on top of which stood the temple. At first he had looked up to see the temple but his eyes became focused on the cliff itself. Caradec was a very observant man and as a mason was familiar with the appearance of rocks and stones. Now he noticed a change. Across the cliff base and well below the temple was a line which displayed the horizontal strata and exuded water. "Strange" he muttered, perplexed. "I've never seen that before, even in the heaviest of rains! I've heard the river's behaving oddly too. It seems to be drying up. Drying up in weather like this? Does it explain our water shortage? Yet there must be torrents of water dammed up somewhere. It won't affect my plans. My task will soon be done."

... ...

Gradlon, King of Ys, was in his Great Hall which had an upper room with many windows. Through them he could see the city and the countryside beyond. Even when ageing he had maintained his habit of early rising and just now he was looking out with a sharper interest than he had shown for some time. There was a break in the rain. Not that he had ever minded rain storms. The rains had briefly purified Ys. The houses shone brightly from water left on their roofs, the ordure in the lanes had been washed away, the cobbles cleansed. The only signs of bird life were two vultures that quartered the skies above the city, searching for carrion. They soared high above the temple, waiting for prey.

Gradlon could see clouds lying like a shroud over that part outside the city walls where lay the burial ground. Mist there rolled in like wreaths as if to offer a tribute to the dead Koneg. Koneg! How well he had known and respected him long ago! In that sudden moment of memory he felt his kinship with the dead, the honourable dead who had lived their lives without blemish. He, too, would soon be with them but at present no gloom oppressed him at the thought. His own spirit and mind were wakening as if from a long sleep. He knew he would brood no more and would become again a man of action. He would rule Ys with rectitude, tempered by mercy. Beyond Ys he could clearly see the forest. There, far beyond, dwelt a man with whom he had once felt common feelings of belief. Guenole, the saintly Breton, who had spoken to him of Kristos and his wondrous works. Would he ever see him again? He longed to ride into the woods and seek Guenole. Yet he felt he was close confined within Ys until his death.

Opposite to the Hall were the stables. Once they had held a score of destriers. Now there was only a single war horse all that was left to Gradlon. He could see the groom, a devoted slave both to himself and his steed, sweeping out the stables, bringing food and water to the horse and rubbing him down.

Gradlon's eyes glowed. There was a great affinity between himself and this animal. He could interpret every mood of the horse before outward signs appeared. He knew when it was angry, frightened, irritated by flies, or just bored. It was much more than an ordinary relationship of rider and steed for the horse in its turn knew when Gradlon was ill or in one of his fits of melancholy. Just now the horse, with the strange intuition of some animals, knew that the man himself was changing. His eyes were brighter, his voice clearer and his orders to the stableman were incisive. Even his back had become straighter.

There was a knock on the door and the groom entered. On his slave collar the two dolphins of Ys had been set in bronze but there was also the image of a horse. This denoted that he was Gradlon's own personal slave. He was a short man with strong arms, a prominent nose, and full lips. Rather like a horse himself, thought Gradlon. The groom was apologetic.

"Is there anything wrong?" Gradlon spoke almost as if to a friend.

"I wouldn't have troubled you but the destrier isn't really himself these past few days."

"He's not eating?"

"He seems to be a little off his food but it's not that that's worrying me."

"I'll come down and look at him."

Gradlon was glad to leave the cold chamber where the damp wood spluttered in the brazier. The door of the stables was out of sight but long before they had reached it Gradlon heard the sounds, a prolonged whinnying that could be the cry of a horse in distress. It was followed by a tremendous clatter as the hooves smashed against the stable. It appeared as if the animal were trying to get out.

"How long has he been like this?"

"It's come on gradually. He became a little restive about the time of our feast day. Nothing then to worry about. Yet in the last few days he's become really violent as you see. I can't understand it at all." The slave's brow was deeply wrinkled. He was a loyal servant to Gradlon and felt keenly his responsibility as head groom.

"Let me see the food and water. Also the bedding. I must see the grain as well as the ground oats."

Gradlon took the food in his cupped hands, sniffed at it, let a few grains run through his fingers, crushed the hay and bedding straw and smelt at it intently. He took a mouthful of water from the spring whence the horse buckets were filled, swilled it round his mouth, tasted it, then spat it out.

"Nothing wrong there. You're giving him food only from my barn?"

"I would not give him food from elsewhere, not after

what happened to those people on the feast day!"

Gradlon frowned. "I'll talk to him then we'll look at the stable itself." He walked up to the half-door, making clicking noises with his tongue. Then he spoke endearingly to the stallion. The great white horse strained his head out of the half-door eager to see him. He stroked the sensitive nose, peered into the dark eyes that stared back at him uneasily and patted the glossy neck with his soothing hands, so experienced at gentling animals. He took out of his pocket a mouthful of corn which he offered. The horse nibbled at it for a moment, then lost interest, nuzzling hard up against his arm as if all it wanted was contact with him or was begging him to stay with it.

Gradlon went on speaking to the horse but gradually began to move away from it. Its eyes became troubled. As he walked still further away it began to prowl up and down the stable, whinnying in a piteous manner and reared right up on its massive hind legs to bring the full weight of legs and body onto the building that was its prison. The stable thundered and quivered from the impact; dust eddied from the walls. Yet the builders had constructed the stables of large rocks embedded in mortar, reinforced on the inside by huge oak timbers with diagonal bracing and they stood quite firm. The horse could not escape. It burst out again in that strange whinnying, so foreign to it.

"Have any other animals been in the stables to frighten the horse?"

"None at all? The rats left Ys on the feast day. A sparrow will sometimes snatch at the food but the horse accepts that. You see he's not nervous of that one there."

"I'll enter the stables with you and look round. I'm sure the horse has no vice. Does this happen at night as well?"

"Yes, it does."

The horse became quite calm as soon as they opened the half-door and walked in. The stables were broad and commodious and the groom kept them very clean. Above them was his own loft where he slept; it was approached by a ladder from outside as well as steps from inside. Gradlon went round everywhere, peering into every corner, lifting up the bedding, and peeping into the stalls. Nothing escaped his attention, not even the condition of the polished metal bits, each with the dolphin of Ys at the side.

He turned his full attention to the body of the horse itself. Gradlon knew a great deal about war horses and farriery. The groom lifted up each hoof for his inspection, made very minutely. He placed his head against the broad chest and listened to the breathing. "It's quite normal!" he exclaimed, feeling too the muscles and the bones of the powerful legs. The horse underwent this close examination without the slightest wince, so kind were the hands, so soft the soothing voice. He even tapped the skull, breathing into the nostrils; he opened its mouth to see its clean, formidable teeth. He patted its glossy coat and well combed mane. The groom kept the horse in perfect condition. Then he left the stables with the groom. At first the horse seemed to be quiet. It poked its head out of the half-door, looking out at the forests. There was an intense longing in its eyes. When Gradlon moved away, there began again that ferocious attack on its stable.

"Has this trouble affected other horses in Ys?"

"One of our wilder beasts broke down the door of its stable, galloped to the Bridgegate which was open at the time and was last seen running into the forest away from Ys. The captain's horse was also affected but was caught. The men who roped it said the animal seemed mad with terror, though a beast as healthy as yours."

"Keep the doors fast closed. They should hold if bolted. Enter cautiously. I don't think the horse has any vice but if he turns nasty call me without delay for a stallion's bite is worse than a spear thrust. I'll come and see him more often. Perhaps the horse is like myself, tired of being cooped up by the rains and needs a good gallop to stretch his legs!"

He went back to his seat in the Great Hall in a reflective mood. What could cause a healthy animal to behave thus? The beast had pawed at the earthen floor as if he were nervous of the ground itself. "And your eyes, my steed! What is the message that you want to tell me? You're close to me. What animal intuition tells you of something menacing to both of us?" He looked up at clouds that were overhanging Ys once more. They were at their darkest where they touched the temple on the cliff above. A fear of this unknown mystery that affected the horse came over him!

... ...

Dahut sat in her room, listening to an armed man, the captain of the guard, who stood before her. "I've heard your reports and others, too, have given me their versions of what happened on the feast day. It's taken time to sift out any truth from the hysteria that then prevailed in the city. The people are quieter now."

She smiled. "I think the rains have damped down their lust for disorder, but I'm most concerned over security in the city. What actually happened in your opinion? Some say that Gwendaline was put to death for poisoning the bread?"

The captain spoke briskly. "The mob seized the woman and rushed her down to the harbour to burn her. Malek rescued her from them but decided that the only way to save her was himself to administer to her the Trial by Water. His own men bound her for her Swimming. His hope was to save her from burning for the mob had set up a stake and were eager to see her in the flames. Malek and his men made Gwendaline do her Swimming legally. She drowned without showing her face above water and thus proved her innocence. I went early to the harbour to see if I could find Gwendaline. There were remnants of clothing but nothing else. The body had gone. Malek appears to have vanished though we have looked everywhere for him."

Dahut stared at the captain keenly. "The woman's dead but what really disturbs me is the crowd violence. The fact that a mob dare take to itself powers of life and death! Any effective rulers must retain entirely in their hands, and their hands alone, the power of life and death. No one else must ever inflict death. The woman should have been arrested, then interrogated by me. Only the official executioners under my orders are empowered to Swim a female accused of fatal witchcraft and burn her to death if guilty. Yet on that day law and order vanished from our streets. Mob rule took over. Why?" she shouted.

The captain bowed his head.

"It was very difficult. Under normal circumstances

there would have been no trouble. The woman would have been accused, arrested and tried. There have been times in Ys, unfortunately, when the more unruly humiliores have taken matters into their own hands and executed people without trial. I realise that such behaviour does cast a stain on Ys. But on the feast day almost all my men were in the market place and our hands were full."

"This is no explanation! You are soldiers. You had spears and swords! Yet your men took so long to gain control! You let the madmen run wild and terrify the populace! If you had exerted yourselves you might also have prevented the drowning."

A flush appeared on the captain's cheeks. "My men don't lack courage but were appalled by a situation which had never before happened in Ys. The demons afflicting the sufferers gave them, for the time being, supernatural strength. Short of stabbing them to death, which we were reluctant to do, all we could do was to try and restrain them from hurting themselves."

"You weren't very successful!"

"Twenty five died from their injuries or from the poison that affected them. Six ran out through the Bridgegate and into the forest. They've never been heard of since. As you ordered, I've burnt all the remaining stocks of rye flour lest the demons cast another spell on them as well."

"There was the monk, too?"

"Guenole? I don't understand." The colour was deeper still on his bronzed cheeks.

"You know what happened, surely? Two of your guards arrived too late to witness the Swimming but saw the drowned woman. Guenole came up and poured abuse and curses on our city but these guards let him depart unscathed. They were under your command. Could they not have done something?"

"Dahut, this man, Guenole, came to us that day 'under our peace', a safeguard signed with the double dolphin so that he could work without molestation. All my men were specially ordered not to lay a finger on him when he had such authority signed by you."

"He had been authorised to find water not to criticise the city! Why didn't your men at least rebuke him for his insolence?"

The captain's voice grew sharper now. His cheeks were scarlet. He looked Dahut full in the eyes. "I know something of this man, Guenole. No one would accuse my men or me of flinching in the face of danger! This man may be a shaven-head, but he's a born leader of men as good as any soldier of worth. I've been in the Mediterranean, I have seen an island from which huge flames exploded into the air. I've seen that terrible fire that comes from the bowels of the earth. I tell you this man's eyes, when he is angry, are a living volcano that can overwhelm all flesh. He has tremendous power and courage. That's why they wouldn't arrest or challenge him."

Dahut shook her head. "I'm still not satisfied with the situation. The mob wanted someone punished for the crime of poisoning the bread. Gwendaline was definitely not the criminal. She was made to do her Swimming properly and the results completely proved her innocence. I think", she spoke slowly, "that people are uneasy with what happened. They think that the real culprit lurks among them, waiting for another chance to harm them. The true culprit must be found. I must find a woman who can, with good reason, be accused of witchcraft. She must be Swum publicly in my presence and burnt alive. That would satisfy those lusting for revenge. I will never again permit a mob in my city to take the law into their own hands. I will find a culprit."

"Now, what of the man Jahaan and the woman Ana?"

"We apprehended them under our law which says that any stranger found here after sunset shall be put to death. They are in prison, pending your decision. They are in chains and receive bread and water only. The other man was handed over to your guards as you requested."

"How are they behaving? Surely the woman fears death?"

"No, they're unusual people. After the shock of their arrest they are recalcitrant. When a guard as he chained them suggested that Jahaan might be one of your guards, he laughed and said 'I should be a very dangerous one'!

"He'll be tamed all right" said Dahut. "We'll get at him through the woman. These Bretons are stubborn but we'll break them. How is she?" The captain replied "Her appearance is very different from the ordinary Breton woman. She is taller and her eyes look strange, too. She is a Kristion. I'm told she breaks their bread while they say the patter the Kristion call prayers."

The captain's voice grew lower. "I don't want this repeated but a rumour has got around Ys that Ana is a Woman from the Sea whom the Bretons fished out of the waves. Some say that her imprisonment will bring evil from the sea god on the city. He may destroy us if any harm comes to her."

"That's ridiculous" exclaimed Dahut. "I've seen her and I've no doubt she is flesh and blood and finding it unpleasant to have iron rings tightly round her hands and feet. A little hard treatment will bring both of them to their senses. For the moment let them kick their heels in gyves, I've other matters to attend to."

The captain bowed. The audience was over, yet he stayed. "There's one more matter. If the Bretons get to know that we are forcibly detaining two of their number, there will be trouble for us." Dahut put up a white hand to reassure him. "No Breton can know of their imprisonment, except one and I shall deal with him. Guenole will think that they left the city before him. The Bretons can't know about the arrest." The captain bowed again and went out.

Alone in her room, the princess stood by the window thinking. "If it were a witch" she whispered, "she must have been close to the bread for her magic to have poisoned it. Which woman, apart from Gwendaline, was close on the day of the festival?" Dahut sat down, her eyes alight from thoughts within her. Then she got up and went down the stone steps to the room where she had first met Avel. She unhooked a lighted torch from its sconce and entered, locking the door behind her. She set the torch in a wall cresset and looked around. A thick branch of ashwood hung, upright and creaking, from a rope which passed through a smooth ring-bolt grouted into the ceiling above. This oiled rope continued to another ring-bolt on the wall to which it was held by a slipknot. A rock was lashed to the base of the branch as a weight to keep it steady. A man, naked save for a cincture, was bound to the ash branch by fetters round his neck, waist, hands and feet. Though he desperately tried to extend his toes downwards so that they would touch the floor, it was just out of reach and his entire weight was held by the pole. The branch, freely suspended, swayed to and fro gently over the flat surface of a wooden trap door in the stone floor. The man could only utter an inarticulate sound when she entered for a gag sealed his mouth.

Dahut went and stood by the dragon image on the wall; she carried a leather polaire. She remained silent for some moments. It was hard to say whose look was the most terrifying, that of the dragon on the wall or that of the woman by its side. Dahut's lips curled in derision. She loosened the bosom of her dress.

"This room will be familiar to you, Avel, for it was here that I first met you and you told me of your life and plans. You always insisted on secrecy. You have it now. No one in Ys, thanks to your hood, knows who you are, or if you are here. Only my personal guards who fastened you up and they will never say a word. They had a struggle to secure you but they did their job very well. Don't try to free yourself! You'll only exhaust yourself and wound your wrists. Those fetters have been put on you by an expert. They're cunningly riveted in place. They'll stay there long enough. Just think of your Kristion martyrs! They enjoyed being crucified, burnt to death or torn by lions! All for their false faith! We're more civilized here! How you glare at me! You'd slay me if you could but I've better plans for you."

Like a cat with a mouse, she was playing with her victim. From some aperture in the room a breeze was pouring in. The only sound from the prisoner was the rhythmic creak of the rope as the ash branch moved backwards and forwards, pendulumwise.

"There won't be any words from your lying lips. Let me begin, however, by giving you a meed of praise. You did that piece of work I wanted you to do. You told me in time when Jahaan and Ana would be coming to Ys. They were captured by my guards for breaking the law and could be put to death. No, they're not dead but both safely in prison as well, chained as you are. They await my pleasure. Your faithless mouth is sealed. No one in Ys is interested in their fate, or in yours."

Unconsciously, she was swinging the polaire on her arm in time to the movement of the ash bough pendulum. Drops of sweat poured down Avel's cheeks as he stared at his tormentor. In her other hand she was holding a wand of some light-coloured wood. "It could have been a plain commercial transaction, shall we say? Some men, for this work, would have been happy with a purse of silver and no questions asked. You wanted greater rewards. A house in Ys, perhaps our citizenship, even possibly immunity from the pursuit of your fellow Bretons if they ever got to know what had happened to Jahaan and Ana through your actions. You were obsessed by that wench, Ana, whose body you wanted to enjoy. You, a celibate cleric, were caught in such a wicked snare!"

The eyes of the helpless prisoner were burning like those of a trapped tiger in the twilight.

"So you thought that, unscathed, you could eke out the rest of your wretched existence in this city, Ys. Did you not realise that we do not like strangers, Avel? If we have ever in the past admitted one to the cherished privilege of living among us he must have been a man of honour and probity and of accepted worth in all aspects of our life as well as of his." She was swinging the polaire as if she would throw it at his head. "You Kristion! You obviously thought we're pagans, ignorant people, suckled in a creed outworn. You're a treacherous devil, Avel! Your heart is black. You were prepared to despise your own faith! Reject your own people! Our gods don't permit us to do that. They demand that we shall be unswerving and steadfast to them as we are faithful to our city. I, too, Dahut, am used to men giving their total loyalty to me for their entire lives. Your own kin were not safe from your hatred. You have betrayed them to chains and prison! And how do I know that you won't turn traitor to a city that might have been foolish enough to accept you?" She quickly ripped open the polaire and tore out the contents, documents, meanwhile never taking her eyes off the man. Her gaze held his eyes more firmly than the chains his body. A groan escaped him.

"However brief your visits to Ys you made use of them for your foul aims. You thought we were fools and couldn't understand Latin. Well, we can and we've read every word of what you have written here. All our little secrets that you could ferret out. The way from outside up to the postern gates, how many men usually man the Bridgegate. How many soldiers you estimate there are in Ys. The way up to the temple. The condition of the harbour wall – were you planning a seaborne invasion? What did you intend to do with all this secret information? Return to the Kristion in your plou and tell them "I've been a wicked person but you'll receive me back, won't you, if I tell you how to conquer Ys? Why, you even noted down the names of our leading men, to suborn them, I suppose! We're not going to let you return to the plou. I have you in my power and I'll make sure forever of your silence. Before we part let me talk to you a little about women, especially about Ana whom you hoped to possess. You don't know anything about our sex. I'll give you your first – and last – lesson."

She stripped off the upper part of her robe and stood with naked torso before him. "This is the body of a beautiful woman! Feast your lustful eyes on it! You've not much time to do so! I'm the woman who is the fairest in Ys. I brook no rivals and expect all men to know and be enslaved by my loveliness. There have been other young men besides yourself who've seen my breasts and been captivated by my body, but they never lived long after that!"

The strange icy wind quickened, bringing with it a stench of decay and death. She thrust her bare body against that of the helpless prisoner. He moaned trying to swing himself away from her, but in vain.

"This is what you hoped to find from Ana, wasn't it? That mysterious contact with a female body which you emaciated geldings deny yourselves for your false god, Kristos! What fools you monks are, bags of skin and bone, nothing more! Think hard about Ana all that you wanted to think! Think about her coming fate, the destiny to which you have condemned her! The blacksmith is already forging the slave collar with the double dolphin on it. My proud emblem and the proof to Ana of her slavery to Ys. It will soon be riveted round her neck. Her body will be the property of some virile man for breeding slaves for Ys. Her lovely belly will soon be swelling out with offspring but not with the fruit of your withered loins. Yes, her breasts will suckle many slaves for we have a great need of babies in Ys."

On her scarlet lips a light foam had gathered and as she danced round the room, her steps were quick and jerky. She seemed almost to have forgotten the man. Her face shone with an unearthly light like a corrigan waving her fairy wand to bewitch men. She danced up and down on the points of her toes.

"I'm the fairest woman in Ys! I'm the loveliest woman in the whole world! Jahaan, I'm going to bewitch you! Like other men, you'll be seduced by my body, the magic of my fairy eyes, the clasp of my arms round you and the mystic spell that I shall throw over you with one touch of my hands! Will you resist me? Of course not, how could any man resist Dahut? Jahaan, you shall know me fully when you are in my power, chained naked on a bed of flowers you'll endure all that feminine arts can inflict on you. Arts to make a man surrender." She laughed, a high pitched laugh. "What an ordeal for a virtuous Kristion trying to save his virtue! Sweeter even than the fragrant flowers and herbs shall be the aroma that you shall breathe in from my body and limbs! They madden even the strongest men as much as the poisoned bread crazed those who swallowed it. Then, when I've finished with you, it'll be the end of your life!"

She suddenly stopped and looked up at the rope and then at the tethered man. "Fah! I waste my time on carrion such as you! Now you must go!" She kicked at the trap door. It slid back on well greased rollers. Below the man now yawned a well from whose depths came up a noisome reek of dank weed, earth and tidal waters. Far below was a faint gurgle. The sea was moving quietly, crying for its prey under the city of Ys.

Dahut threw a small pebble into this cavity and

waited, counting "One, two, three!" Deep down came the sound of a splash. "There lies the water – your black grave! It's very dark and is always waiting for victims! There's plenty of it. Drink your fill, Avel! Drink! Drink deep, monster!"

Deftly she gave a sharp tug to the free end of the slip-knot. The rope, now loosed from its belay and tensed already by the weight it was holding, slithered like a snake through the ring-bolts. The heavy stone bore man and pole straight down the well.

There was a slight splash below but nothing more!

CHAPTER 20

Ana slept little during that first night in the prison of Ys. Although she was tired physically, her mind remained active as she thought over the events of the past few hours and what was to come. She recalled with an element of grim humour how pleased she had been when Jahaan asked her to come with him to Ys. How proud she was that she was able to row as well as any man. How excited she had been when he told her about the ancient city of Ys and about the people and the children. She had looked forward with immense pleasure to this visit to the strange and mysterious city. And now, after a few hours, she and Jahaan were in chains in the prison, awaiting their deaths. Her mind was not blunted by their past experiences or dulled by thoughts of what was to come. She thought intently about the preceding events. The handshake that Norah had given her, the food they had munched in the curragh, the last she had tasted, and the death of Gwendaline which had made such a deep impression on her. Then came their capture. She wondered if it was an accident that they had been so delayed in the crowd like so many people or whether some enemy had purposely arranged their capture. The guards who had captured them had simply said that they had broken the law and would be put in prison. They had not said who had informed Dahut about their presence in Ys and Ana wondered why they had not somehow or other slipped out through the lane before the soldiers saw them. It wasn't much good thinking about that. There was the matter of escape. But how could they escape without outside assistance? Then there was Guenole's prediction, as he stood by the body of Gwendaline, that Ys was doomed. She wondered if everyone would suffer in some terrible destruction of the city. Everything seemed perfectly safe and enduring.

Ana glanced at Jahaan sleeping soundly on the prison floor. With a rusty nail he had already scratched a large cross on the cell wall. The night passed in thought and with the dawn came men in dark clothes and with sombre countenances. There was the vergobret, the Captain of the Guards with his soldiers, some members of the curia and the slave master. The vergobret interrogated them. He wanted to know if Jahaan had any ulterior motives in visiting Ys other than to sell fish. When Ana was questioned she explained clearly her work in the plou, her nursing and her care of the elderly, then added bluntly "I am needed there, I must go back at once." The vergobret said nothing at all nor was there any change in his countenance.

After a while he went out with the Captain of the Guards and talked privately with him. Then he came back and said "you have both been guilty of a very grave crime for which the punishment is death. Dahut and the curia have carefully considered the matter and have decided to grant you a pardon on certain conditions which must be strictly observed at all times and in all places. First, Jahaan. Dahut considers that he would make a valuable member of the Guards. He is strong and fearless. He must take a vow of loyalty to Dahut, Ys and the Guards after which he will be a member of the

Guards and serve in them. We know that you Kristion respect a vow as much as we do in Ys and if he takes the vow he will observe it. Secondly, Ana. She is not your wife by our laws but a female stranger who also broke the law. She will be regarded as of slave status to be handed over to a suitable master in the presence of a number of witnesses. Like Jahaan, she will swear loyalty to Dahut, to Ys and to her master. The iron slave collar will then be riveted around her neck. Kneeling she will suck the breasts of her master in token of her full submission to him. She will bear children to him and to Ys." The vergobret paused briefly then continued, "I will give you an hour in which to consider this offer." He left the cell leaving behind the slave master and the Captain of the Guards.

The slave master was to examine both chained prisoners to see if they were really fit to perform the tasks likely to be assigned to them. He spent little time over Jahaan. He said briefly "He'll do. He's tough enough." With Ana it was different. He always took longer in examining women slaves as he was blamed if the slave died in childbirth or produced sickly offspring. Despite her protests and Jahaan's loud Breton curses, he tapped her back and buttocks very carefully shaking his head meantime. He looked at her mouth and her ears but spent most time of all looking deeply into her eyes. Then he stopped his examination and went outside with the Captain of the Guards. He was shaking a little. "I have looked into this woman's eyes. They are deep blue with a peculiar tinge of green like that female slave whose body we fished out of the water. I won't have this woman as a breeding slave" he whispered hoarsely. "There's no tail about her but they discard them when they come ashore."

"You mean she is a Woman from the Sea?" the Captain asked quietly.

"I mean just that and so do the gossips of Lower Ys. What kind of children will she bear? Creatures with webbed feet and hands and these odd eyes? There is another point which is most important Captain. We have our troubles in Ys. The gods have sent us the marsh fever which takes away our children. The gods know we have our troubles. If this woman suffers the slightest harm the God of the Sea will exact a fearful vengeance from us. The sea is our enemy Captain, not our friend."

"It's the responsibility of Dahut" said the Captain, "Not yours." Then they both departed and the vergobret returned.

"What is your decision?" he asked the prisoners.

Jahaan spoke first. "We are both Bretons. We belong to an independent people and you must let us go or you will bring a hornet's nest about your ears."

"And you, Ana?"

"I am a Breton and we are both Kristion. We have no wish to live in Ys which is a pagan city and a wicked one. You must free us."

"I cannot free you" said the vergobret, "but I will give you tonight and tomorrow to reconsider your decision and, if possible, to change your minds. If you remain obstinate your blood be on your own heads. The curia and Dahut will meet tomorrow to decide your sentence."

After the departure of the vergobret and his men they were left alone. The jailer did not appear and they were given neither food nor drink, but a little spring of water trickling down the cell wall slaked their thirst. That day and the next they maintained a close watch from the window. There was no human activity to be seen. The house opposite, close-barred, seemed uninhabited as did a ruined cottage further down the lane. The first hours of the second night they slept well but were awakened by a terrific clap of thunder and lightning flashes. Then the rain came in torrents. While Jahaan was watching from the window Ana suddenly had a strange giddiness. She did not fall but it seemed to her that the cell and all in it had vanished. She said nothing to Jahaan. Immediately afterwards she made a discovery. Her manacles were so loose that she could slip her hands out of them. She put them back quickly lest the jailer should see her hands were free.

They had been somewhat silent up to then but after a while they forgot where they were and talked much of the past, especially of the time when Jahaan had found her on the rocks and of her baptism. Now, very soon, they might be in the presence of God. "Let us pray" said Ana. "We might soon be facing a barbarous and cruel people. Then let us say the Lord's Prayer and those words 'Father, forgive them, for they know not what they do'."

It grew colder. An unusually strong wind blew through their lane and shook the walls of their prison. The torrents of rain had ceased but massive, dark clouds driven by mighty winds were rushing across the sky. Jahaan stood by the window. This storm had aroused his instincts for survival at sea and on land. He muttered "the wind is coming right off the sea and its strength is increasing. Look at those heavy branches being hurtled along. It's a gale now but I'll wager by morning we may see a true hurricane." As he spoke a long branch with a brown bag tied to its tip tapped against the window sill and a low voice in broken Breton said "Take the bag quickly. It is death to aid a prisoner." Jahaan took the bag. Ana hid it. The visitor at the window was Theodora the pregnant Greek slave. "It's near my time" she gasped "but I think sometimes it would be better if both of us were to leave this world. Blessings on you." She crossed herself and slipped away in silence. Ravenous, they devoured the food that was in the bag and it gave them strength for what might come.

The noise made by the wind rose to a wild howling. Yet by now they were fast asleep. Ana had a vivid dream. Crowds of people, ragged or naked, were screaming in fear or running in panic. Far above them emerged the figure of an angel her face shining in glory. Her hand pointed down to Ana and she cried out "Awaken! Awaken! Don't sleep! Awaken!"

Ana awoke. Jahaan too was stirring. It was still dim in the cell and only a little light filtered through the window. They heard the storm still roaring and the waves pounding on the cliffs. "Awaken!" The voice was just outside the window! Someone was tapping on the sill. They moved to the window opening. "It's a good friend who speaks now to you! I have an acquaintance in the curia. He has told me the sentences have already been arranged. Ana is sentenced to death but Jahaan will be spared."

"How strange that because I made my first visit to Ys and was delayed there I must die for such a small fault!" exclaimed Ana.

"No. They will not execute you for breaking that

law but for another quite different crime" said the stranger speaking always in Breton. "You must know that Gwendaline the witch proved her innocence in her Trial by Water by sinking and drowning! All – Dahut, the curia, are now convinced that another hitherto unknown woman was guilty of poisoning the bread by her magic. That woman was close to the bread! You, Ana, were that woman! You cannot deny that fact. They believe you laid a spell on it. You will be judged and if found guilty burnt to death."

"I am wholly innocent" said Ana quietly. "God will give me strength to endure all that may be inflicted on me."

"You don't understand what will happen to you" said the man quickly, a note of urgency in his voice. "At dawn tomorrow the guards will come here and take you to the harbour. There a stake with chains has been set up and faggots piled below. There will be two braziers with hot coals – one for kindling the faggots the other for the red hot irons customarily used to brand a convicted witch. They will bind your great toes and thumbs together crosswise. Bound, you will then undergo the Trial by Water to prove whether you are guilty or innocent. Meantime a vast crowd will have gathered and Dahut will sit in the Chair of Justice. Your Swimming can only have one outcome. The executioners will make sure that your head does not sink at any time. After you have floated with your face out of the water for a short time the verdict will be clear and Dahut will call out 'the prisoner floats! She is guilty!' The crowd will call out 'Guilty! To the fire with her!' The crowd will watch enthusiastically as they carry out your body, dry you and chain you to the stake. Their cruelty will know no bounds as they see the executioners thrust their glowing irons onto your breasts, branding each with the double dolphin of Ys. Then the flames will slowly consume your limbs and body and rob you forever of the power to inflict your evil magic on Ys again."

"And Jahaan?"

"Chained to a post nearby he will be forced to witness both your Swimming and your burning, after which he will be placed 'in the mercy of Dahut'."

"Give me strength, O Kristos!" cried Ana, "to accept all for your sake!"

"Kristos does not intend you to burn!" said the visitor. "You shall escape. You must escape from Ys."

"How?" asked Jahaan.

"There are tools in that bag to cut your chains, a dagger, two cloaks and some bread." They heard the bars creak under very powerful hands. "They're no problem. But work fast. You have not a moment to lose!"

He pushed the bag through the opening. All the time the unknown man had kept his face, except his eyes, hidden deep in his hooded cloak. "My name doesn't matter to you! Only heed my last words. You must be right out of Ys well before daylight! When you've forced your rivets and cut the bars go straight through this lane and to the Bridgegate. Once through that, over the bridge and well up the ravine, you will be safe. Your jailer is dead drunk. I've seen to that."

"But the guard at the Bridgewater?"

"I've primed the man with cervoise and something much stronger. By the time you get there he will be unconscious. If by chance you meet anyone in Ys at this early hour they won't know you for you will be wearing cloaks with large cowls. Keep them fast round your faces! You must hasten! It's your only chance of escape!"

He was gone suddenly, silently into the surrounding darkness and the shrieks of the storm swallowed him up and stilled his footsteps.

CHAPTER 21

Ridna smiled as she woke. She was with child by the officer. She'd bear it in the summer. She'd love it, suckle it! It would be healthy in the sea air. She would no longer be chained to wooden beams at night. Outside the waves crashed down on the shore and the wind howled. Their hut, wrought by honest labour with roof ropes storm-set, withstood the gale. She peered at the sleepers. At the entrance slumbered two slaves. The old woman slave had gone for water. Then she would unchain all of them.

Ridna did not know that the old woman would never return. Struck down by heart failure, she lay dead, the keys still round her neck.

The storm increased in strength. The hissing of the surfs grew louder and ghostly wraiths of spindrift floated over the harbour. The mighty waves broke on the land with terrific force. Ridna had no fear. Their hut stood on a slope up which any flooding must come before it reached them. By then they would have escaped to higher ground.

Suddenly her heart beat fast. Water gleamed close by. It was a very high tide! The flood came in slowly but already she smelt wrack and saw spray. Ridna knew that Romans before battles chained slave rowers to their galleys. If a ship sank they drowned! If not quickly unchained they also were doomed! Now the flood was flowing at the threshold! All woke and stared, wide-eyed, at the incoming death. It was fate! The gods had chosen the two slaves to display first to the others how they all must die! The water oozed under their beds, swirling round them. As it deepened their bodies rose too, with limbs anchored by chains. Floating well, the two believed they might sustain this position and did not cry "help!"

The waters rose higher. Fetter-restrained, they sank beneath the surface. They had one hope. By straining their heads upwards their nostrils might remain above water and so they would survive. This hope was denied to them. The water soon grew deeper. Their companions heard them take one last deep breath before their mouths were awash. For a half minute, like diving maidens, they frantically held their breath but their bodies, unable to bear the strain longer, compelled them, gaping mouthed, vigorously to expel their air as gleaming bubbles. Now, forced to breath in, they filled their lungs with water, writhing in their last struggle for life while their chains clanked passing knells.

Gradually all there similarly perished, most uttering few words. Ridna was the last. As the waves covered her she cried "Woe is me! I asked Dahut to chain me! I drowned them! I, too, must die and my babe with me!"

The sea was not content only with their deaths. Strong eddies in the hut loosened the two timbers until the backwash dragged them out into the open sea. The corpses, naked save for slave collars, remained firmly chained between the beams and floated helplessly at the whim of every wave. Yet the swell which affected the movements of these bodies created images that had a certain grace about them. But in death, even as in life, the slaves were in fetters.

CHAPTER 22

Near the coast was a small hut shielded from the wind by a heap of stones. In the semi-darkness within were two women. Theodora the Greek slave lay upon a bed of straw. Her face was drawn from the pain she had undergone. Opposite to her was apparently a bundle of old rags which lay on a piece of jetsam wood. Above it was a cross made from branches tied together with straw rope. During the night she had borne a man-child but he had died at birth.

Outside a puddle reflected what feeble light was coming to the troubled land. The wind thrust fiercely at the derelict hurdle that barred their door hole. "It's been a long night for you and you must be weary, Ismene" Theodora said to the woman who knelt by her side. The harlot's cheeks were tear stained. "I did all I could for you. I know a little about birth and it's a woman's lot to have pain. Theodora, I've lain with many men but I've never had a child that I could call my own, no small life that I might cherish. That's why I wanted so much for you to bear this baby. I would have helped you to rear him and even in this accursed city of Ys I would have brought him up to be a good man. Yet you know what we Greeks say 'it was not so written', so he died."

For moments while she spoke, the savage wind ceased to howl as if even its ferocity were hushed before the small corpse on the crude wooden bier. To these women nothing outside really mattered. Only the peace that emanated from the dead baby. "There's no sadness in your eyes, Theodora, only contentment. Is it because you know that your baby died in the Kristion faith? That faith which you would never give up despite the sneers of pagan people, the honeyed arguments of the young heathen priest or the sharp lash of your master's lash on your bare back". Her Greek, quick and pure, sounded so strange against the background of the alien skies above their fragile dwelling. The wind had resumed its murderous assaults on the land. Sometimes her voice was drowned in the turmoil.

Theodora's eyes brightened. They bore triumph in them. "Yes, 'it was not so written' as you say. Death took him from me at the moment of birth but I thank God that I remembered the due rites. I gave him to Kristos. There was no priest of my religion here but that didn't matter for you assisted me splendidly and what was more you understood what it all meant to me. It was so good of you to go out in the storm and get water for me which you left lying under the holy cross that you had made. Above all it was so considerate of you to take him up and hold his little body so close, so very close to me for I was very tired. Yet thus I was able to sprinkle him with the holy water which had been sanctified by contact with that cross. So I baptised him, though born in pagan Ys, with the words 'In the name of the Father, the Son and the Holy Spirit'. I couldn't remember any more but I'm sure the good Kristos will understand. Had the boy lived I would have called him Niklas."

Exhausted, she fell back on the pillow. Ismene wiped away the sweat from her brow. The double dolphins eyed her slyly from the slave collar that hung slackly from the neck of the sufferer. "I feel worn out now" whispered Theodora, "but prop me up so that I can see the sea. We Greeks have no fear of the sea no matter how terrible it appears!" Her wan face brightened. "Isn't a ship like a great womb that carries safely within it human lives on long voyages?" Supported by Ismene's strong arms Theodora managed to sit up. She gazed with profound longing through the door. At the harbour mouth the battle between the sea and the open land was growing in intensity. All along the coast the waves were breaking in tremendous bands of foam and clouds of white spray drenched the inner harbour walls.

"It was on a day like this that our ship, caught in a White Squall, was driven hard before the wind into Massilia. I was only a small girl but I remember all those times very well. A slave in that city, I grew up to full stature and figure. Then my owner, a rich merchant, decided to make a journey to the north-west of Gaul. We were nearly there when raiders attacked the caravan, slaughtered the merchant and dragged the booty and me away. I, already with child, bound by my neck and hands in a slave coffle, was brought here with other young women slaves whom they had captured. Ah, there won't be any more journeys for me for I feel I am near the end of my earthly road. Tell me now, for I can't see much from my bed, where those sounds are coming from?"

"It's been a stormy night, Theodora, and the gale is still increasing in strength. Can you hear the heavy beat of the waves as they crash on the cliffs and the sea walls of Ys? You can also hear the hissing of the surfs as they draw back like serpents cheated for the moment of their prey but only to gather more strength for heavier attacks."

"There's another sound coming to my ears. It's music and so close by."

"It's the old harper who dwells near the quayside. He has risen in the night and is now playing his harp. Above the roar of the waves it sounds melodious. Now I can see him clearly. He stands upright, body bent a little to meet the force of the wind. His white hair streams out behind him."

"How does he play?"

"He plays in different ways. Sometimes he plucks his strings quickly as if he would reflect in his music the angry mood of the seas. Sometimes he just touches his strings with the tips of his fingers, pausing a little between each string and listening as if he would embody the very sounds of the sea, the great waves, within his notes. Mostly he gazes out to sea but once he turned round and looked at the houses of Ys where people still sleep. When he turned back again and faced the waves, I noticed that his music had become very sad. It were as if he were saying a long farewell to his people."

"What do you see when you yourself turn right away from gazing at that raging sea?"

"I see the city of Ys. It rests, secure and firm on its narrow steep neck of land which is overlooked by the great temple on the high cliff above it. The roofs of the dwellings bathed in moisture shine brightly but no one can be seen now on its streets. Whatever the people may have done they have no concern about the morrow. Rich or poor, young or old, they sleep away the last hours of this night. Soon they will waken again to another day and live their lives, many of them in wickedness. Let me turn away now and gaze once more at the old harper who is so devoted to his music and lives apart from all other dwellers in this city. He is a man who lives a good life."

"I've lost much blood in my travail and I must lie down again for I am dizzy and cannot sit up much longer. Soon I know I shall be gone from you." Ismene put her arms round Theodora and lowered her gently back onto the bed. Theodora spoke again. "The wind is making an uncanny soughing as it blows through the trees. It shrieks almost as if it were a human being. Yet why don't I hear the purling of the river?"

"The river's become barely a trickle. It almost seems to have stopped flowing. You wouldn't recognise it, Theodora. It's very strange for we've had so much rain these last few weeks." Ismene grasped the ailing woman tightly to her. "Let's forget about the storm and everything else. I want to be so near to you, Theodora. Ever since you came, a woman slave, to this awful city you've been such a good friend to me."

"I've done so little for you in the past and now this long night you've worn yourself out for me."

"No, no, you've been such an example to me. You were ill-treated right from your arrival here, yet you bore your sufferings so patiently. You made me want to learn more of your God, this Kristos whom you worshipped so faithfully. How did he strengthen you to suffer silently the squalid life here, the blows, the constant degrading servitude of a bondwoman to these people with their loathsome gods? You, who are so young, don't even fear death! You, whose life has been so brief and harsh for you've had so little pleasure in it!"

The whisper from the woman on the bed was so low that Ismene had to bend right over to hear what she said. "What I know about Kristos came to me first when I was a young girl in Massilia. I talked to a Greek priest there. He told me much about Kristos and though since I left Massilia I've had no contact with people of my faith I've tried to live my life as Kristos would have lived had he been here. Yet there are certain things which I must tell you now I am leaving you." She paused for breath. Then Ismene gave her a sip of the holy water. It seemed to revive her.

"I learnt above all things that Kristos was the Soter, the Saviour who came into this world to save all men from their wickedness and to help them to live upright and good lives."

"Even the people of Ys so steeped in cruelty and evil?"

"Even the people of Ys. The slavemaster whose scars are on my body, whose offspring I would have had to bear had I lived any longer. The raging mob who would have burnt Gwendaline after her Swimming if they could. He will pardon them, he will save them from the fires of Hell if they truly repent of their sins and come to Him. Kristos has great all-conquering power in His message to us. Not the might of armies or of princes but the power of love – 'Agape'."

The eyes had that look in them which told the watcher that Theodora was about to pass to another world. "There's nothing left for me now but Love. His Love! As the tide surges over the oceans so my life here is pouring fast away. I've lost all that humanity would value. My kin, my freedom, my child. Now it is time for me to yield up my own life. I do so gladly."

"There's nothing for me now except Love – His Love – 'Agape'."

The speech had become sighing and indistinct, the voice was growing very faint. "Don't weep, my friend, because I have to leave you here in Ys. I know that Kristos will soon come to you and you'll learn at last the meaning of His Love which forgives all men. His Love that gives you Life Everlasting. Don't bewail my passing for I go to a better world than this. I grow so cold. Put your arms around me and hold me close. Keep me close to you until the very end!"

When first light came to Ys, Ismene lay asleep on the bed with the now still form of Theodora clutched in her embrace. Neither heeded the increasing thunder of the giant waves as they roared in to threaten the city of Ys.

CHAPTER 23

Their lives depended upon escaping, their escape on tools. All the things needed were in the bag. Scotching hammer, files, crowbar, dagger, cloaks and bread. They set to work. Ana pulled her hands free and held Jahaan steady while he prised the rivets away. She forced the rivets from his manacles and he freed his feet. They toiled briefly, pausing often to listen. Could they be heard outside? Luckily the howling of the wind covered all other sounds and soon their chains were off. Then the window! The crowbar levered one bar, the others needed cold chisel and file. While Jahaan worked Ana listened for footsteps. No one came by. They cut the last bar and scrambled through immediately throwing on their hooded cloaks. Panting, they rested against the wall, eyes straining to see through the mist that shrouded the lane, ears tense for footsteps, the clink of arms or a voice. The keen winds blew through their cloaks.

Their part of Ys was silent. Yet far away, borne faintly on the wind, came a friendly sound. It was the sound of a harp. Who was awake at that hour, playing? The music came from the Lower City. The sounds, heard when the wind back-gusted, had a pleasant, familiar tone about them, almost as if the harper played to encourage them as they set out, bare feet making only a pitter-patter on the cobbles. The lane was narrow and split by a long gully between the stones. Always they moved furtively like animals eager to escape their hunters.

There was no glow from any house. Although the wind was blowing so strongly that they could barely keep their footing, it was also a blessing to them. People would not want at night to face the mounting fury of the storm. Ys could have been a city of the dead, its inhabitants sunk in uncanny quiet.

A dark building loomed up and from an arrow slit winked a faint light. "The Hall of Gradlon!" breathed Jahaan. They crept along quickly, crouched down to reduce their silhouettes as they crossed the market place. There now came to them the roar of waves striking on rocks. Above, stars fitfully struggled against clouds that tore past at terrific speed hastening inland. "Pray God there are no ships near this coast" whispered Jahaan. "The sea is breaking on a dead lee shore."

A thin ribbon of grey, a sign of the coming dawn, was visible in the east. It was already lightly tinged with crimson. They must not lose any time. They must be out of Ys before daybreak.

In the uncertain light they trudged along feeling cautiously with their feet lest any careless stubbing of heel or toe against loose stones might arouse some light sleeper. They came to the lane where they had been captured. They were very near the Bridgegate! Suddenly a door opened and a pencil of light shone out into the lane. They froze, pressing their bodies flat against the wall and keeping in the shadow.

A man stepped out onto the cobbles, his buskins making a clicking sound on the stones. His back was towards them but the light fell full on his helmet and the sword dangling by his side. A voice from within shouted "Must you always be in such a hurry? We've had such pleasant hours this night throwing dice. You must give me my chance of revenge!"

"I don't want to go stumbling along the streets in this accursed dark" cried the swordsman. His voice was tinged by cervoise to a mellow tone and he swayed uncertainly. The watchers sensed the ambience of hesitation in his voice. Jahaan felt for the dagger pommel.

The hidden voice bawled again. "You can spare a few minutes! Why, it's still dark. There's enough time to take some sips more! What's the hurry man?"

"I've had orders from Dahut to take the man and woman from prison and prepare them for their fate. The woman will Swim then be burned alive. As for the man, Jahaan, he will be in Dahut's dungeon and you know what that means."

"I'll see you're not late! Come in and shut the door for it's cold in that wind!" The man yielded and the door closed on him. The fugitives scuttled along out of danger.

The last hazard loomed up before them. The bridge. Already, hearts throbbing fast, they could see its slender arch over the ravine. The formidable jaws of the Bridgegate tower yawned up before them. On tip-toe they approached and from behind a buttress reconnoitred. The sentry lay on his back on a bench. The man's breathing resounded, loud and stertorous. They paused for a moment, took heart and walked right up to him. The bridge showed through the arch and as they passed the sentry they looked at him more closely. His eyes were half-closed in a fixed stare, the pupils narrowed to black points. He made no movement.

The Bridgegate had been well built for a stubborn

defence and they had to turn sharply before they passed through the outer gate. It was wide open but they nearly tripped over an obstacle in their way. A body sprawled, partly on the bridge partly in the gate which it almost blocked. The haft of a long poniard stuck out from the man's spine and there was a red stain below his tunic. His sword had dropped beneath him. He must have been stabbed without warning from behind. Over him stared down the massive stone dolphins built into the tower. The threatening insignia of the power of Ys!

Then they were out onto the bridge, half running, half walking in their haste to get clear of the city. The loose timbers of the footway creaked loudly but they did not heed the noise. Soon they were off the bridge and on the other side of the ravine climbing up its steep slopes, away from Ys at last. They could have shouted for joy!

Their troubles were not yet over. They were still in view of Ys. Nearby was the hall where Dahut would be waiting to hear that her orders had been carried out. Though they were beyond the city walls it was possible that she could send out a search party to recapture them.

Ana stared at the inner harbour. Her heart beat quickly at what she saw. Everything was ready for her execution. There was a tall stake, faggots, branding irons, chains and the tar with which they would coat her naked body beforehand. The tar, clinging tightly, would burn slowly and prolong her agony. She said nothing to Jahaan of her feelings. It was better for him not to worry on her behalf as he had enough to do to find a way out.

A voice came to her inward ear "Death hath no terrors for you."

They scrambled up the ravine sides dislodging stones which slithered down with loud scraping sounds. They were conscious that they were visible to watchers, if there were any on the city walls, for the ravine sides were almost bare and so steep that they had to cling to tussocks of grass and scrub to help them.

Breathless, they talked about their next move. The only way was to creep inland hugging the ravine until they could make for the forest and the paths there from which they might reach the plou.

Suddenly their luck seemed to have deserted them. A wide gap yawned in the ravine sides and loose earth and water were sliding down it making crossing impossible. For the moment they must try to control themselves and hope they could thus evade any pursuit. They would have to linger there until the hue and cry had died down. By the crest of the crack they found a clump of bushes big enough to conceal them. Lying flat on their bellies and gasping for breath they rested while they munched their bread. The clump protected them from the wind and in their hideaway they now looked at the waters far beyond Ys.

The sea in the grey morning was a remarkable sight. Colossal waves as high as houses were advancing in long lines of battle against the cliffs and against Ys. The white crests took what little light there was but in between were hollows blacker than the darkest night. In whatever direction they looked were only to be seen enormous billows whose foaming peaks were often blown clean away by the savagery of the wind and tossed, mangled, into the air. As the waves approached the cliffs their lofty summits began to curl over in majestic arches and they broke in thunderous roars which echoed from the precipices. At times clouds of white spray blotted out the land then momentarily it would clear and they saw again this spectacle of remorseless, unbridled power. It was a scene of the utmost desolation and gloom.

Yet through all this turmoil as the sea attacked the land, there sounded the music of the harp. Sometimes the gusts would block the sound but in calm intervals between they listened to the slow, repeated notes. Far below them they could see the tiny figure of the harper and his instrument. There was no sign of other human life in Ys where the people still slumbered on.

The defences of Ys against the sea were in its lower part. The mouth of its small harbour had long been closed altogether to boats. The chain gangs over the years had carried heavy rocks there. The rocks had been thrown into the gap to try and seal it off though sometimes the waters did seep through. The harbour waters thus usually remained placid. The two arms of the harbour up to the mouth now appeared like the mighty fist of a boxer stretched out to fight their foe, the sea. The waves had not yet really broken on the central part of the harbour but had struck its walls with sideways blows and as the tidal flow increased and the waters rose the pressure on the coast and the harbour defences grew more and more intense.

The sea in this battle was like a living human being with a will and a mind of its own. It was cunning and deceptive too. In its first assaults it had appeared to ignore the weakest spot of all, the gap at the harbour mouth. So it did not break on the mouth at all preferring the strongest parts of the defences, the walls to the right and left of the mouth as if to deceive the harbour that it was only playing a game and would soon retreat. These earlier waves effected little damage only giving off massive sprays as they broke.

Eight of these lesser waves had broken thus when there came a rogue wave, the ninth. It was a gigantic wave and it came steadily and slowly towards the land seemingly too lazy even to crest in the wind. At the same time, another huge wave approached on a diagonal course. Both waves met at the weak harbour mouth. They broke with terrific ferocity exactly at the same moment. There was a roar louder than the heaviest thunder. When the rogue wave receded, the destruction it had done could clearly be seen. The stones in the gap had been all torn bodily away.

The breach had been made! There would be no respite now for the harbour or for Ys. Wave after wave poured remorselessly into the opened harbour and with each wave the opening was widened still more. The only feeble protection left to the land was a very low inner wall near the quayside behind which huddled the dwellings of some poorer inhabitants and the huts of the slaves. The conquering waves surged onwards, forming a phalanx of irresistible strength rapidly flooding all low lying land and dwellings.

Jahaan for a long time had looked at this scene of desolation measuring the height of the waves with a sailor's eyes. Soon his gaze was focused not on the harbour but on the sea cliffs nearby. "My God!" he cried to Ana, "do you see what is happening? The sea level is rising!"

"You mean there's a high tide?"

"A high tide but more than that! The sea is higher than is usual. It will overwhelm all the lower part of Ys.

See those cliffs! The waves are right above high water mark. I've never heard of such a thing before."

Ana was looking back at the land. In the upper part of Ys, high above the water, the superiors slumbered on in their luxurious beds heedless of the threat to their hapless fellow citizens down by the shore. Above them, firmly rooted on the cliff top as it had been for centuries, splendid and enduring, was the great heathen temple. Neither rain nor storm could affect it. For Ana and Jahaan it was a symbol of the everlasting power of Ys which had seized them in its clutches and which even now might reach out and arrest them unless they could flee from it.

The landscape was changing. The ancient oaks by the temple were leaning over, hard pressed by the gale. There were brown stains on the cliffs below the temple and from them water was trickling. As she looked she felt that strange aloofness that she had experienced in the prison. The temple, the city, the cliff appeared for a second to be places in a dream. The city seemed to have no human life at all save the harper faithfully playing near the harbour. Only the sea and the wind had voices now.

Just below the temple, underneath the colonnade that overhung the precipice, was a row of small holes. Wisps of vapour began to come out of these and at first were blown away by the wind. They thickened until each vent was pouring out clouds of dense black smoke which the wind could not quell and which blew upwards round the colonnade. Then spurts of yellow-red fire burst from the holes until the colonnade above was itself clothed in broad flames. The temple was on fire!

Cracks appeared in the base of the temple. The fire

mounted upwards until that part of the temple was engulfed in great sheets of flame. The colonnade tottered slowly outwards, swaying. The movement became rapid and vertical. The temple collapsed, striking the cliff in two places before it fell sheer onto the house of the young priest and those of three superiors almost immediately below. Dust rose in blinding clouds to be snatched away by the winds. Huge fragments fell. No one caught beneath the giant stones could have survived.

The two watchers, nailed to their hiding place, gazed in horror at this scene of destruction and death. If one link of a chain is given a blow the force of the blow is transmitted, link by link, along the length of the metal. The cliff itself had been wounded by the impact of the falling building. Deep hollows had been gouged out of its surface. These rapidly grew into immense fissures that opened out like the gaping jaws of dragons. They widened still further. There was a sudden roar that drowned the sound of thunder claps from the clouds above where lightning flickered. Tens of thousands of tons of soil and uprooted rock, sliding on the now released waters of the river, crashed down on Upper Ys. Some houses were submerged at once, others crumbled and cracked like dried oak leaves crushed beneath buskined feet then were embedded deep beneath this avalanche. All was destruction. The wet, weary soil long hidden for centuries, the outthrust of imprisoned river water, the wounded rocks torn from the bosom of their age-old resting places – all these things stunned the senses of the watchers.

So shocked were they by this disaster that they fell on their knees, hands clasped in prayer while they went on mutely gazing at the destruction of the city.

As the landslide spread fast down the steeper parts of Ys it assumed the shape of a dragon whose jaws gaped at the untouched houses. A shockwave, greater than the first, brought the remainder of the mangled cliffs with its full weight to bear on all in its path. As the second landslide hit the first it assumed a rotary movement so that for an instant it appeared as if the earth were moving uphill! Yet all the time the enormous mass of earth and rock and water was forcing its way downhill, this time into the lower city and towards the sea. Perhaps because the slope there was slightly less steep it came more slowly but its force was overwhelming.

Only two buildings had so far escaped destruction in the upper city. The Hall of Gradlon with its stables still stood on its isolated rock and the Bridgegate with its bridge dominated the ravine though the landslide slithered round both buildings like the claws of the dragon it resembled. There would be no epitaph for those who had died, lost to sight beneath many feet of water.

The landslide began to advance into the lower city. Those few people who were already awake saw the immense tongue of the dragon swaying above their dwellings. Crazed with fear they rushed out heedless of the shrieks of those left behind to die in the crushed houses. They stumbled, not knowing what they did, to what they thought was safety, that part of Ys bordering the sea. Over them, indifferent to their distress, hovered flocks of seabirds, and ravens quartered the air high above where the temple had once been.

Those living by the sea came tumbling out of their wretched cabins, wild-eyed at the prospect of sudden death and running hither and thither like so many ants whose nest has been disturbed. Women feverishly grasping infants to their breasts screamed in high pitched voices or stood mute at the awful thing aimed at their lives. Above them began to loom the limbs of the dragon now encircling all of the city. There was no way out. Behind them advanced the landslide. In front was the angry sea. On the very edge of the waters was an ever-narrowing space crammed with people pitiful and naked just as they had jumped from their beds.

The implacable waves rose like lofty ramparts to oppose the escape of the people of Ys from their doom. The landslide advanced down behind them onto its shivering prey with steady, ruthless precision.

One man only was unmoved amidst the turmoil and panic. The old harper sat, impassive even when the sprays soaked him and the surfs grasped at his bare feet. His eyes were fast closed and absorbed in his music he played on. While his fingers touched his beloved strings, he was unaffected by the fury of the sea. The notes of the harp floated up and above the dying city. He was playing a lament for Ys. As he played, the stormy petrels, fearless in the gales, wheeled down as if they would pay homage to him. Yet their voices, strange, unearthly, seemed a mockery of human life. Vultures, sweeping slowly from the cliffs, inspected men, women and children with impartial, aloof eyes. Dawn was coming but only to shine on a scene of utter misery and annihilation.

Suddenly amidst the shrieks and the grinding of the rocks came another sound, the clatter of a horse's hooves. An old man, naked, with hair streaming out in the wind, was riding bareback away from Gradlon's stables. Behind him ran a woman frantically waving her arms and screaming to him to stop. Dahut, her body naked, her face soiled by earth and thighs flecked by blood. He halted for an instant, she jumped up and clung to him. He galloped away but the stallion needed no spur. Its eyes dilated by terror and mane flat on its neck, it charged straight for the Bridgegate. The tower was already cracked and crumbling. It did not hesitate but careered right through and out onto the bridge itself. The tower collapsed behind it.

The bridge was still intact but was shaken repeatedly as its foundations were sapped by the landslide. Below it was the gorge, black and formidable and filled now by the foaming waters of the sea.

At the far side, standing on a rock spur at the end of the bridge and clad in an abbot's robes, was a tall man. One of Guenole's hands held a great cross that towered up high in the air. His other hand held a wand of ashwood. The stallion halted abruptly right back on its haunches before this apparition that barred its passage. Dahut gripped the flanks of the steed more firmly with her legs and grasped her father's waist. Necklaces of jewels fluttered around her neck.

"Save me! Save me! she screamed. "Save me! I will give you all my jewels if you'll grant me my life!"

She cowered down behind the front rider seeking to hide herself from the piercing eyes of the saint. The horse made no attempt to move. It appeared paralysed by terror. Guenole extended the great cross right out to Gradlon.

"Do you wholly accept the faith of Kristos? Will you follow one God, the God of the Kristion, for the rest of your days if they are spared?"

"My God, I do" said Gradlon. "Give me my life!"

"Then let that heathen woman who has committed so much wickedness go!"

"I can't do that! She's my daughter!"

Thrice Guenole expostulated with Gradlon. After the third time he stretched out towards the woman his other hand that held the ashwood rod. At the touch of the wand her body convulsed, her hands suddenly lost their grip and she let go, falling head first into the whirlpool below. The horse with its solitary rider bounded on to the firm ground just before the bridge fell down below its rear hooves.

"In manus tuas!" cried Guenole, leading the quivering stallion away.

In the lower city only one building still resisted the pressure of the landslide. The church, so far entire, was leaning over as if better to combat its worst enemy. The morning light shone with an ethereal brightness on the tiny figure of the white stone angel. Always she stretched out her beautiful, loving arm towards the city that was now only a torrent of mud, rocks and swirling water. The bell at the tower slowly swayed and began to toll the last hours of Ys.

By now the sea had breached the remnants of the inner sea wall and was flooding all the land by the harbour and beyond. The last of the few living were forced inexorably into a very narrow space between the landslide and the fierce waves. Some, their limbs paralysed by terror, could not move and were crushed deep beneath the mud and rocks. Others, maddened by fear of the landslide more than the waves, threw themselves into the sea and were dashed to pieces on the stones.

There was now only one inhabitant left in Ys. The

harper. He stood on his tiny flat rock. Above his head crouched the overhanging mouth of the landslide. At his feet the waves rose higher and higher still to devour this ultimate victim. Ana and Jahaan heard the clear notes go up the strings of his harp then down again. Yet before he reached the bottom note it was suddenly cut off. The sea had taken the harper to itself.

The church tower was swaying drunkenly. In the lower part great cracks appeared. Yet the bell went on tolling, the angel still stretched out her arm in deep compassion over the holocaust while the sea swallowed the foundations of the building. Finally the tower heeled over with a horrible sucking sound. Church and bell still ringing loudly fell into the sea.

The struggle of the dragon had not yet finished. It had destroyed the city of Ys and thrust it below the waters. Now the landslide began to reach out into the very waters themselves as if to contest possession. The battle had begun with its most terrible enemy.

The raging sea fought desperately with this impertinent interloper. Enormous waves overwhelmed the writhing mass of mud and rocks, white surfs cut into the tentacles of this creature, biting it away constantly here and there and everywhere. Earth and mud fell like great waterfalls into the teeth of the billows and vanished. In this contest of the giants the waters around what had been Ys became the hue of dark blood, the life blood of the martyred land.

The sea was a victor, countless masses of water being constantly poured into the breach. Gradually the very land on which the city of Ys had been built disappeared. Houses, temples, church, cornfields were all under the sea. The seagulls, wheeling overhead, cried out their harsh farewells to the city that once had been.

So shocked had Ana been by this tragedy that at first she couldn't even accept that the city had gone out of existence. It were almost as if she had experienced this cataclysm in a dream from which she would waken to find that Ys was still there. However, her memory still held all too vivid pictures of those last hours. People, crushed like grotesque dolls, their mouths gaping in their last screams. A woman throwing her baby clear as she fell beneath chunks of masonry. The head of the decapitated slavemaster pinned to the ground. Only one person, Gradlon, had survived.

How impersonal had been the strength of the earth and rocks that made up the landslide. How powerful had been the raging sea that had become a tomb for humanity. The falling cliff, the avalanche of mud and rocks had no link with the lives of the people of Ys. All the savagery and hates, the lust and the cruelties that had given Ys its notoriety as a wicked city had been as nothing to these powerful natural forces that acted so blindly. Was it true as Guenole had prophesised that the people were destroyed for the sins of their city? If so, what of the innocent Theodora? There must have been others like her who even in Ys had lived good lives. Why did they have to perish?

Everything and everyone in Ys had been annihilated. Only Jahaan had been left to her and the land of Armorica to which he belonged. Neither she nor he could see from where they stood that on the fringe of the forest armed men were advancing in the direction of what had been Ys. Men who spoke Breton and who carried a great banner on which was emblazoned a cross. By the banner trudged an old woman.

Jahaan was walking closer to the cliff on the seaward side and he was saying "I must look if the curragh is still there." Ana began to feel a dizziness come over her at the sight of the waves striking on the base of the precipice on which grew some tufts of sea-pink. Her hands touched them, grasped a tuft or two without her knowing why, while she saw the massive waves spreading a shroud of white and green over Ys. Cities might pass away and the people who dwelt in them. The sea would remain forever.

"I must see if the curragh is all right" he repeated.

"Surely you won't look for the curragh? It'll be badly damaged by now. Mustn't we try to get back to the plou?"

She knew what she wanted at this crisis! To be quite secure, to know his love now that they had gone through so much together. Her body was waiting for him, ready to bear children to whom she'd tell the story of Ys, the city overwhelmed by the seas. Oh, how proud I shall be to have children whom I, the triple-breasted, shall suckle as Guen suckled Guenole! Yes, children who will overcome death when they, too, have children as well.

"Let's go back to the plou!"

Why did he look at her now as if she were a foreign being, not from this world, his world? Why did Claudia's words come back to her mind, "Sweet is God's love. It reaches to us over the long centuries. *Quis separabit?* Who shall separate us from the love of God? ... you are from the future!" Was she, indeed, a stranger to him now? Had the destruction of Ys altered their relationship to each other?

He was slowly going down the cliff and she was following him as she always did. There were cracks where the vibrations of the landslide had broken the solid rocks. He halted for a moment, stretching up his hands to hold hers and smiling to encourage her. She saw his eyes gazing at her. He held her close to him for a short while then released her. He walked on ahead. She felt giddy once more and called out "Jahaan, be careful, the cliffs are dangerous – they're breaking up!"

He only laughed and went on downwards. They were now much closer to the tips of the waves as they broke on the cliff.

He called out her name, "Ana", putting the stress on the first syllable as he always did. There was no fear at all in his strong voice but she foresaw with a woman's intuition that he was going away from her forever. He was going to another kingdom, the kingdom of the sea. The great sea of Armorica would take him to its bosom. He would die there and be transmuted into those waves that broke on the Armoric shores.

Again he called out her name with that stress on the first syllable. His voice was filled with hope and joy toward her.

Then the cliff began to crumble beneath them and Ana no longer heard the voice of the man who would love her forever.

EPILOGUE

September, 1926

"Ann! Ann!" it was the voice of a young woman tense with anxiety and fatigue. "Thank God you've come round at last! After all this time! It was just sheer chance that Yves got to you in those first few minutes! A little while more in the sea and you'd have gone from me forever!" Tears mingled with sweat glistened on Mary's face. She was exhausted from the long spells of resuscitation treatment. Her red nightdress, soaked by immersion, clung to her body.

Dawn was coming slowly to the Bay of Douarnenez. The young sun faintly gilded the far distant clouds floating across an azure sky. It clothed the scattered white cottages in a gentle light. Yet it showed up as pallid the weary faces of the people clustered round the woman lying on the sand.

Dr le Brun straightened his aching back and with his fine-woven handkerchief wiped his smooth brow. His sensitive fingers held Ann's hand delicately in his while he read the pulse once more. For him also it had been a long night. First, that difficult early evening obstetric case in Douarnenez. Fortunately it had very quickly turned out all right. Then there was this. It was lucky that at the right moment he had stopped his trap to speak to Yves about his mother's asthma. Still more luck that, before he left for Douarnenez, he had dumped that new oxygen cylinder in his trap. After a very prolonged struggle it had got Ann's breathing going again normally but it had been touch and go for such a time!

He certainly couldn't take all the credit due. That English woman, the swimmer, had learnt her First Aid stuff very well and started resuscitation even at sea while he was running down the beach to them.

His face was still grave. It wasn't a case of simple drowning. She'd barely swallowed a mouthful of water. It was her prolonged unconsciousness that had baffled him. Often he had had the feeling that she didn't want to come back from that world of darkness in which she was plunged. Was it some form of catalepsy where the soul appears to leave the body for hours or even much longer and experiences another form of existence? Perhaps in another human being? Where the physical body remains living but quiescent as it were? He had heard of this phenomenon but himself had not come across it. Anyway, her colour was gradually returning to normal and she smiled faintly at Mary.

His Parisian gaiety had to erupt to the surface as he wagged a reproving finger at her. "Well, Mademoiselle, are you better after your crazy escapades? You've no right to your life, you know." He smiled, an affectionate smile of compassion and encouragement. "No more midnight bathes by yourself!" He touched her forehead, her chest and looked intently into her eyes. They drew his attention like a magnet.

"Mon Dieu, how lucky you were! Our friend Yves just happened to be rowing past and fished you out before you'd time to set up your ménage at the bottom of the Bay. There, too, was Mary splashing frantically to you, not knowing what you had done. Breathe deeply now and regularly! Your lungs are made for fresh air not sea water." His banter concealed the black care he felt always over drowning or near-drowning cases. The fisherfolk had too many of them. Mary and Yves were rubbing her hands, her feet.

"Apart from a small bruise on your forehead where you must have hit the rock and a slight tear in your costume de bain, you've not even a scratch. Yet I find it strange that your fingers, when we found you, were clutching tightly a dried up fragment of sea-pink. It looked so old as if it had come from a long way off! That plant, you know, grows on cliffs not in the bottom of the sea!" He really wasn't quite happy with that distant look in her eyes as if she were still remote from them and from life too. He checked her breathing again with his stethoscope. They had no stretcher but when he had finished the young fisherman picked her up and carried her back to her room.

It was a slow journey for her over the uneven ground but all the time Ann was conscious of Yves' strong arms beneath her, of his warm body, so close, of his face, so grave and reticent, that betrayed nothing of his feelings towards the woman he had saved from death. She was deeply grateful to the doctor but just now felt that the most important person for her was Yves as he trudged carefully trying somehow to protect her against the roughness of the journey.

She couldn't remember anything of the accident only that she had gone into a great blackness at the rock. Her thoughts were more for Yves. Before that night they had met so seldom yet now it were as if she had known him for a very long time.

Fortunately their hostess soon had very hot coffee waiting for them and they all drank it with much sugar after Ann was settled in her bed. The doctor was now even more loquacious and compliments gushed from his lips. "Mademoiselle Mary, you ought to be a nurse, especially a night nurse. You've an instinct for guessing when someone is in trouble. That's why you woke up and ran to the beach after your madcap friend. As for you, Mademoiselle Ann, we must keep you still and as warm as we can." He nodded professionally at their hostess; he was in his element with womenfolk.

"I'll see you again tonight Mademoiselle Ann, and perhaps tomorrow. We'll discuss the chances of your returning to England, say, in a day or so. I must be sure your lungs are not infected and I think you should take it easily for a while after your return to London. Still, our Bay waters are clean and you're young and healthy." He snapped to the hasps of his case, gave a colossal yawn, and was gone. Morning surgery was at 8.30 and he had another long day before him. It was all in a doctor's life!

The next day Ann rested quietly between the white sheets while Mary fussed around packing books and clothing, for the doctor had pronounced her fit enough to travel. The sunlight shone so placidly through the mullioned windows while she made an attempt to recall what had happened to her at the rock. It was impossible, for between her and that past event some wall seemed to have been erected. It was also strange as she was at times overcome by feelings of unutterable sadness.

Mary had gone out for a while and Ann was alone.

She fell asleep, a light dreamless sleep from which she was awakened by a gentle tap on the door. A brief, tentative knock. "Entrez!"

Yves came into the room slowly as if he were not used to visiting young ladies. A shy man, he held his beret in his right hand in an embarrassed manner as if he did not quite know what to do with it. His left hand grasped a small object carefully wrapped.

The breath of the sea drifted in with Yves. The tang of salt air, the smell of damp ropes, of fish, of boats. His eyes had that faraway look that comes from gazing over the wild wastes of the ocean or peering into the darkness of stormy nights.

He spoke in Breton mixed with French, picking his words with deliberation. "I'm so sorry to disturb you, Mademoiselle. I have to go out on a fishing smack tonight and we shall not be back for some days, by which time you will have returned to Angleterre. So I – I wanted to see you again before you left." He stopped, uncertain of how to go on. Yet he held the little object very gently in his upturned palm as if it were an oblation he were about to offer at a sacred shrine.

"You've not in the slightest disturbed me, Yves! It was very good of you to come when you're so busy with your work. I owe my life to you. To your skill with your boat in coming so fast to me, to your great strength in dragging me so swiftly from the water. I could have died then. I shall always be deeply indebted to you."

A flush appeared on his bronzed cheeks. "It was rien – nothing. I just happened to have been there that was all. Any other man would have done the same." His eyes looked into hers with that same piercing intentness that they had shown on that bathing day when he had warned her to keep away from the Rock. He sighed, "Yes, it could have been the green grave for you. I know these waters. They are deep and dark and hold the mysteries of many lost lives." Then he smiled and said more briskly "I mustn't depress you, Mademoiselle. How do you feel? I notice that the colour's come back to your cheeks. Now you'll forget everything and go back to your studies. I feel sure that you're contented with your life and work. My mother and I will give thanks to the Virgin that your life was spared for a good purpose, God's purpose. At our next Pardon we'll kneel down and say prayers for you." He crossed himself, bowing slightly.

"I'll never forget Brittany or the Breton people or you, Yves."

The little package was quivering in his hand as if he were irresolute about something. His face had gone a deeper red. The next few words were stammered. "Mademoiselle Mary told me that while you were in the water you lost something you greatly value. Your silver cross. I've been out in my boat several times and searched carefully all round the Rock but couldn't see it anywhere. I – I think the currents must have carried it away. I know – I know that you must be grieving for the loss of your precious cross so I – so I brought this – I made it myself – it's a mere trifle – but I hope you will accept this gift from me."

He placed the little package on the bed close to her hand and unrolled the covering, glancing at her sideways as if he sought her approval. Then he held up what had been so carefully wrapped inside. On his calloused palm now rested a small wooden cross. It had been made with great care. The proportions were perfect. "I carved it myself from a scrap of Breton oak. It has been very well seasoned and is as sound as a ship's timbers. I assure you it will never split with the passing years. I know that compared to your silver cross it's only a trinket but will you accept it from me?"

Ann's tears began to flow, drops coursing down her cheeks. "Of course I will, Yves. I'll value it more than the other cross since it comes from you."

There was a loop of fishing line fastened to the top of the cross. She unlaced the front of her nightdress and then looked up at him, beseeching. "My hands are a little shaky still Yves. Would you do me the kindness to place it round my neck?" Deftly, he obeyed. The cross now rested exactly where the silver one had been, its dark brown shape standing out in contrast to the deep white valley between her breasts. Through her tears she smiled up at him.

"I'll wear it always and in that place in perpetual remembrance of the man who saved me from the sea. Who brought me back from certain death."

He was shifting his feet uneasily, clutching his beret more tightly. He would have to leave her now. His work was a stern taskmaster. He could not stay any longer. Yet, with her woman's intuition, Ann perceived that he would have to be the one to say the very last words of farewell. He bent over and seized her small hand in his powerful grip, gazing hard into her eyes as if he would imprint upon his memory forever that last impression of her and her lovely face.

"Au revoir, Mademoiselle Ann – Kenavo er Baradoz – until we meet in Paradise."

Then he was gone. Ann listened for the footsteps on the stairs, the door banging to, the crunch of the gravel beneath his wooden sabots. She was alone once more. Alone with her tears, her thoughts, the cross of Breton oak which Yves had made and given to her. Ann cupped it in her hand, fingered it, gazed at its beauty, pressed it against her breast and thought of the great faith it symbolised. The faith of the Bretons through their long and sometimes bitter history. Feelings of unutterable pain and loss came to her in her great loneliness. In a lightning flash of revelation she now knew that never more in her life would come to her ears the sounds of that faraway harper or the mysterious voice that had called out her name so urgently.

While in this agony of mind she cried to God for help, she knew how profound her brief experience of Brittany had been to her and how it had changed her life and outlook. She had found that Time no longer really separated her from the people who had lived and suffered in the past. She saw all humanity, including herself, as one vast unity. A feeling of great love for all who had ever existed overwhelmed her. It was a love so deep that it would persist throughout her life.

Her immediate future was still to be revealed. With renewed vigour she would go to her studies. She would work. She'd probably remain a single woman for the Great War had cut down so many young men who otherwise would have married. She had intelligence and courage and she knew above all that her understanding of people had grown so much since she had come to Brittany. She would make friends wherever she went.

Yet – yet – there would sometimes be yearnings within her. Longings for someone, something far, far away in time and place. When she felt those powerful yearnings, she knew that she would murmur to herself those words that had come from Yves' lips in that little Breton room.

"Kenavo er Baradoz – until we meet in Paradise"

GLOSSARY

cervoise	beer
cincture	loin-cloth
clepsydra	water clock
cophini	baskets
curragh	skin boat
destrier	war horse
dominical	veil for women for use in church, etc.
francisca	throwing axe
Kristion	Christian (adjective or noun)
llan	small community of religious or building in which they worshipped
metropolitan	bishop in charge of a province
nemet	sacred grove
plou	parish (settlement of Bretons)
polaire	satchel or bag
quern	hand mill for corn, etc.
swimming	trial by water ordeal
tripeccia	three-legged stool
viaticum	Holy Communion given to those in imminent danger of death

Place Names

Aquilonia	Near Quimper
Armorica	"The land of the sea" – somewhat larger than modern Brittany
Burdigala	Bordeaux
Lugdunum	Lyons

ISBN 1-4120-2657-1